THE ART OF HIDING WHAT EVERYONE CAN SEE

THE ART OF HIDING WHAT EVERYONE CAN SEE

AFTEN BROOK SZYMANSKI

Brooks Books

The Art
of Hiding
What Everyone
Can See

Aften Brook Szymanski

To all those who have something they think they have to hide.
Please know that you are seen and loved.

1

A cat in the middle of the road doesn't move. There's an unreal stillness to it before I realize it's not going to move. The neighbor's curtains keep fluttering across the street as they spy our abnormal behavior. For one thing, we've never lined up Sound of Music style—standing on the lawn at attention like we're about to undergo some military inspection.

"Remember to be culturally sensitive," Mom warns at my side. Her house-brown mouse-hair static clinging to her face in the August heat.

Even Dad with his 'not just any rag will do' lecture not ten minutes earlier when Howie spilled his milk on the table. Not any rag, no—in our house the hand towels are for drying hands, the dishrags are for dishes, and the paper towels collect spills. There's no towel for the mess of us standing, waiting, spilling over with expectations to meet our Japanese exchange student for the year.

Korean Kpop and Kdrama along with Japanese comic obsession at my high school have definitely tainted my idea of how kids dress and apply make-up from that part of the world. Instead of the fold out from the latest KBop magazine, a regular girl, with an unfortunate choppy haircut, and eyes red from jet lag stands before me. She doesn't exactly look exotic despite her porcelain skin and blue-black hair. Not even her name sounds super international. Tami Watanabe (her last name sounds Native American more than Japanese—not that I have a clue). I mean, there are kids at school—local ones—with names like Acura and Zipper. We're freaking naming kids after vehicles and clothing parts in

America, and my family gets the exchange student that sounds more boring than American-average.

Her melodic soft toned voice, with unusual breaks and pauses at certain sounds reminds me to control my expression so I remain 'sensitive looking' instead of 'judgy'. At least I try, until her greeting before me comes out. "What's wrong with your face?"

Apparently, no one warned Tami about international manners. I should expect this question since I've grown up with a portwine stain like a saber strike running from the top left side of my face across the bridge of my nose and extending down the right side of my chin, even onto my neck. It's my defining trait. Or it used to be when I was in first grade, but in small towns people get over things because they see you all the time. There's an unspoken general rule: you get less and less interesting and different the more exposure you get. Everyone I know got over my face a long time ago—this interloper has no right to act like it's a big deal, because it's not.

But now this new person must get used to it and I didn't expect that. Probably how she must have expected a normal American family—as defined by television, which has no actual normal Americans on it at all. I guess we're mutually disappointed by each other.

I fully expect to be defined by Tami living with my family from here on out. There's something identity-sucking about her. I'll be 'those guys hosting so and so'. Not even a person. I'm destined to be a conglomerate of 'those guys' for the rest of the year, I know it.

The placement coordinator stammers for a second, her hands twitch toward Tami's mouth as if she's considering clamping them over her face. I wish she would.

Worst idea ever. An exchange student? I'm not sure if it's Mom who needed this, or if she thought I did. Since Bevan left home we've all been searching for something to take care of. My older brother has the more extensive Sturge-Weber syndrome associated with portwine stain. But, lucky for him, his birthmark hides under a headful of brillo hair. Like some kind of deal made in the gene pool. Unlucky for him, he also has mental delays and seizures to go along with it.

All I know, the second Bevan announced that his high school senior special education advisor arranged a work-study opportunity away from home upon graduation, none of us knew what to do with each other. Bevan's seizure medication has been stable for over a year, but that doesn't mean we don't hover. Hovering: a family trait. And now we're still like a bunch of dupes waiting for a cue regarding what to do with this new human we want to hover around, but also don't know if that's a normal response.

The coordinator, Hellen, finally speaks. "This is Lowry, your exchange sister. You'll be attending high school together." A forced smile can't hide the wide panic in her eyes. Under her breath Hellen adds, "I told you about her," with her back to me and a gesture of one arm crossing her face, in what I assume isn't supposed to be an obvious reference to my birthmark, but totally is.

Tami's expression remains flat. Not even a wrinkle of emotion. It doesn't make her any more exotic—it makes her distant in a non-foreign sense. Tami blinks at Hellen. "What's wrong with her face?" she asks again. Maybe she's worse at English than we all assumed or we talk too fast to follow.

Hellen turns away from Tami, arms stretched wide and looking at us. Her entire face almost the same shade of red as my birthmark. "Let's get her bags inside." She turns again, with all the flourish of a fantasy character and unlashes the bungees holding down several pieces of hard-cased luggage in the back of the truck. One pale pink case slides toward me. Before I'm out of earshot she says to Tami, "Placements are tight, don't blow this."

I spot the flattened animal in the road on my way back in the house. It's not the worst thing about this morning, which says something.

Tami catches up behind me, like she doesn't want me beating her to the room she will stay in—inside *my* house. Like she has any claim over the space. Her face never shifts to a smile or any semblance of gratitude for providing her free room and board. Host families don't get compensated, at least not with the program Mom and Dad agreed to. Every good deed deserves a stab in the back, I like to say. At least I might adopt the saying.

Tami invades Bevan's room, which my parents refer to now as 'our spare room' down a long hall from mine in the basement. I drop the large case on the floor at Tami's feet—considering she's at my heels.

"Do you need any help getting settled?" Mom squishes in behind me with the last of Tami's luggage.

Tami doesn't speak.

"Okay then." Mom pushes her hands down the front of her pants like there's dust to wipe off.

I feel that way now. I'd like to brush Tami out of our house like gathered dust, I don't like her. I'd much rather have Bevan to remind to wear his seizure helmet.

Mom backs out of the room. "Lunch should be ready in an hour, and dinner's at seven."

Mom grips my arm and pulls me out of the room with her. The second we clear the doorframe the hallow panel door closes inches from our noses.

I roll my eyes up to Mom in a 'well this was a terrible idea' fashion. "How long is this arrangement?"

"A year." Toothpaste and face wash mix in the air as she waves her head, as if she can shake off the weird first impressions. "Cultural differences...Also, jetlag can affect people in all kinds of ways—when you're over tired—you know how it is."

I've never experienced jetlag, having never traveled anywhere farther than Houston to visit an aunt once. I have no idea 'how it is'.

We stand together for a moment. For me it's the foreboding clarity of a year's long mistake. "Where's Howell?" We ask together. Because we hover when we worry. It's what we do, and right now we need reassuring habits.

Howell sleeps upstairs near my parents. He woke early today and ended up having a morning nap, so he wasn't there to greet Tami. I've never envied my three-year-old brother more.

His unmarked face is the most heartbreaking thing I've ever seen—especially when he sleeps. I can see it on Mom's face too. The ache of gratitude at having a perfect child. I know it's not supposed to hurt to see her smile down at Howell, but it does. So much.

Without Bevan around, all that hovering transferred to Howell—the youngest. A surprise baby thirteen years after my parents stopped having children out of fear they'd keep coming out with a perma-bruise and mental disorders. But, Howell is perfect. So perfect, I vowed to hate him for the first year of his life, but couldn't stick to it. He's too adorable.

School doesn't start for another fifteen days. Tami has been with us for three days and I've barely seen her outside the room we're now calling hers, but used to be Bevan's. It probably still smells like him too. Bevan always smelled of icy hot and sweat. Like an old guy trapped in jock's body. I miss Bevan.

It's not like we have a large home. The main floor consists of my parent's room, which doesn't even have a real master bathroom. There are two doors on their bathroom, which is why I hate using it. I'm terrified Mom or Dad might walk in from their room at any moment—too much stress while trying to relieve myself. I stick to the basement bathroom, which used to be mine.

The kitchen stretches hallway-style between the dining room and living room. I'm not sure that qualifies as open concept, or poor planning on the part of the home designer. The basement has two bedrooms and a large living space no one uses. In short, our house isn't somewhere a person can get lost or hideout—it's small. A wanna-be trailer.

None of my efforts work to get Tami to come out of her room. Standing in the dark hallway in the middle of the afternoon I consider flipping on the light, which goes against Dad's 'no electric lights during daylight hours' policy.

"Tami." I knock three times, not a demanding knock. More of a light rap I can't imagine any polite person would ignore. "Some kids from school are going to the fair tonight." I let my fist fall a little harder against the door. "You're invited." Bronze Town, New Mexico county fair isn't much to brag about, but it's something to do in a town where there's nothing to do.

As far as duties done, Mom can't get after me for not including Tami. I tried. It's not my fault she's anti-social. I walk away from the closed door, slapping the wall one time for good measure—marking the fact I've been here.

"Did you try opening the door?" Mom blocks my exit.

How long has she been standing there? "That would be an invasion of privacy."

"Lowry, I swear..." Mom lets the rest of the sentence smolder in her lungs as she pushes me aside and turns the knob on Tami's door. "Tami?" When there's no answer, she opens in further.

Curiosity gets the better of me. Peeking over Mom's shoulder, I see Tami's bed isn't even slept in. "Where is she?"

Mom shrugs and pushes the door until it hits the wall. When she steps in, I follow. We give the room a visual scan. It appears empty aside from the luggage on the floor. Tami hasn't moved any of it since she arrived. The large hard case lays open with a shirt hanging over the edge. It's the only sign of life.

"Tami?" Mom hesitates, like an unseen force prevents her from exploring more. I feel it too. Some energy that says, *you don't want to know why this room feels like a ghost town.* Mom faces me, or blocks me from the creepy space, I can't tell which. "Did you see her leave?"

I shake my head, no.

"Did you see her at breakfast?"

Again. No.

"Well. That's odd."

That's an understatement.

"I think we need to work harder to include Tami in family things," Mom says.

I gesture to the room with wide stretched arms. "How? We don't know where she is."

"She has to be somewhere."

I let my arms fall back to my sides, because Mom's right. Tami does have to be somewhere. The fact that none of us knows where that is, nor saw her go anywhere, concerns me. "Is this normal?"

Mom pulls her mouth to the side. A gesture I'm familiar with. It's her, *yikes, I should know this, but I don't, and I'm not going to admit anything because I'm the designated adult,* face. "Cultural differences, I bet." She shrugs like that's as good an answer as any. I can tell I'm going to hear that a lot.

I look around the room again and ache for a stronger icy hot scent in the air. I walk back to the door, the closet slides open the second I'm in the hall. Scraping in its track like the sharp end of a nail across a window pane—I expect something to break, yet it's quiet.

"Tami, what are you doing hiding in there?" Mom asks.

I stay in the hall, moving against the wall, where my clothes cling to the eggshell finish, and stick more than slide closer to the doorway. I can better eavesdrop.

I don't hear the broken English response from Tami, but the scuttle of her feet dragging on the carpet makes me suck in my stomach in an effort to be one with the wall. I feel like I'm standing on eggshells instead of merely pressing my back into the flat finish of the taupe paint.

"You don't have to be afraid. It's only a birthmark," Mom says from inside the room.

My face. Tami's afraid of me, like I'm some kind of monster? That's probably the reason she hasn't come out of her room for three days. I should be used to it—people being afraid of the way I look, but I'm not. Because usually people don't hide from me—it's not socially acceptable these days. Besides, I'm likeable most of the time.

With my back against the wall, I pound both fists so hard, that it pushes me forward. Both Mom and Tami pop their heads around the corner. Tami's eyes are so wide, I imagine them falling out of their sockets. But, I'm too upset to give it much more thought or really savor the horror of the idea.

I can tell Mom is stuck. She needs to smooth things over with Tami before she can make excuses for the person I now feel is our home invader. I stomp down the hall—wanting the sound to bounce around for hours—reminding everyone of the injustice of appearance-based judgment. The basement floor absorbs my anger into the carpet padding. I'm muted by my own house—betrayed by where I sleep.

I slam my bedroom door—happy with the wall-shaking tremor sure to short a few lights from wires shaking behind the walls. Dad's going to be pissed. That's the last thing I need. I text Bevan.

Did you have to leave? I hate it here without you.

Bevan never was good with his phone. I imagine him poking at a black screen once he gets the chime that he has a message. I doubt I'll get a response, even if Bevan does figure out how to open his message app.

I cover my face with a pillow and fall face first onto the bed. It's not long before I hear knocking at the door. "Lowry, make sure to include Tami with your friends tonight." There's a pause before Mom taps her nails against the door. "It'll be good for you both to spend time together."

I doubt that. Besides, there's enough going on at the fair, I can avoid Tami all night. If I'm lucky, we'll lose her in a crowd of tourists and my year can go back to worrying about Bevan and Howell.

Is there room for Tami, my family's exchange student? I text Sara.

Sara's family, the Nelsons, have six adopted kids from Haiti, in addition to their two biological kids, and a thirteen passenger van we use for friend outings. I know there'll be room, but secretly hope Sara gained seven new friends over the summer, one for every unclaimed seatbelt.

No prob. It'll be great for her to get to know more kids before school starts. Good thinking, Lowry. You're the best. <3

It's so like Sara to give me credit for something my mom's forcing me to do. Sara always sees the best in people. I wish what she thought of me was always the truth. Sometimes, hanging out with Sara, I feel like a better person. Like she's some sort of fairy godmother of goodwill. I could use some of that magic tonight.

A new text from Sara comes in, making me jump because I thought our exchange was over.

Head's up, the boys are coming with us too.

'The boys' means Derrick Faulkner and his best friend Nathaniel Holme. Derrick's on everyone's 'datably-hot' list. Nathaniel isn't. However, the fact Derrick is best friends with the most annoying Junior in high school, Nathaniel, adds even more hot points. I'm a sucker for good looking guys with heart. I roll onto my back, keeping the pillow over my face so it traps the sigh that escapes when I think of spending the evening with Derrick.

What this really means—I should be on my best behavior. I don't want to be caught complaining about weird-Tami in front of someone like Derrick. Knowing him, befriending culturally backwards exchange students tops his to-do list.

No pressure.

However, if anyone can see past my face-stain to the heart of who I am on the inside, it's Derrick. I wish I was good looking on the outside too, like him. The whole package. I text Sara again.

Sounds fun.

What I really mean is, *sounds like a chance for me to humiliate myself.*

We'll split a funnel cake and laugh if any carnies try to hit on us. A whole new start. And it feels like it really could be. Thank goodness for friends like Sara. I know tonight will be good. Better than good—it'll be great.

Fifteen minutes before five I get a text from Sara.

On our way.

She must already have a van-full, including 'the boys.' Nerves strike before I'm ready for them. I have no plan for how not to act like an idiot in front of Derrick. I want him to like me, not pity me because of my face and the new person who seems to have a problem with it. There's a big difference between liking someone for their personality and *liking someone.*

My stomach growls. Not wanting to embarrass myself in front of Derrick, I pour a bowl of milk and a glass of cereal. I hate soggy cereal. I add cereal to the milk three times before emptying the glass.

"Tami!" I shout, while finishing off the bowl.

Tami slinks from behind the wall at the top of the stairs. Like she's been watching me this whole time? My spine tingles.

"You look cute," Mom says entering the kitchen from the living room. Mom nods toward Tami, cuing her to speak. It's like living in a marionette stage with Mom pulling all our strings.

"I like your shoe." Tami sounds like a robotic compliment program.

I have on my rattiest Chuck Taylors. It's the fair after all. My feet are going to get muddy. It looks like I'm wearing huge mud clods as it is. Mom forgot to talk about how to pretend to sound sincere when they discussed giving compliments. "Thanks," I say after way too much time for anyone to believe I mean it. Then I notice how Mom eyes me expectantly, leaning and twitching toward Tami while staring at me. I look from Mom to Tami. "You look cute."

Awkward doesn't fade. Every pause, pregnant with an expectation for one of us to speak. No one does. It's a nightmare. Why isn't Sara here yet?

A honk sounds. "That's got to be Sara."

Mom puffs a stale breath of relief. "Thank the stars."

Tami stands stiff-backed and walks out the door before me.

"This is going to be fun," I say to Mom.

"Be nice."

"Me?" I tip my head to the road, because how on earth does she think the weirdness originates from me? "Don't you mean single-white-exchange student over there?" (Referencing an old movie my Mom thinks is scary and loves to watch every Halloween called 'Single-White-Female,' where some crazy chick moves in on some other chick's life).

"You need to let it go—" Mom shakes her head and puts up both hands. "Have you even seen the movie you're referencing? You never watch it with me."

"If it hasn't been remade in the last two years, then no." The point in making an old-timey reference is that Mom gets it, how does she not know that?

"Well. I guarantee, that movie is not what this is."

I close the open front door even though Tami's already in the van. Everyone is waiting on me, staring at the side of my face to see what kind of parental-warning I'm getting right now.

"She's homesick," Mom says.

"Did she tell you that?"

"She didn't have to. And—and." Mom leans closer like she's confiding something, which she isn't. "It's scary being in a different country around different social norms, and where everyone speaks a language you barely understand. Not to mention jetlag."

"Mom, Helen said they've been stateside for two weeks going through some cultural prep—unless jetlag lasts a month."

Mom chews her cheek thinking.

A car door opens, I peek around it to see Sara standing in the driver's side—up on the floorboards so she can give me the 'what's up' arm gesture over the top of the van. I put up my hand and nod to Mom, but only to end this now. "I get it. Point made. I'll make sure she has the best night at the county fair any foreigner has ever had."

"You don't have to over sell it."

I'm already out the door. In the van, I see Tami has selected the backmost seat—where no one else sits. Very a-social, if you ask me. I have no idea if I'm supposed to climb back there with her, choose to sit between Derrick and Nathaniel, or squish next to Lacy, Violet, and Jenn. Sara's brother Max has the passenger seat, he's in our grade, but he's not twins with Sara, he's adopted. And he's hot. "Max, can I have shotgun?" Please save me from this bench seat roulette.

"Sure." He hops back with Tami, making me look like a jerk. I'm hoping I only feel like a jerk and no one else thinks I'm the worst person ever—avoiding sitting next to her at all costs.

Sara raises her eyebrows at me. I put a hand up and her brows go down. The topic of van seating will come up later. Maybe I can use my crush on Derrick to explain. Throwing crushes around usually works for an excuse whenever I act stupid. And, I can trust Sara not to say anything about who I'm fake-crushing on. In this case it's real, but I'm using it in a fake way.

We pass the sign that says, 'Welcome to Bronze Town.' I often wonder if the name of our town was a joke, or a dare. We aren't far from Silver City, where they mined real silver once. But, bronze isn't mined, it's an alloy made from copper and tin.

We're a self-made town that never got larger than twenty-six thousand people. The fair likes to capitalize on the bronze theme. Everything gets treated like an alloy. We mix different ethnic foods and slap rap with country twang for dance music until everything shares the same qualities.

Sara takes two parking spaces even though the thirteen passenger van claims the same length as an extended cab truck and totally fits in a single spot. We all pile out and discuss where people want to eat.

"Funnel Chinese," Nathaniel says referring to a booth that offers Chinese rice, funnel cakes, and jalapeño poppers.

I cringe—wondering if using the term 'Chinese,' though it's about food, offends or not. It's not Japanese so it shouldn't upset Tami because it doesn't represent her, right? I have no idea what's okay or politically correct. Her face remains inscrutably passive.

"How about BBQ, fries, and everything fatty," I offer. The name written across the banner literally makes up the cuisine. BBQ sandwiches served alongside other fried things, including Twinkies, Snickers, Oreos, pickles—everything.

"I want ice cream, that's it," Sara says. Most of the girls coo and nod in agreement with Sara. "I'm pretty sure there's a non-GMO ice cream booth."

"I've been starving all day so I could gorge here," I say.

"You eat three times," Tami says holding up her fingers in case no one understood her heavy accent.

"No." Have I mentioned how Tami is the worst? She's the worst. "I had one bowl of cereal, which I poured milk into three times, because I can't stand soggy cereal."

"She does that," Sara confirms, then laughs. "She's eaten breakfast at my house before." Everyone else laughs too, because for some reason, having an aversion to soggy breakfast food equals hilarity.

"How about we split up?" Derrick suggests. "Everyone who wants Chinese and jalapeño poppers come with Nathaniel and me." Dang it. Me and my big mouth, I already declared I didn't want to go there. I was sort of hoping we'd end up at the same place—like we'd be the only two people who desperately needed BBQ and bond over it or something romantic. "BBQ is with Lori." He doesn't even know my name? "And ice cream—follow Sara."

Everyone files into three groups. Somehow, I end up with Max. Just Max. Without Sara... weird. Even though Max is my age, I feel like I'm hanging out with Sara's hot younger brother. Gross.

Also, Derrick doesn't know my freaking name and no one bothered to correct him. Not even Sara, who usually has my back. She probably didn't notice because she was standing across the whole group from Derrick, but still.

I consider going with Sara to get ice cream and bailing on solid food, so I can complain about the whole 'not knowing my name thing' to Sara, except Tami's there and I can't. Also, I'd be leaving Max without a chow buddy. I can't whine to Sara about it until much later.

He doesn't know my name...

"Come on, Max. Let's fill our sorrows with well-seasoned meat."

"Now you're talking," Max says.

Please Fate, don't let me have more in common with Sara's hot brother, Max than with good-looking, kind-hearted Derrick. Nathaniel waves to everyone as they stride toward the, likely culturally offensive, Chinese food. I still have no idea if it's offensive or not, but after the day I've had, I don't want to risk it by eating there in front of Tami—who isn't Chinese.

Being culturally sensitive, as Mom warned me, is a major burden. It's destroying my potential-dating life.

4

"How's life at the UN?" Max asks. He doesn't have an accent per se, but he always sounds like he's on the verge of yawning whenever he talks. I figure it's the Haitian in him and it only adds to his hot factor, which I'm doing my best to ignore. We grew up together, he's practically my brother. He and Bevan used to spend as much time together as Sara and me, except they were always in trouble while Sara earned recognition for charity work.

"Huh?"

"You know, since you guys are now an international household—sort of like our house, but less permanent."

I hadn't thought about how adoption compares to exchange students. It doesn't, does it? I can't imagine Sara once thinking of her adopted siblings the way I've been viewing Tami—*an invasion*. Max is adopted. His midnight skin used to stand out to me in this mildly tanned town, but I've spent so much time with him, I only see Max now.

"I'm no diplomat." I order the philly pulled-pork cheese and peppers with horseradish dressing and a side of home fries. I hesitate a moment, watching Max stare at the items listed for sale and add fried pickles and snickers to my order.

"Nice." Max slides a fifty-dollar bill to the window clerk. "I'll have the same exact thing," he tells the kid taking our orders. "I'm paying for both meals."

"No way, that's a twenty-five-dollar order," I say. Fair food costs a buttload, but it's only once a year, so we all suck it up and fork out the dough.

Max shrugs and doesn't ask for change. I'm grateful, but also, I loathe feeling like I owe people. Money is one of those uncomfortable things.

"Your order will be ready in fifteen minutes," the window attendant says.

"Cool." Max walks to a covered pavilion where people eat on picnic tables. The evening sun makes the whole 'covered' section pointless, shining with August heat below the roofline. We sit with our backs to the sun. "So... Tami..."

My friends are all super nice people. The kind of people who can look at the purple mark across my face and not cringe. They aren't the kind of people to badmouth others, which means they aren't the kind of people who tolerate that either. "She's alright."

"She doesn't like me," Max says.

I sit a little taller. It's not like anyone in Sara's family to speak this way. "Why do you say that?"

"I'm pretty sure she made the Buddhist equivalent of the cross when I sat next to her in the van."

"I don't think there is one."

"Yeah, I was being polite. She scooted away from me and stared out the window without speaking when I tried to start a conversation."

"My mom says she's homesick."

"Has she ever been around a black dude before?"

My eyes go wide and I look around the area, like the word 'black' threatens to flag us as bigots. "You can't say that."

Max leans in and speaks in his quietest pre-yawn tone. "I'm black. I can say lots of things."

"Honestly, I have no idea what she's been around." I take a second to contemplate what Max will think of me if I continue this conversation. "She called me a monster."

He pushes the table so hard I think the seat, bolted to the table top, might break away. "She what?"

I put a hand on his shoulder, and then remove it as quickly, because yikes—this is Max, not some guy from school. "It's nothing. She just..." I point to the deformity across my face. "Has never seen anyone like me before."

"She's lucky Bevan isn't home. He'd pound her for talking to you like that."

"No he wouldn't." Bevan's the gentlest person on earth unless Max influences him, partly why Mom and I hover. He needed protecting and probably still does. Worry stirs inside me at the thought of him out on his own.

"Maybe not. But he'd tell me, and I'd pound her."

That I believe. "You're not going to do anything," I tell him. "She just got here, she's still adjusting." I hear my words and wonder if Max somehow tricked me into sticking up for Tami. Maybe I drank too much Neilson water over the years. I'm giving people the benefit of the doubt.

Max nods and stands up. "Our food's ready."

He returns with two overflowing paper baskets. It doesn't look like fifty dollars' worth of food, but it still looks like more than I should eat in one sitting. The heavy grease aroma hangs in the air, coating my skin in oily heaven.

"Thanks for dinner. I'll get your tickets for the rides."

"No need. I have a job now." He smiles. Max's teeth are extra white. I don't know if it's the toothpaste he uses or the way his skin contrasts against them, but he seems brighter than most other boys.

"Oh yeah? Where are you working?"

"Apprenticing with the Johns. Drywall work."

"A trade. Nice." Around here no one holds a grudge against the less educated so long as they work hard and can support a family. Trades accomplished all that. Lots of family men work trades in our town, serving the bigger cities filled with people who frame law degrees and medical licenses. "I'll know who to call if I ever punch a hole in the wall and don't want my parents to find out."

Max lifts his eyebrows and laughs. "Yeah. Definitely I can help."

"I'm still covering your carnie rides."

"If that makes you happy."

We bite into our sandwiches and stop talking, because it's that good. I finish mine before Max, a little embarrassing, but he doesn't notice. I wait for him to finish before digging into my fried snickers. It's been sitting a while so the chocolate inside isn't as gooey as I want, but it's still sinfully rich. I eat my fried pickles after half the candy bar sweets-me-out, and then return to the fried sugar to end on a sweet note.

My name pierces the buzz of the crowd—causing both Max and I to look up from our food coma. Sara and Violet come running toward Max and I panic-hollering my name. My first thought: Tami has done something to offend everyone.

Sara reaches us before Violet. "We lost her." She stops to catch her breath. "We've looked everywhere we can think of."

"Lost who?" Max asks.

I've already guessed: Tami.

"We were standing in line—it was huge," Sara says before Violet cuts her off.

"It's so hot, of course ice cream is going to be what everyone wants to eat."

"And we were all talking about which classes we have in common this semester," Sara says.

"It's not like we didn't try to include Tami. We did. Sara asked questions and everything, but she turned her back to us and watched people walk by."

Sara nods. "Yeah, and so I kept talking to the other girls because I thought, maybe I was overwhelming her by talking too fast." See there's Sara giving Tami the benefit of the doubt again. I definitely need to be more like Sara. "But, then when I turned back to try to include Tami again—she was gone."

"Like vanished," Violet says swiping both arms in front of her to show how absent Tami was when they turned around. "In seconds, I swear."

"Have you checked with Derrick?" Max asks.

"No," Violet says.

"I thought you said you checked everywhere." Max grabs my basket along with his and walks to the trash like there's no emergency.

Sara follows Max, but continues facing me, like she can't figure out who she has to explain herself to. "We checked the women's bathrooms, the van, the ticket counter."

"That's hardly everywhere," Max says and walks back.

"The fair is huge." Violet throws her arms in the air again.

"Let's check with Derrick first."

Sara looks at me. "First? First what? What's second?"

"I don't know—losing our minds, and me getting grounded, or arrested, or whatever happens when you lose a foreign exchange student."

"Oh my gosh, I'm so sorry, Lowry." Tears glisten at the corner of Sara's eyes. Max gives her a side hug.

"It's not your fault." I hope Mom doesn't think it's mine. "I'm sure she's fine." Then I consider the time. We waited forever in line, waited for our food, and had time to eat it. "Did you finish ordering and eating your ice cream?"

"Well..." Violet stammers. "The line was so long, and at first we thought she maybe went to the bathroom and would come back."

"We seriously thought she'd show up." Sara interjects.

"That line. I did not want to start the wait all over again for ice cream," Violet says.

"It's okay," I say, but to be honest, I'm a little upset they stayed in line after they knew Tami was missing. "Where's Lacy?"

"She volunteered to check with Derrick and Nathaniel." Sara gets very excited all of a sudden, while I'm miffed she never mentioned that part until now. "Maybe Lacy found Tami and they're all laughing about it right now."

"That'd be great." All I can think about is Derrick and Lacy winning homecoming royalty. I shake my head and remind myself that this isn't about me, at least it isn't up to the point that we really can't find Tami. If it comes to that, it's about how badly I failed at international relations three days in.

Nathaniel runs up to Sara before the group merges. "Did you find her?" He's breathing so heavily I wonder if he's personally been running around the fairgrounds searching for Tami.

"No. We were hoping she was with you," Violet says.

Nathaniel runs both hands through his hair and scans random directions in a haphazard circle. Lacy and Derrick walk up together. I notice how their hands almost touch when they swing their arms, not where my focus should be right now.

"Has anyone contacted the authorities?" Derrick asks.

"Lost and found." Nathaniel sticks his hands in his pockets, but it doesn't help. The night has triggered his anxiety. His whole body shakes like a ball of nervous energy.

"Nathaniel," I say. "I'm so sorry you're upset, but this is my fault. I should've mentioned that it's not okay to wonder off—that it's too easy to lose someone in big crowds—and." I spin and scan the overcrowded fields and booths. "She doesn't know anyone. I mean, where would she go?"

"It's not your fault. It's mine," Sara says.

"Taking blame won't help." Max steps forward. "Right now we need to find Tami."

"I should've stayed with her." I ignore Max, because there's no way I'm letting Sara claim blame on this. "What was I thinking?"

"I know what Max was thinking," Derrick jabs an elbow toward Lacy the way two guys joke with each other and I relax a little more than I was two minutes ago.

"Hey, not my fault you two can't do math," Max says with both hands up in surrender.

"What does that mean?" Derrick's smile drops along with his jabby elbow.

We are obviously not experienced at panic-mode productivity. Time keeps ticking by, but I kind of want to know what Max means, so I don't rush anyone.

"It means there are two girls to every guy in our group, yet I'm the only one who had dinner with someone of the opposite sex who I'm also not related to."

"Yeah, but you're practically like her brother," Sara says giving me the side-eye.

The best comfort I can offer, a different subject. "Should we split up? Or... I don't know, call an amber alert? I have no idea what to do right now."

"We'll check the rides," Derrick offers.

"We've got booths and free events," Sara says slapping my shoulder. "Violet, why don't you and Max check the animal barn."

"What do I do?" Nathaniel shifts from one foot and back to the other.

"You're with me, Nathaniel," Derrick says. Nathaniel sheds a layer of anxiety like a winter jacket.

"If anyone finds Tami, text the whole group, okay?" I lift my phone in the air, like it's some kind of game plan. Everyone nods and we break.

Sara and I walk from booth to booth asking if anyone has seen a short Asian girl who doesn't speak much English. None of us knows much about Tami as a person, so we lack a lot of detail in how best to ask questions. Other than stereotypes, like the fact she has a digital camera and a phone, which I want to avoid, I don't know how to describe her other than 'Asian' without sounding like a culturally insensitive jerk. It's not easy.

After inquiring along an entire row of booths, Sara asks, "So, what's with you and Max?'

"Max?" My voice cracks a little and starts way too high. "Like what? What do you mean? *Max.*" Now my voice drops so low it cracks again. "Nothing's with... Nothing. Why? What do you mean? I mean... He's Bevan's best friend, and your brother. So, if you mean, what's with that..."

"I mean, you're acting weird."

"No. Weird. Me? Weird? No."

"Okay cool. Just wanted to make sure."

"I mean, he is like—Olympic sprinter hot."

"Lowry, I knew it. You think my brother's hot. Gross."

"No." Yes, I do. Everyone does. But, Sara's more important to me than her hot brother. "I'm just saying, he's not the worst. You know?" The truth is, if she'd have asked me earlier today via text if I thought Max was hot, I would have said 'gross' and meant it. But, after spending some one-on-one time over dinner, it's hard not to think about how Max has muscles that flex with every movement he makes. Even his muscles have muscles, smaller, tighter ones that stretch across each other in a way that only professional athletes have developed.

"Actually, he has gotten into running over the summer." Sara says. "He's pretty good probably. I don't know, the track coach said he should train for a running scholarship or something."

"Way to make college sound like torture, Coach." We both laugh then continue down the rows asking about a missing girl. I'm putting off texting Mom as long as I can, but my phone weighs bricks in my pocket.

We make it through all the booths, which goes faster than I thought it would, then move on to check the free events under the big top. It's really a massive overhead cover tethered to the ground like a picnic fly with rows and rows of wooden pews, like the kind in a large old-fashioned church building, set in front of a portable stage.

Sara and I walk the middle row as if we're attendants in a wedding, step-stopping to glance down each row of benches. Some people look like they could be Tami from the side, then turn to reveal facial hair.

"We're never going to find her in this crowd," Sara says.

"Unless she knows we're looking for her—or if she was looking for us."

"What do you mean?"

"We announce over the loud speaker, that she's to meet us." Why didn't I think of this before? "We post someone at a single location and announce for Tami to meet there. The rest of us can continue searching."

"Why would we need to keep searching? If we tell her to meet, she'll meet right."

"Unless she can't hear the announcement."

"Or if she's been kidnapped," I say.

"Not helpful."

We locate the booth in the center of the grounds. The announcement goes over the loud speakers at the same time I push send. The guy at the booth says he'll replay the announcement every fifteen minutes for one hour.

Derrick responds that they'll meet us, having finished checking the rides. Max texts that they'll meet up once they're done with the animal pens.

"This'll work," I say, then grip Sara's arm. "What if this doesn't work? I'm in so much trouble. What do you think the punishment is for someone who fights with, ditches, and then loses an international visitor?" I imagine Mom's wrath slicing through driving privileges, nights out with friends, homecoming—maybe as far out as prom, which isn't until Spring. "I'll be grounded forever. My life is over."

"We won't let that happen," Max jokes as he and Violet appear next to us. Soon we're all huddled together going over the next game plan on 'where in the fair is Tami Watanabe.'

"Someone said they spotted like five Asian kids hanging out near the animal pens, all hush-hush or something when they walked past." The way Violet shares information resembles an undercover informant who could be discovered as a double agent any moment.

"Tami doesn't know anybody except us. There's no way she would have been with a whole group of people," I say.

Violet throws her arms in the air and lets them fall back dramatically. Max bites his lower lip, but says nothing to dissuade Violet's irritation with me. "I've explained this to Max like five times already—what is wrong with you people? She must have run into more Asians."

Sara's eyes get very large—like we're all standing in a spotlight and we have taboo slime all over us. "I don't think it works like that, Vi."

"How do you know she doesn't know anyone else?" Violet asks.

"People don't magically know everyone who hails from the same country as them," I say, trying to avoid any red-flag words, like 'race' or 'culture.' I'll be honest, I'm not even sure what a no-no word or term is, I'm fairly certain there are some and I'm trying desperately to avoid them.

"Maybe being similar is a conversation starter and then they become fast friends," Violet says.

"I think you described a movie," Max says. "'How to pick up friends without the complications of a sit-down relationship."

Lacy slaps Max lightly on the back of the shoulder. Her fingers linger a moment longer than necessary. "That's silly." Does she have to touch every guy here?

"Nothing." Derrick shows empty palms as further proof. Nathaniel does too.

"We can't stay at the fair now," I say. "I have to get home and face Mom—find out how much trouble I'm in and how to organize a search party." I'm half-joking, or hope I'm joking. I silently pray it doesn't come to that, but now it's all I can think about. "This is awful."

"Worst night at the fair ever," Violet says. I'd like to make fun of her 'fast-friends' remark, but it would only make things worse.

"I'll drive you, and I can come back to pick up anyone who wants to stay," Sara offers. "That way no one's night has to be ruined."

Violet glances toward Max and brightens, and Lacy stares at Derrick without apology for how obvious she's being. Blink, Lace, blink. Sara must notice the pairings as well, but instead of disgust, there's that 'aww' look on her face. I'm betrayed! Sara gives these couples a chance to hang out, one-on-one, like a date-date. No! We're a team, a group.

There should be no pairing off, besides where does that leave me and Sara? Splitting Nathaniel? We might as well buy leashes and give Derrick our leads for all the good that would do. ... That's not a terrible idea.

Neither Derrick nor Max seem to notice what's happening with Violet and Lacy's longing gazes. I could hug them both.

"There's no way I could enjoy the fair without everyone here—one of us is missing." Max includes Tami with 'us.' "We either find Tami, or the night is ruined for everyone." Sara kicks Max's shoe, and I don't think it's because he lumped Tami into our group.

"I agree," Derrick says with a forceful nod, more of a head punch then a nod. Nathaniel copies Derrick's head-butt style nod and the other girls kick the grass and trudge along behind us.

Sara unlocks the van. A wave of hot air spills out as the first door opens. Once two are open a nice cross draft alleviates some of the furnace affect.

"Why doesn't Max drive?" Violet asks, hopping in the passenger seat.

"You want to tell them?" Sara asks Max with a snicker. She retains the keys and sits behind the wheel.

"I'm grounded," Max mumbles.

"He backed over the mailbox yesterday," Sara says. "He's grounded from driving for a week."

"I paid for the damages—Mom and Dad are being completely unreasona—" Max stops talking mid-climb into the back of the van. "I found Tami."

We all freeze—remembering we're at the van because of Tami and not there to joke about driving privileges. The seriousness of the moment feels dirty somehow because of our laughter seconds before.

"Tami?" I hold back an accusing shout—my words still come out strong. "What the heck? Where did you go? Why didn't you say anything?" I take Max's place in the vehicle doorway. "You can't take-off without saying something. What is wrong with you?"

"Whoa," Sara says. She's come around the van and stands behind me. "Let's not accuse her of doing anything wrong."

Sometimes Sara's good nature borders throat-punch worthy—like right now. "Who does that, Sara? Who takes off and doesn't say anything, and just... Never comes back?"

"She's in the van." Sara points out. "She came back to the van."

"Maybe she couldn't find us—I mean, we did just meet," Violet says.

"I don't believe this," I say.

"Didn't you lock the van?" Max asks Sara. She looks at the keys in her hand, then at the open door, then at the keys again.

"Yeah, I think so. I usually do."

"How'd she get in?" I ask. "She obviously got inside a locked vehicle —isn't that breaking and entering? That's wrong, isn't it?"

"Maybe I forgot to lock it." Sara continues to give Tami the benefit of the doubt.

Right now, I'd like to give Tami a one-way ticket back to wherever she came from. "You forgot an annoying habit like locking your Mom's van?"

"How is that an annoying habit?" Sara asks.

Max pulls me out from the door and playfully shoves Sara back with his other hand. "The point is—we found Tami, and she's safe. Now what?" There's still a sliver of sunlight on the horizon, plenty of romantic-evening fair left to enjoy. Violet and Lacy both suck in a hopeful breath.

"I'm done. I'm going home," I say.

"It kind of feels over," Derrick says with a shrug.

This time Max nods along with Nathaniel, much less forcefully than Derrick had earlier. Lacy rolls her eyes, probably having forgotten that there's still enough light for all of us to see her face. We pile in the van. I sit next to Tami, though I don't want to. Once home, I thank Sara before escaping inside my house.

When we arrive home hours earlier than expected, Mom stands at the door with her arms crossed. For a second I think she won't let us inside until we've spent the undeclared, undefined, and impossible to achieve 'approved hours of fun' together. Tami walks passed Mom, to her room, and shuts the door—not a slam, a nice quiet closure. Mom uncrosses her arms and focuses her eyes on me.

"I didn't do anything."

"Something happened."

Something called Tami. "She hid out in the van the whole time."

"In that heat?" Mom's voice rises to panic level. I hadn't thought about that. Sitting in the van in that heat, that long—I'm pretty sure it wouldn't be good. People have died in overheated vehicles.

"Is she okay?" Mom asks.

"I don't know." I really don't. I didn't even bother to ask Tami if everything was okay, or why she ran off in the first place. I was so busy being mad at her, that I didn't do anything right. Sara was right about not jumping to conclusions. I have no idea why Tami did what she did, or if she's okay now.

"I better go check on her." Mom grabs a water bottle from the fridge and trips in her rush down the stairs. She catches herself and continues to Tami's room.

I stay upstairs and check on Howell, who's sleeping peacefully. Waking him, so I have someone to talk to, would be the wrong thing to do. I wish he would wake up all on his own. I need a Howell hug. Instead I close his door until right before the latch clicks and turn on the living room TV. I don't want to go to sleep with all the weird ideas rolling around in my head and not knowing which side of the line my actions are on.

Am I the bad guy tonight? Why'd Lacy keep touching Derrick and Max? Can't she pick one guy? Is Tami okay? Was she really in a dangerously hot van for over two hours? Where else would she have been? Is all of this because she's foreign and I'm misreading her social norms, or is there something fundamentally wrong with her? I don't even know if I'm allowed to think like that. I'm certain I can't ask any of my questions.

I let the cold glow of TV wash over me until a commercial comes on and I can't recall what program I'm watching, and then go to bed.

School starts next Tuesday. It's in the air like a weight filled with explosive-laden standardized tests. Except, No one sets off fireworks celebrating school starting. Being grounded, I'm barred from pre-torture teen-debauchery.

Other than responding to overly concerned texts from Sara, to which I assured her that *school will be fine, class schedule mix-ups will all be ironed out the first week, no one dies of test-pre-anxiety, junior year is probably not the defining chapter in our lives upon which all other chapters will be judged...yes I'm fine and Tami's fine,* (like I would know).

Tami returns to a room dweller. I only see her at evening meals, and even then—it's not like we talk. I have no actual connection to anyone at the moment. Being grounded equals depression and closed doors and embarrassment.

Thursday night during dinner Mom announces. "Dad's off work tomorrow, so we're taking a girls' day."

I let go of my fork. It falls on top of my chicken and rice. "A what?" Mom has never taken me on anything called a 'girls' day' before. I suspect it's some ploy to try to get Tami and me to spend time together.

Mostly I know I'm right about this because fifteen minutes later, when Tami returns to her room and we all hear the door close. Mom turns to me and says, "She's hiding in her room all the time because she doesn't feel welcome." Mom—expert at reasons people do weird things,

I guess. I'd ask her for more clairvoyant insights into life, but I'm too peeved. It's like Mom thinks it's my fault Tami's a whackadoo.

"That's not my fault."

"Partly." Mom takes my plate, even though I'm not finished. Dad doesn't do a thing to save my food from the disposal. He's too busy battling Howell to eat. "You haven't invited her to spend time with you or your friends since that night at the fair."

Stomping my feet, shoving my chair back until it hits the wall, I shout, "I've been grounded."

"Keep your voices down," Dad says in a bored tone like he's used to Mom and me fighting and doesn't want to invest in either side.

Howell takes advantage of the fact Dad's distracted and shoves his plastic plate off the table. It crashes to the floor, flipping rice bits and chicken chunks in a wide spray.

"Howie!" Dad yells, jumping away from the mess.

"You're going shopping with us," Mom points a finger at me, ignoring the mess all over the room. "We are going to find bargains, and bond, you hear me?" She drops dishes into the sink and leaves the kitchen.

"You're not going to help?" Dad calls after her, referring to the chicken and rice mess. "Abby!" I stand to retreat to my own room while he's calling Mom back. "No way, you grab a paper towel and help me clean this up."

"Ugh. Howie!" I get a paper towel from the sink. "I wish I could act like a three-year-old again."

"Who says you ever quit?" Dad asks. He tries to hold a straight face, like he means it, but ends up cracking a smile and I know everything's fine between us. It's Mom I'm unsure about.

All night long I worry about how strained it's going to be shopping with Tami-the-non-English-speaking-robot. I can't sleep. When I do sleep, I dream about Howell choking, coughing, gagging. I reach out to find him, help him, save him... But he's never within reach, or a glass wall slips between us creating a barrier.

"Howie." I wake, sweat sticky against my neck, catching my hair. This is what happens when the first half of my life is dedicated to worrying about Bevan—invented reasons to worry when he's gone.

My phone shines five am when I poke it.

"Five? Seriously? Why am I awake?" My brain stalls on Howie, like some kind of bad omen has alerted me to his need, and if I don't check on him some unknown horror will fall from the sky directly into his room.

I throw the covers aside and stumble to adjust to the darkness. I don't want to wake up the whole house. When I open my bedroom door something is immediately off. Light. Window-light. I peek back toward my room—the curtains drawn, only a chalk line of moonlight brushes my floor. Tami's room down the hall floods with moonlight—even weirder—her door gapes wide open, bed made, it looks never slept in, and a cold breeze from that direction ruffles my pajama pants.

Everything inside of me screams NOT to go down the hall and check what's going on. So I don't. It's freaking scary down there. Leaving the lights off, I take the stairs two at a time and run through the kitchen without stopping to peek under tables or around corners. I have to make sure Howie's okay. Then I can sleep.

His bedroom door hangs open too. Mom never leaves his door open, because he wanders out when she does. My feet stop moving before my head tells them to, jarring the upper half of me.

Why is Howie's door open?

Moonlight creeps over his toddler bed, stretching toward the top of the covers. I step, one foot in front of the other trying to prevent any sound from escaping between the sole of my foot and the carpeted floor. My hands pat the air. I mouth 'sh,' 'sh,' sh,' with every step.

Straining my eyes into the darkness, I try to determine a Howie bulge under the space-themed covers. I'm almost to his door, close enough to see the lump on his bed is a pillow, not a three-year-old. My heart pounds so fiercely against my chest I think for sure I'm having a heart attack at the age of sixteen.

My ears fill like I've shot too high in elevation and all that's around me are screaming winds. I want to call out to Howie, but I'm scared. And I don't want any part of my dream to come true, except I was scared in my dream... So maybe it already has.

"Howie." My loud whisper comes out hoarse and angry.

Scuffling and movement within his room brings me back to that one-time Mom made me watch Labyrinth where creepy little Muppets steal a whiny girl's step-brother. Nobody has permission to come anywhere near my baby brother.

Contemplating what to do next, my throat seals up. My voice so tight, I shake the words out. "Howie, is that you?"

A small shadow slides into view as if hinged to the curve of the wall.

"What the..." I stop myself from pouncing—my monster-filled brain continues to conjure terrors in the darkness, but it's Howie. Standing in his room in the middle of the night, with the light off. Yeah, it's still a little creepy.

Howie's silhouette points a chubby little finger toward his bed.

"Yes, buddy. You need to get to bed."

He shakes his shadowed head no and points again to his bed.

"You want me to tuck you in?" And draw your curtains? There's something eerie about moonlight.

Howie shakes his head no again. His fat fingers extend out toward the bed.

"You afraid?"

His hand drops.

"Here's a deal, Bud. I'll check under your bed and in your closet for luck, and then you'll go to bed."

Howie nods.

I flip his light on. "Why are you out of bed anyway?" I walk to the edge of his bed and grab a hunk of covers to lift, before bending to check underneath. "Don't you know what time it is?" Cold black eyes, not fully open, and angled in a way that makes me feel I've had daggers pulled on me, stare back from under the low bed. I scream and drop the covers.

Lifting Howie, and not thinking, I run him to the living room in the dark, and set him on the couch—*because that's way safer... A thing* is in the house. Nowhere remains safe.

Feet pad against the floor behind me. I stand straight and spin, in time to see Tami turn a corner and disappear. Next I hear the thunk of her feet descending the stairs, followed by the forceful, yet not slammed, closure of a basement door.

My mouth open—my chest rises and falls like I've run three miles. I side-step to a wall and flip the living room light on, even though there's nothing there anymore. Howell rubs his eyes, and climbs down from the couch. He kisses my thigh, because that's as high as he can reach and rests his head on my leg before uttering his version of 'love you, good night,' which is more 'wuvooniygh' than anything. He then returns to his room at a slow trudge.

I can't move.

Minutes pass before my breathing regulates. I back up until the couch hits my calves and collapse onto the cushions. Howell's door closes. I stand and rush to the hall, knock on his door, open it a crack. "Hey, Buddy, are you alright?"

His speech ability so latent, it's hard to know if he responds, "play' or 'pay' or 'pray'... It doesn't really matter, does it?

"I mean. Bud." I pause for him to look at me. "Are you scared of Tami?" I drop my voice to a whisper. Knowing her room falls directly below his and right now I'm paranoid she has a glass to her ceiling, listening to everything I'm asking. Howell shakes his head no, rubs his eyes again—really demonstrating fatigue—and pulls his covers all the way over his head.

"I'll get your curtains, Howie. You don't have to sleep under the covers." At the window, I see the glow of light stretch across the lawn from the window below. I pull the curtains—wishing there was a second set to close. I want to shut everything about Tami out of this house.

I return to the living room and stop before going into the kitchen. I'm not sleeping downstairs tonight. I want to guard the hall and make sure Howell's room remains undisturbed. I hope he can get some sleep before official morning. I know I won't.

7

The couch is deceptively uncomfortable to sleep on. Before last night, I never noticed the wooden beam where the seat and back cushions meet. Granted, I never had a reason to sleep on our couch instead of my bed either. I kept getting sucked into that hole with the hard-wooden bar against my hip.

"You slept on the couch?" Mom's voice is the first thing I hear in the morning.

On the verge of explaining the whole 'Tami is a weirdo night-stalker', I hear dishes clinking with use. One glance at the kitchen table reveals Howell eating breakfast next to Tami. Tami doesn't look at the spoon entering her mouth—she stares at me without blinking and still lands the milky-drip coming off her spoon inside her mouth. "Yep—the couch," I say. "I'll probably sleep here for a while, actually." Hopefully Tami hears me. I say it loud enough.

Mom gives me the *that's weird, but I don't want to 'get into it'* look. "Shopping!" The car keys clink-slap as Mom claps her hands together while holding them.

Shopping. Mom's cure-all for when people aren't getting along. No one does dressing room montages in real life. Why can't she get it through her head that trying on outfits doesn't lead to laughter, lattes, and solutions? "Can't I stay home?" I ask. "Howell didn't sleep well, and..." I realize I'm giving Tami the side-eye and open my eyes up, weirdly wide, to try and recover the accusing glare.

"I was so tired, I didn't even notice him crying until Tami knocked on the door to ask if it was okay if she read to him last night." Mom beams with appreciation.

"What? Howell wasn't crying."

"He cry. Bove my room long time. I read story." Tami holds up what must be a Japanese comic book. From the front cover, I can only guess the interior content isn't three-year-old appropriate.

"Are you kidding me? For a toddler, you chose that?"

Mom tilts her head to the side and lets out an embarrassed puff of morning breath in my face, like I've done something wrong in this exchange. "Of course, she read picture books to Howell—the ones on his dresser."

"This my. I read, we drive. How have book he room."

Not to be rude, but I really expected exchange students to know more English. It takes me several minutes to piece together what Tami means sometimes. Probably why she only speaks around Howell and Mom. Yesterday she didn't say three words to me—even after I found her crouched under my baby brother's bed like a creeper. But Mom thinks Tami saved the night reading to Howie who was crying, or whatever. There's no way she'll believe that Tami freaked me out, when Mom thinks she's a hero. Knowing Mom, she'd probably say Tami jumped under the bed because I scared her by snooping around in the dark—when it's totally the other way around.

The three of us continue to walk out to the car while this conversation takes place. Like we're resigned to this stupid shopping idea no matter what comes out of the discussion.

"She was hiding under his bed!" I shout to Mom. "Like. Weirdly." I can't even say what I want to say, *'How did she read to Howie, when she can't even say three words in English?'* because I'm pretty sure I'm already in trouble and Mom's liable to slap me.

"What are you talking about?" Mom waves her keys at us, like sweeping us both toward the door, and out to the car. It works.

"I went to check on Howie, and Tami was in the dark, hiding under his bed." I look at Tami, expecting her to look exposed or caught in the act of oddity. Instead she blinks—flat and without concern.

"You probably scared her."

Oh my gosh, Mom! "There weren't any lights on—any! I'm the one who turned on the lights."

Tami sits in the back seat of the car before I can even offer the front. Mom takes the opportunity of Tami getting in the car to nod at me like I'm being a jerk. I pop my shoulders in the air like *'What do you want me to do?Force her to sit in the front seat?'*

Mom hoarsely whispers, "You're ruining shopping."

"I don't want to go," I whisper back.

She leans away the tiniest bit and I know I'm not winning—nobody wins when Mom gets that determined look on her face—the one she's giving me right now that says, *'You did not challenge me,'* but I accidently did. *'Now you shall know my wrath.'*

"Get in this car and do not say anything—unless it is thoughtful, kind, and—" she leans toward me once more in a more cautious whisper. "Culturally sensitive." Because heaven forbid Tami have any clue we're tiptoeing around the fact that she's not my friggin' twin sister. Is it culturally sensitive to avoid any and all topics of differences? Or unusual behavior? I think that's stupid.

I slide into the car, slam the door—Mom hates that and I know it—and buckle my seat before Mom can say anything.

"Tami, you're very patient, putting up with our family," Mom says before turning the key.

If I wanted to apologize for thinking last night was weird, I would've. But I don't. It was weird okay. Tami is weird. No one speaks for the rest of the drive.

Mom pulls into the mall, finds a space, and shifts into park. We idle between a mud-crusted green ford and a yellow slug bug. "Have you ever seen anything like a mall?" Like one of the wonders of the world lies out the front windshield.

"They have stores in other countries, Mom." And she thinks I'm lacking international awareness. "If you really wanted to impress her, you should have driven the extra forty-five minutes to Silver City." I unbuckle.

"Very nice," Tami says. I half expect 'Your American mall is so impressive Mrs. Dodds' to come out of her mouth. Except I don't think she knows that many words.

I turn to see her face, wondering if she ever places an expression there, and find the slightest of smiles—and she nods. It's fake. All of it—a show for Mom. The car chokes before the engine cuts out. I wish I had the luxury of coughing my distain at having to be a part in this ruse, but that's reserved for vehicles. There's no way shopping in Bronzetown mall holds the key to an appreciation for whatever personality is locked under Tami's expressionless face.

When we arrive, it's like we can't get out of the car fast enough—needing to distance ourselves from each other. But, now what?

"Where do you want to go first?" Mom directs her question to the entire building—not us. No one volunteers a store name. "Okay, how about American Eagle?"

"That's not uniquely American, either," I say.

"Stop that."

"What?"

"Stop being such a downer." Mom looks at Tami, like she's considering how much she's willing to discuss in front of her. "I know things haven't gone as smoothly or sensibly as you think they should, but..."

"Sensibly?" I look between Mom and Tami. No show of emotion on Tami's face emboldens me to speak my mind. "Try weird, Mom. It's been really abnormal, and not culturally."I use air quotes around Mom's new crutch word. Tami doesn't respond in any way that would signify she's following the conversation. "The fair, hiding in her room all the time, and last night... That's a whole lotta strange."

Mom lifts a hand toward Tami, as if extending a life raft of excuses. "She obviously can't explain herself very well."

"Don't you think that's weird? Who would send a seventeen-year-old to another country to study without knowing enough English to say anything more than, 'Hi, my name is...?'

Mom points at me, her mouth opens, but no words come out. Several kids from school walk past us. "Dodds." Amberly waves—she's the kind of girl who knows everybody, the exact opposite of what I need right now. Great, all we need, an audience. "Who'd you get for English? I totally have Masterson, who is the worst, am I right?"

"I've got Sorenson," I say.

"Whoa AP. Nice." Everyone knows Sorensen teaches strictly AP English. Amberly looks from my Mom, who stands there, to Tami, whose only expressive thing is blinking, and back to me. "So..." The friend that's with her nods toward a designer store. "I'll see you at school." They walk away.

"Don't you think you should have introduced Tami?" Mom says. "They were obviously waiting for you to introduce who you're with. People are going to be curious, you know."

How does Mom expect me to know all this? It's not like I've had a class on exchange student politics. "Why didn't you say something then?"

"I thought you knew. I didn't want to be the lame Mom butting in."

"Next time, assume I don't have a clue." Not wanting to enter the store where those girls are, I point to Old Navy. Mom nods. Tami trails behind us as we walk, like a puppy. If we stop, she stops, never quite catching up. It's almost like she doesn't want to be associated with us—also weird.

In the store, I find three shirts and two pairs of jeans that fit perfectly. Tami's pile consists of a belt, socks, and one sweater.

"Don't you need more clothes?" I noticed she only unpacked two pairs of pants, one dress, and a small stack of shirts when she arrived.

"I mail. I shop mail." Tami waits with me in the winding line. Back-to-school sales and late shoppers add to theme-park sized lines winding back and forth through ribboned posts, filling the mid-section of the store.

"You'd save money buying clothes here, not having to pay shipping." I don't actually know if that's true. What do clothes cost in Japan? Everything in the states says, 'made in China' or 'India' maybe it's cheaper to buy overseas and ship it here.

"I clothes mail."

"Okay. Cool." Not wanting Tami to stare at me the whole time we wait in line, I let her move ahead of me. Mom catches me rolling my eyes behind Tami. I know I'm going to hear about that later. I'm failing this 'bond over shopping' outing.

Once we reach the register, the click chirp of cards being chipped ahead of us stops its rhythm. Tami pulls a plastic card from her wallet. I notice the name on the card begins with 'K' and strings too many consonants together. The last name's short—not like Watanabe at all. Maybe it's her mom's card, and they have a different last name? "Is Tami short for something else? Or like the American version of your name?" I ask, reading over her shoulder.

Tami slides the card back in her wallet and walks away from her small stack of items without purchasing anything. The cashier looks at me confused. What did I do?

Mom talks over my head to the cashier, "Just ring it up altogether." The cashier sets her face to the rhythm of pressured-long line with a sour smile in shared condolences to those waiting behind us. Then Mom grabs my bicep and squeezes. "We will talk about your attitude toward Tami once we're not in public," she whispers in my ear.

"Let me guess, I'm grounded some more?" Mom tightens her hold. I take that as a yes.

Tami walks out of the store toward the car.

After Mom pays for my and Tami's stuff she swipes the bag with my items out of my hand. "You'll get these back when you make things right with Tami."

"I don't even know what's wrong."

"Figure it out, if you want new clothes to wear."

At least we're done pretending that this day is going well.

8

When Sara texts me to hang out the weekend before school starts, I respond, *Grounded.*

Still?

Again, I text back.

Sorry.

I wait for the *dot, dot, dot* to wiggle while Sara types another message.

Do you think it would help if we invite Tami to come?

If Sara asks whether Mom will let Tami go without me... Ouch.

Invite Tami. It'll be good for her. Even before hitting 'send' on my text I feel better inside. Like the simple act of giving my permission for my friends to invite Tami to hang out, without me, fixes something I didn't know was broken.

Do I call her? Do you have Tami's number?

Huh. I know Tami has a phone. I never thought to ask her for her number. I peek out my bedroom door and see Tami's door closes. Not already closed—it moves into the shut position once I look out from my open doorway. Too weird—like she's been listening to me this whole time. I'm not breaching the hall barrier between us.

Just come by and invite her. I text. Because, no one can say 'no' to an in-person invite. And I'm not going to be the one to extend it.

I run upstairs where Mom's watching daytime TV and folding laundry. A news update teases today's top stories in commercial form *"The wall between the United States and Mexico has not proven to reduce immigration to our nation. Flash floods from early summer leave one small town community up a dry-creek with fall looming and population booming. More on one community banding together, our alien-infiltration, along with weather and sports highlights tonight at five."* "Sara wants to invite Tami to go dirt-biking tonight."

Mom looks up from her television fog, shakes wrinkles out of Dad's shirt before rolling it into a tube, the way Dad prefers his clothes stored. "Is this some attempt to get out of being grounded?" She looks at me over the top of her work.

"I told Sara I couldn't go."

Mom shakes another piece of clean clothing. She really hates wrinkles. "Because I'm not going to unground you."

"I know."

"The lawn needs mowing."

For my good deed, I get chores. "Fine." Sunblock, and a large brim hat, and I'm outside mowing the front lawn when Max pulls into our driveway. I kill the motor on the mower so I can at least say hi.

"You're not coming?" Max asks getting out before Sara. Then I realize Sara isn't with him, making it weird that I'm standing by Max without Sara, or anyone else, between us—except the car of course.

"Grounded."

His dark skin looks like a welcome shade to the beating sun. Whoa! Don't think like that. The fair messed with my Max-perceptions or something. Or maybe it's being out in the heat so long.

"Huh. I thought you were coming."

I shake my head no.

Max closes the driver's door and walks around the car so that there's nothing between us except air. I walk around behind the lawn mower. There, something between us.

Max watches me move and tilts his head a little to one side. I can only imagine what a dork he must think I am. Good. He should think of me like a big dork. I'm his adoptive twin sister's best friend. He scratches his forehead and points to the house. "So... Tami's coming?"

"Yeah." I point a thumb over my shoulder toward the house. "Go ahead and knock."

"Good seeing you," he says. Like he won't see me the whole rest of the time he's knocking, and talking to my family.

"Yeah." I notice in that second how good Max looks. His jeans fit perfectly, not too tight or too loose. He has on a snap front shirt that highlights the natural V shape from his waist to his shoulders.

Oh no. Am I staring? I move the brim of my hat low to cover my eyes, and reach for the motor pull. Max turns, giving me a clearer understanding of how perfectly his jeans fit in the back, like they were tailor-made for his rear-end—again not too tight, but...

I can't believe my brain right now. Stop. It's Max. I like Derrick.

I pull the cord, hoping the motor will start right away for once, and drown out the sound of Max inviting Tami out. I'd mentally prepared for Sara to do the inviting and had no idea how hard it would be to say, 'I'm grounded' in front of anyone else.

Max knocks three times. Mom opens the door. I try not to eavesdrop, but I totally am since the motor won't engage.

"Is Tami here?"

"Just a moment."

Max looks over his shoulder—catching me watching him. Dang it.

"I'm just." There's no way to recover from the fact I'm staring at him. "This mower is a piece of crap." I yank on the cord to demonstrate —so of course it starts right up.

Max laughs over the roar of the motor. I could die from embarrassment. I push the stupid machine which has betrayed me, and keep one eye on the door. Tami appears in the doorway in front of Max. I see Max's hands gesture what I assume is the sign for dirt-biking. He points to his car, then to the hills in the distance and even leans inside the house for a minute. I imagine he's trying to enlist Mom's help in getting the point across to Tami, who knows less English than any foreigner I've ever met in my life. Not that I know a lot of international travelers.

I turn a corner to continue the line I'm mowing and double back. Straight lines, how Dad likes the front lawn. In the back I can mow shapes, or whatever I want, but the front lawn must be 'done right,' which means having exact lines, or Dad will make me do it over. Tami shuts the door in Max's face. My hand lets go of the gas lever without thinking. The engine dies as Max stomps down the steps.

"What happened?" I ask.

"Your house guest." He gestures one hand behind him toward the door, doesn't even stop to explain, before opening the driver's door like he's going to leave me standing in the middle of lawn, totally confused and curious. The worst way to leave me.

"But," I say—stopping him from disappearing inside the car. "What happened?" I ask again—at a loss for what other questions there are to possibly ask.

"You're already in trouble, right?" he asks. Max is Bevan's friend, his trouble maker friend. Max is the main reason Bevan knows what being grounded is. It's not like Bev would ever break a rule on his own.

I look at the house. With all the doors closed and Tami in there, it feels like the most unwelcoming place on earth. "Yeah."

"So, what's a little more?" Max smiles mischievously, ducks inside his car, reaches across the seat and opens the passenger door from the inside. He then pops up standing on the floorboard of the driver side. "Come on, let's get out of here."

"Uh..." I stare at the mower, then the lawn, only one-third finished. I know why Mom was always a little upset with Max's influence on Bevan—and why Max always seems to be losing his car privileges...

Max bites his bottom lip, rolls his eyes, and slides into the car, not waiting to see if I'm coming too. Not wanting him to leave me behind, I throw the hat to the ground, turn my phone to silent, and rush for the still-opened passenger door. I pull the door shut, and reach for the buckle. Max's hand touches my shoulder and I freeze, despite the fact hot zings spark from his fingertips into my whole body.

"Don't let anyone tell you you're not good enough," he says.

I let the chemical surge and whatever the heck I thought might have been happening between Max and me reshape into what it really is. I'm Bevan's little sister and Sara's best friend. Max looks out for me—

nothing more to his interest. I must have twisted everything from after the fair so far out of proportion in my head...

Tami has problems with anyone who looks different, me with my birthmark across my face, and him with his skin. I sort of thought colored skin was an issue of the long past, but I guess some people are unschooled in the 'things that don't matter anymore' part of life. Some people, being Tami.

Mom opens the door before we speed away, and I know I'm in So. Much. Trouble. when I get home. But, for now, I'm here with Max. "Did she say something?" I ask while Max backs out of the driveway.

"She said I'm dirty. Like that. And then slammed the door in my face, like I'm not worth speaking to."

"I'm sorry."

"It's not your fault." He flips the turn signal—not toward the hills. "I don't feel like biking. What do you say to a night in the big city?"

"Silver City? Are you serious?" My clothes are NOT city-standard. I look like I ran from a grass factory explosion. "I smell like motor oil."

"I kind of like it. Perfume de'la'motoure'."

Pfft. I'm pretty sure Max failed basic French, and he was born in Haiti. "Won't Sara be upset when you don't show up?"

"Don't tell her okay? She gets really protective when anyone gets judgmental with our sibs." He moves his jaw around like he's grinding on more words. I don't press him. "And she's smaller than me—I can't have her defending my honor." He smiles, like that's supposed to be a joke. We both know there's a small grain of truth in there.

He's right. Sara hates it when people treat her adopted siblings different than anyone else. I admit I sort of want to see Sara go 'equality-justice-patrol' all over Tami, but Max is right. It's not Sara's fight. I don't want her wagging a finger at Tami for continually treating me like a deformed beast because of my birthmark. It's my battle to fight.

It takes us an hour and a half to reach the city limits. It might've been faster, but we got stuck behind a tractor for several miles on a two-way highway with double yellow lines down the center of the road and no pull-off lanes in sight. That cut a thirty-minute chunk out of our fun.

In Silver City every light shines, even in the daytime like the added electricity can overcome the desert dust, a sad attempt to sparkle in the sun covered in a layer of sand. "Now what?"

"Food?" Max turns onto the main road, not Main Street—it's Bullard Street, where we pass several 'food' options. We can see the University from Bullard Street. "Did you know that school was originally named New Mexico Normal School? From a town with less than one percent African American population now, I can only guess how well I'd be welcome in 'Normal' back then."

"We're not living then though. They'll pay you to go to WNMU today—I've seen the letters begging you to attend." Max had a million track scholarships already. I have a big fat stack of nothing in the scholarships department of life. "Tami really got to you, didn't she?" I don't want to make this a big thing, but I can tell something more bugs Max. My guess, Tami was the topping that tipped the scales on how much he could handle today.

"Just tired of being type-cast, that's all." Max pulls into a bakery and turns off the engine.

"This is food?"

"I want pastry. Fatty, unhealthy, ruin my splits time, screw my arteries, pastry. Lots of it." Then he looks worried. "But, if you want something else, I mean..." Max bends as if he can see down the road from where we're parked.

"No."

Max stops leaning toward the main road, or the road that is mainly used. It's amazing how flash floods were once so common in this dry climate that flooding forced shop owners to use the back door so long that it turned into a main door, and a new main street. It's amazing what a fleeting force can accomplish.

"I want to ruin my appetite—like destroy it for a week in one sitting," I say.

"That's my girl." When he opens his door, Max walks around the car to my side.

I'm too busy wondering how to reframe 'my girl' into something brotherly and failing majorly, to think about opening my door before Max does and I fail at that too. "Uh. Thanks."

"Don't mention it." Max waves a hand, brushing off the gesture, and completely confusing me. I need to stop reading into anything he says or does. How can I make myself think of Derrick? It's so much easier to obsess over someone who doesn't know my name, than someone who knows all my nicknames—especially the embarrassing ones.

A ding announces our entrance into the bakery. A buttery aroma and the unmistakable scent of flaky carbs waiting to attach themselves to every fat molecule in my body greets us before any sales person has a chance—like they need a sales team with a business that smells this good. Behind a pale blue counter stands a single employee in a flour-dusted apron as if they really did some baking today. I can't help but wonder if it's a staged look.

The shop teems with coffee drinkers and people who own laptops instead of lapdogs. Dim lighting on each table compliments the dark-painted walls and rope lights throughout the space. "Hipster Donuts?" I ask.

"Be right with you," someone shouts from the back, where several more flour-dusted employees emerge.

"I'm ordering everything with filling," I say. Then pat my spandex pants—I was mowing in a workout getup... I have no money on me.

"Don't worry. I've got this covered."

"I'll pay you back, I promise."

"Please don't. I want to get you something." Max steps to the counter, wallet in hand.

Am I on a date? Or not?

While Max orders everything with filling, I check my phone. Seven messages. All from home. I'm so dead when I get back. "Is your phone on?" I ask Max.

"No. Didn't want to deal with Sara yet. Not sure what to tell her without setting her off." Max pulls his phone from one pocket. "Yikes." His face pulls into a grimace. "Isn't this your mom's number?" he shows me his phone. There are ten calls from a number listed as 'You're All In Trouble,' which I recall being Mom's most common greeting when Max would drop Bevan home after a night out last year.

"We're so dead."

"Your parents are going to ban me from hanging out with Bevan ever again."

Seriously? He's with me right now and complaining that he won't be allowed to chill with my older brother when he visits at Thanksgiving—three months from now?

"Your donuts." The cashier holds up a bag. Max runs a bank card through the reader and takes the bag.

"Pick a table," Max says. There are only three available in a tight space.

I pick the one closest to a window, bumping a Saturday afternoon donut consumer fiercely clacking on a tablet. "Sorry," I say. The person doesn't even pause, but raises their shoulders to acknowledge my words. Max and I exchange a look trying not to laugh. "What about our angry families? Shouldn't we get back?"

"They're already angry. Might as well enjoy our food."

He has a point. Of course Max doesn't see me as a date. I'm like Bevan, a pet he needs to look out for—and feed apparently. Being friends with Sara is emotionally-twenty-times easier than being friends with Max.

Max passes me the unopened bag. "You get first pick."

"Thanks." I pick one with chocolate icing, orange and yellow sprinkles—an early homage to fall, even though it's still ninety degrees outside. Max waits for me to take a bite before choosing one of his own. Bavarian cream oozes from the center when I bite into it. "It's good."

"I'm glad I got two of everything." He pulls out a copy of the donut I'm eating and sinks his teeth halfway through the entire circle.

I tip his hand and the pastry filling squirts up toward his nose. We both laugh. It's not the worst being Max's friend, even though it hurts a little on the inside.

After eating three donuts each, *thank goodness I did some yard work to counter balance all those calories*, Max drives around Silver City. We pass a bowling sign, movie theater logo, and hiking trails, doing our best to pretend we didn't see anything. It's clear neither of us feels like exploring any activities.

"You want to head back?" Max asks.

I nod. "Anything good to listen to?"

Max puts on a Black Keys album. We start the rock jazz album two more times, and eat the entire bag of donuts, before we're back in Bronze town. A heavy dread settles into my outlook along with the setting of the sun. It's not Tami and closed doors I'm coming home to, but parents who won't take my side in any future arguments or personal issues with Tami.

"Sorry if I got you in trouble," Max says pulling into the driveway.

A curtain parts and falls back, sealing light inside. "I did it to myself."

"I guess I won't see you until Tuesday."

School starts on Tuesday in our district. I can't remember a time when the school year started on a Monday, there must be a rule about it somewhere.

"Have fun training." I know Max. He'll be running the rest of the week, if only to burn off all the donuts we consumed in the last four hours.

Max turns off the car and goes for the handle. I think he's going to open the car door for me, until the house door opens and yellow light spills around the silhouette of my Dad with his arms folded across his chest. Max pulls his door closed, no longer gentlemanly—fear of someone's dad can do that to an otherwise decent guy. "Good luck in there."

I open my own door. "Tell Sara I'm sorry I missed her thing." Fresh-cut grass fills the air. I scan the yard—low cut, straight lines. Dad must have finished what I started.

"Don't worry, I'll absorb that one—it's pretty much my fault."

I kind of want him to offer to absorb Dad's wrath too. I close Max's car door, listen to the engine turn over, and watch him back out of the driveway. I'm on my own the rest of the way to the house.

"I'll be in my room," I say, attempting to squeeze through the slight space between Dad and the doorjamb, hoping to get by before he has a chance to say anything. The scent of Tide rises through the mudroom. Clean laundry adds to my list of things I didn't do today.

"You didn't answer your phone." He doesn't move from the doorway, blocking my path—forcing me to talk as my toll. "Did the battery die? Help me understand what you were thinking."

"I wasn't."

"You've got that right." He shifts his feet, and for a second, I think he's going to let me through. "I just..." Then the shift closes to a solid block again. "We never had this kind of problem with you when Bevan was here."

Because it was Bevan out with Max, and for some reason that's less of a concern. Bring Bevan back home—that's a great solution. He won't care about losing independence... Right? I want Bevan, and Howie and no Tami. I want to copy Dad and fold my arms across my chest. Instead I lift my shoulders, going for the rebel-without-a-cause pout. "What do you want me to do?"

"Grounding doesn't seem to be working. If anything, you're behaving worse."

"Does that mean I'm no longer grounded?"

Dad drops his folded arms. He's never struck me, and I've never been afraid he would, but in the moment, with the sudden shift of his arm, and the weirdness of the day, I flinch.

The warm glow of the porch light combined with the hot evening air softens Dad's features. His brows draw together as he slides to the side, his head hanging like he's lost something.

Now I stand in the doorway, not filling half the space Dad occupied. "I'm sorry."

He shakes off my apology and pulls the door closed, a single moth sweeps inside before the evening gets shut out.

"I'm tired," I say—trying to tag it onto my sorry. Like that will lighten my wrongs tonight.

Dad rubs one eye with his finger, as if showing that he too is tired, too tired to say so much in words. And I realize my flinch cost me something worse than being yelled at—he's so hurt he can't even talk to me.

"I should have answered my phone."

Dad doesn't speak. He doesn't move away. He only waits. I look at my shoes, my hands, the door. The dryer rattling against the uneven tile. Still, he doesn't engage me. He turns and walks into the dining room. Strong and silent—a personality I will avoid when I get married.

Finally, I nod, fold my arms like I wanted to anyway, but this time it's more of a self-hug for the Dad talk I lost, and walk out of the room. Down the stairs. Tami's door remains closed at the end of the hall. It better stay that way all night. Nobody reads scary foreign comics to my baby brother and survives to make the same mistake twice. Except. I wasn't here all day, hovering over Howell. I have no idea if Tami spent time with him. If she did, was Mom there supervising? Mom's usually a great helicopter parent, but since Tami arrived, it's like she forgot how to be overprotective.

Mom seems to have her spotlight on all my mistakes lately, instead of possible three-year-old hazards. Suddenly, I feel guilt. So much guilt, because leaving was selfish. Not only had I left Howell unsupervised, I diverted Mom's attention even further from the real threat. Instead of making sure Tami's not a psycho, Mom was calling my phone every seven minutes. I need to be everywhere Tami is, so that in the very least, Mom looks in the right direction.

Max, I text. Is it weird to state his name? I mean, I'm texting him, he knows who he is, and if I'm texting, he'll assume I know who I'm texting... Right? I delete his name from the text. *I'm going to be wherever Tami is from now on.*

Usually it's Sara I'd message in a time like this, but today feels like a Max day. It's strange to rely on her brother. I wonder if it's strange for either of them, and then push the thought away when I see Max respond.

His reply comes in three separate messages, one for each sentence. *How much trouble are you in? I'm so sorry. I should have talked to your dad.*

He really should have talked to my dad, but not because of this—I mean, he's the one who suggested I ditch mowing and drive over an hour away for junk food. *It's my own plan. I'm not in trouble—or any additional trouble, I think.* Am I?

Max replies. *Sara's pissed. Lacy and Derrick took off without telling anyone. She said the night was a bust. They had five people, one dirt bike, and no fun.*

She didn't text me any of that. I know. I checked for any messages from her already. *I'll text her to say sorry.*

It's cool. I'm without car keys again. First class passenger in the Neilson-mobile for me, from now until forever.

You can run everywhere faster anyway.

True. Little dots bounce, stop, bounce some more. Like he's retrying different versions of what to say next. *Tami-magnet? anything more?*

What do I say? I didn't tell him about Tami hiding under Howie's bed at like two in the morning. Or that my parents are more concerned with my behavior lately to properly over-parent my baby brother? Max and Sara have so many siblings, I sometimes wonder if anyone directly parents anyone. Or maybe they all take turns hovering.

Whenever I'm at their house, I get the feeling they all assume someone else watches the kids who need watching, while the kids who need watching are bathing the cat or something they shouldn't be doing. Do they even understand helicopter-style families?

Is your plan to wear down her defenses? Exposure therapy? Max sends two texts in a row.

I quickly search the internet on my phone for 'exposure therapy' so I can sound like I know what he's talking about when I respond. It's basically dealing with anxiety by facing the thing that makes a person anxious until that thing is less scary. So, it's torture.

Yes. Exactly.

###

The weekend passes like the summer can't wait to get rid of school kids molding in its wake. I stay in my room mostly reading. If I hear Tami's door open, I open mine. When she prepares a meal, always for herself—even though Mom makes massive multi-course family meals these days, I eat too. The bathroom has never known a line before I decided to be a Tami shadow.

Tami commits to the silent treatment. She not only avoids speaking to me, but does a fine job of not looking at me either. Mainly not looking at my birth-marked face, as if the mere sight of me could burn her cornea. At least, that's the impression I get from the few times she's had to make eye contact across the table. One hand shielding her eyes, an emotion-blank squint camouflaging her feelings about me from my parents, who are still so intent on being upset with me that they probably wouldn't notice if Tami donned a big white sheet with the eye holes cut-out.

Tami permits Howell free-reign of her electronics—like candy from a stranger in an unmarked van. He appears unaware of the dangers of Tami—everyone does, which makes me even more suspicious of her.

Tuesday my alarm goes off at five in the morning. "Too early." I must have set it wrong by mistake. I slap the snooze button, but can't manage sleep. All I can think about is the fact my alarm goes off again in an hour. Until I hear the distinctly non-English rasping of one-side of what sounds like a two-sided argument.

I slip out of bed with my blanket around my shoulders against the morning chill. I lean against Bevan's hijacked bedroom door to listen. Sure enough, Tami speaks—not English. I don't know enough languages to know the difference between Japanese, Mandarin, Cantonese, or Korean. But, she sure isn't speaking English, and she isn't happy.

In an attempt to press my ear flatter against the door, I accidentally push the door the fraction of space it wasn't fully closed, and it clicks. Tami stops talking. Thinking my spying mission is blown, I open the door—Tami's emotionless face fills the crack between the door and the frame. I fall backwards, tripping on the blanket I had wrapped around me. It lands over the top of me so that I'm caught in my own comfort net.

"What the?... What are you doing?" I shout, battling my way out of the blanket, when really, she should be the one asking me that question, since I'm the one spying.

Tami's eyes are wide, on me, and so freaking wide. I don't even think I can open my eyes that much without both eyeballs falling out. And her face isn't emotionless like I keep telling myself she is—red circles her eyes and tears glisten at the corners.

Down the hall, behind her looming over me, I can see Tami's bedroom door open, the light on, like she's been up and working for hours. Everything about her demonstrates more alertness than I've seen since the day she arrived.

"It's five in the morning," I say in all the lameness of that statement.

Tami steps back from my room. She backs down the entire length of the hall, keeping her eyes on me, puts a hand on her own door and shuts it without once looking away from where I'm still in a mess of blanket on the carpet.

"School starts in two and a half hours," I say to her closed door.

Tomorrow I plan to start spying much, much earlier. And maybe do a better—less noticeable job.

10

Tami sits behind me on the drive to school, like I'm her chauffeur. She wears a beige shift dress with low pockets and no leggings. If she bends over, she'll be sent home. Before we left the house this morning, I expected Mom to say something so Tami would change her dress—or at least put on pants. Now at school, I expect the principal, a counselor, or teacher to say something. Apparently, school dress code doesn't translate. But, is anyone looking out for Tami and her soon-to-be-memorialized nether regions on Snapsgram? Nope.

Our school is newer. By newer I mean my parents didn't attend high school in the same building. It's a single level with high ceilings in the common areas. The halls stretch out like four octopus legs claiming all the land Bronzetown doesn't know what to do with. I planned my classes better this year, so I won't have to run from one hall to the other to get to class on time.

The first day of school means fashion week. This year the organic trend seems to be teal and salmon at the same time—colored piping to define a guy's hem, and tatted lace for a feminine accent. Except Tami who wears everything beige and cream neutral with exhibitionist hemlines.

I'm obviously a lemming, wearing a plum piping trimmed, gray-geometric patterned, tunic with plum leggings with lace at the ankle. I'm pretty sure two other juniors are wearing the same outfit. My only saving grace—the fact I'm wearing plaid converse sneakers where most girls have on wedges or blunt heels.

Tami appears animated and outgoing the second she steps into the school building. Unlike at home, she walks up to people and smiles. What is happening?

Not wanting to miss out on the nice version of Tami, I approach a group of cheerleaders greeting three other exchange students in addition to Tami. Violet's in cheer, so it's not too uncomfortable to address them. As I get closer, Sara calls my name. She's with Violet in the cheerleader welcome squad.

Sara has on an oversized graphic tee with a fitted-bead belt over the top and dark blue jeans. I wouldn't have guessed the look would work, but somehow it really does. She stands with Lacy, who wears the same outfit I am—almost exactly. That's not something one plans for in high school. Violet has turquoise earrings and jeans to match, which really set off her blond hair and crystal blue eyes cased in heavy black liner.

"Did you join cheer?" I ask Sara. Of course, Violet's in cheer. It's been her life's mission since she was five to be a varsity cheerleader.

Sara waves off my question, she refers to herself as not coordinated enough for cheer. "Wouldn't it be great to do an international week, or something like that. To really highlight the foreign exchange kids?" That's Sara, always finding new ways to be awesome.

"As far as I know, we're only in charge of welcoming," Violet says. "I don't know who to ask about coordinating themed weeks—student council maybe?"

"I'll totally consider that." We wave again before moving to the commons, a large open space in front of the auditorium. I catch Tami motioning across her face to one of the other girls. Mom taught me to never let other people's misconceptions bother me. So why does it? Someone grabs my shoulder from behind and spins me to face him—Derrick. When I turn around his fist rises in the air, like he's going to knuckle bump my nose. Does he think I'm a dude?

"Oh, Lori—hi," he says removing his hand. "I thought you were Lacy." His brows furrow in honest confusion. When he notices Lacy right next to me, in the same outfit, he ruffles his own hair and chuckles to match the movement. "I thought I saw you get off the bus in that."

"It wasn't planned," Lacy says before I can open my mouth. "But, it's not the worst thing ever, right, Lore?" She hip bumps me. "I mean. We both bring our own thing to it." She spins—bringing a whole lot more to her outfit than I can.

I've never had a problem with Lacy. I've always liked her ditzy inability to comprehend personal space, it usually makes me feel welcome in her happy little bubble, but this year something's off. And I'm beginning to wonder if it's only off with me. I swallow back the possibility that I am destined for the nickname 'Lore' this year, because Lacy does something to not embarrass Derrick, in the fact he obviously doesn't know my name is Lowry like 'loud-ree' without the 'd' in there.

"We need to find one more, and our quest as the three-outfiteers is complete," I say. Lacy laughs, lightly touching my shoulder. Derrick decides to touch my shoulder and laugh too. Like I'm some sort of conduit of hilarity. It crosses my mind to try to touch my own shoulder, but that might get weird.

Nathaniel stands behind Derrick, not touching anyone. I like that I can rely on Nathaniel to be himself, and never worry about interpreting how he and I relate to each other, unlike Derrick and Max. Where is Max for that matter? Is it obvious if I ask about him?

"How lucky is Violet? Hanging with the exchange kids—that's gotta be cool." He turns to me—oh panic—don't ask about living with Tami, please, oh please, oh— "How cool is it living with someone from another country? Do you get to eat sushi all the time now?"

New Mexico sushi rivals Nebraskan lobster. It exists, it's not the same as in Maine and never could be. "Not yet, but I'm sure sushi month awaits." I wait for the group to laugh, because—that's funny. Derrick nods along like I'm serious. Sara's already distracted by people she knows talking on the fringes of our group.

Outlier friends from our various specialized interests, such as band, drama, and debate, shout hello, wave in passing, or loiter for a quick 'best of luck to a new year' greeting, before rushing off to first hour.

"I cannot be late," Nathaniel announces. Derrick pounds his fist, despite the fact Nathaniel wasn't waiting on a fist-bump, and slaps his shoulder leading the two of them toward their first class. As they go, I notice females' heads turn in Derrick's direction. I know what they're thinking. *He's such a great guy—and not at all bad looking. See how he's best friends with that socially inept kid? Wow, he's great. I sure would like to date him...* Wait, what?

"I sure would like to date him," Lacy repeats. Apparently, she said that last line I thought I was voicing in my head.

Sara catches my eye, she knows about my fake-real crush on Derrick. "Let's not put any pressure on our awesome group dynamics. Just...hang and have fun."

"Speaking of group dynamics," Violet appears out of nowhere. I guess she's done with her welcome committee duties. Violet has no filter. I'm not prepared. "What's with you and Max?"

"Max?" I look around like the mere mention of him can summon him to my side. Then realize his twin sister stands right in front of me. "What about him?"

"Saturday... With the solo road trip." Violet finally notices Sara and graces us with a little awkward recognition the topic deserves.

"It wasn't like that," I say. Not diffusing the expression on Sara's face as much as I hope. I don't want to throw Tami under the bus, but... What choice do I have? "I was grounded...and mowing the lawn when Max showed up." If I say Tami made a racist remark to Max, Sara will lose her freaking mind. "I was upset about still being grounded..."

"No joke. Isn't that like three weeks straight?" Violet asks.

"Something like that," I say even though it's only a bit over two. "So, before Max could get to the door, I sort of kidnapped him."

Sara's forehead wrinkles in a way that tells me she's not buying it. The only problem, I don't know which aspect of my lie I'm losing her on. The lie that I'm not attracted to her adopted twin, or the fact that Max sort of kidnapped me—and got me grounded for much, much longer. Her brother falls inside her one goodwill blind spot.

"He asked if I wanted to go off-roading with you guys, but I figured my parents would find me there, and I—" Sara looks so deep in thought that I'm really getting worried. "Turned off my phone."

"That explains why you guys didn't answer any calls." Violet leans in closer to me. "Did he say anything about me?"

"Who, Max?" Sara and I say together.

"Sara, don't get mad," Violet puts up a hand. "But, I sort of think Max is hot."

"Come on. No." Sara says with one hand blocking Violet's face from getting any closer. "Uh-uh. No. He's my brother."

"He's hot," Lacy says. "I'd date him."

"You'd date everybody," Violet says before giving Lacy a light push on the shoulder, reminding me of the saying, 'chip off the old block' for some reason.

Lacy smiles, making it impossible for me to dislike her—dang her natural sweetness.

"Max would be lucky to date any one of our friends, but it's too weird to talk about in front of me," Sara confesses. Instead of sharing my mutual crush on her brother—like every other girl in our group—I keep it to myself. Proving I am, once again, not as cool as my best friends.

"So, I can drag Lowry aside and ask her what it was like to be one-on-one with Max for several hours?" Violet claps her hands together.

Sara's mouth opens, but she doesn't speak. I can't tell if she's trying to figure out if Violet's joking or serious.

I, for one, don't want to know. "I better hurry if I'm going to make it to class."

"Me too. Catch you all at lunch," Sara says.

"Meet here?" Lacy asks. We all nod and scatter.

High school as a junior feels sort of like high school as a sophomore. I know most of the teachers and the students. I've never paid much attention to the foreign exchange kids in previous years, demonstrating to myself how junior year differs from former years. Exchange kids are always juniors or seniors. So now they're in our social pool, whereas previous years we never really crossed paths.

Every class change, I keep my eyes peeled for exchange students. It's weird. This year, it appears all the exchange students are from Asian countries. I can't say if that's normal, since I've never paid attention before, which means it's probably not strange that foreign kids tend to stick in packs and don't mingle too deeply with locals. It's almost sad now that I realize it. Or maybe it's the 'find something familiar' phase before we all relax around each other.

I decide to go out of my way to try to befriend more exchange students this year. This decision also helps with the fact I'm practically stalking the group Tami seems to be a part of. There's a group of five girls and three boys, all with the same sleek black hair at various lengths and hair-dye, and perfect skin. After first period, I noticed four of them walking together to choir, and later there are six in the fine arts pod. I've not seen more than the seven at once, maybe there aren't any other exchange students. Is there a limited amount a school permits?

I have no idea.

Whenever I see Tami in the group, traveling the halls, she's happy and energetic. Nothing like when she's at my house. I watch them all hold their phones, take turns showing their display screen in a serious, but not severe, manner before all punching information to their personal devices and continuing down the hall before lunch.

"What are you doing?" Max surprises me, standing directly behind me, looking over my shoulder using me as cover where I'm using the corner of a wall for cover.

"Don't do that!" I slap his backpack, like that'll show him.

"You're the one being sneaky." He peeks around my corner. "What are you spying on? Or who?"

"Tami." He nods, not discouraging me, nor pressing for a motive. "Where were you this morning?"

"Practice."

"Track?"

"Two-a-day distance runs. Track season doesn't even start yet. It's crazy."

"You should have bought more donuts."

Max laughs. "No kidding. We should go back." He takes a turn smacking my bag, with a major difference being his whack pushes all the way through to my back—sending me flying out into the hallway and drawing far too much attention to me.

I spin back toward him, my eyes bugging with annoyance. Tami's pack of friends totally sees me, not at all helping with the stealth befriendment operation I'm planning. I open my eyelids even further, and tilt my head toward the foreign students in a 'dude? Way to blow my cover' gesture. In response, Max steps out from behind the corner, waves to the Tami's group, a massive smile overtaking his face, and grabs my arm so that I'm now facing them too...

Unsure what I can possibly do to recover this moment, I smile and wave as well, walking toward the lunch tables like it's totally American-normal to be creeping around pillars in halls at lunch. If anything, Max and I are painting a bizarre American stereotype for the exchange kids to write home about.

"Want to eat with us?" Max shouts gesturing at me, then himself, then a lunch table. I assume the motions are in case they have Tami level English and need supportive sign language to figure out his invitation.

Derrick, Nathaniel, and Lacy approach Max and me from a side hall—waving hello and motioning for a long table. Derrick has that confident swagger down—the kind that all women notice. Two girls next to Tami elbow her, nod toward Derrick and start walking toward us. The rest of the group follows. We all sit at a long table.

"Is Sara coming?" Nathaniel asks.

It's never occurred to me that Nathaniel might find one of us attractive, or be interested in girls at all, because he's not interested in much of anything other than facts—and none of the girls in our group are known for our 'absolute' nature. I guess Sara does have an absolute sense of goodness, maybe Nathaniel noticed.

"She'll be here buddy, right Max?" Derrick says.

Max nods, but his attention focuses on the newcomers. "So where are you all from?"

"I grew up outside Seoul, Korea," one of the girls says. She has the shortest hair with light blue streaks and soft pixie features to compliment how petite she is. Her accent stays soft, not pronounced or difficult to understand. I would have guessed she was American born with how well she speaks. "My name is Aiko Lou." She pronounces 'Eye-ee-ko Lau' with Lou sounding a lot like the way the first part of my name is pronounced. Maybe Derrick will botch her name too.

"What a pretty name, Aiko Lou," Derrick repeats—the perfect mimic. I notice him leaning in toward Aiko. Lacy seems to notice as well.

One of the other girls speaks next, none of them seems shy like I imagined—no one covers their mouth to laugh like in movies. Movies are so stupid sometimes. "I'm Yi Cho." Yi she pronounces as Yee. Yi has round eyes and high cheeks with a robust waist for how petite she is. She extends a hand toward Derrick, even though Max asked the question. She then turns to Max. "What's your name?"

"Oh, Tami hasn't told you?" he asks more defensively than he needs to, I'm sure. Tami looks up, like she's not following the conversation until she hears her name. "I'm Max." Yi offers her hand to Max, to shake.

Max's eyes dart my way, like he wasn't expecting to be greeted kindly, probably not helped by the fact every girl noticed Derrick first. But the fact is, so far everyone has been warm and friendly since coming over to our table and it's me and him being the big jerks with our expectations that they'd be jerks first.

I give a small smile toward Yi and Aiko, who both smile back welcomingly. I'm the one who should be welcoming them. I totally fail international domestic relations... For a second time.

Sara lands in a jump between Max and me—a smile overtaking her whole face in a genuinely thrilled expression. Nathaniel noticeably perks. Sara can't wait to make new friends, I know her well enough to know she was hoping to be best friends with Tami all along. "I'm so happy you guys sat with us! Thanks for bringing your friends over, Tami."

Tami again, looks up at the mention of her name.

Sara taps my shoulder for me to make space. Then, motions Violet over to the bench section elbow to elbow with Max. I can take a hint. Sara obviously rethought her stance on how weird it is for Violet to crush on her brother. Now Sara's acting like she views Violet as perfect for Max, which isn't a problem for me. It's not. I swear—I'm not thinking about it at all.

The rest of the exchange kids announce themselves. In addition to Aiko from Korea, and Yi from China, is Masato Nashimura a short-haired boy from Japan, Quon Lee a wild-haired boy from Korea, Tung Mun who doesn't say where he's from, but whose name reminds me of the word tongue, and Ishi Fujii, a girl who doesn't take her eyes off Derrick the entire lunch hour.

"You all seem instant friends," Max says. He's apparently taken it upon himself to be the conversation maker, aka interrogator. "Did you know each other before enrolling in BTHS?" BTHS—Bronze Town High School.

Yi opens her mouth to answer, then jolts as if she's had her foot stomped. She glares at Tung, who doesn't meet her eyes. "No," she says after recovering from her odd opening.

Max rubs the skin under his bottom lip, like there could be stubble there, which I doubt.

"I haven't seen any European exchange students this year, is that normal?" Violet asks.

None of the foreign kids has an answer, understandable since none of them was here the year before, and would not know what the average ratio of country of origin by continent from the previous year. Beside the point, it's an uncomfortable question for all of us. It's difficult to know if it makes the students feel less welcome in our company, which isn't Violet's intention, I'm sure. She simply doesn't filter.

"Who cares about that stuff?" Sara's the first to speak after Violet—perhaps a little late on the recovery for her. "I want to hear about all the cool things from where you guys live. Favorite everything. Go."

No one knows who should answer first, or what the question is exactly, based on the looks on everyone's faces.

"Okay, so I know Tami loves noodles based on what Lowry's told me."

Tami looks at Sara, then at me, then at Sara. "Favorite no. House food is no good." Tami, by far, has the worst English in the group. I need to include that in my evaluation of her. How much about her hinges on communicational frustration, and how much of Tami is plain rude?

Tung laughs and fist bumps Masato, then turns toward Derrick, reaching across the table to fist bump him as well.

"Okay. See, I learned something. Tami doesn't love noodles, but given the options at Lowry's house, it's the best thing they have. And Tung likes to fist bump." A bunch of the foreign kids laugh while Tung overly nods like this is his big joke. Sara smiles like we're all bonding.

"Sushi," Masato says.

"Yeah Bro," Derrick raises his clenched fist for a knuckle slam. "Sushi ya." Masato returns the gesture, much to my surprise. Tung gets in on it too. Maybe we are bonding.

The rest of the exchange students nod and echo, "Sushi." Some add "Fish" as if we don't know what sushi is.

"I'd love to try authentic sushi," Sara says.

"I too would enjoy that," Nathaniel adds, which must be a lie. I've never seen Nathaniel deviate from a select few food groups, none of which include fish in any form.

Our time to eat lunch rushes past. Without anyone saying anything, we all focus on our own eating and let the conversing die down. When most of us are done, uncomfortable nods and half-smiles pass between us until it's time to go to our next classes.

One of the varsity cheerleaders, Mandy I think, addresses our group. "Hey cool, you all are befriending the exchanges." She faces Tung, who looks like a K-Drama rock star, which is super hip right now. "Let us know if you need anything. We're still the official welcoming committee." She sees Violet in the mix. "Oh, hey Vi."

Tung seems to notice the awkward moment. A mischievous glint in his eye, he leans over and picks up Violet's hand across the table like he's going to kiss it. Violet turns bright red. His lips almost touch her pale skin. Mandy's confidence is shot, riddled with holes that drop her shoulders and her jaw at the same time. Then, he lets go centimeters from contact, and laughs open-mouthed close to Violet's face, turning to do the same thing to Mandy. The boys from his group also laugh like that was the funniest thing they've seen for days. The girls laugh too, even Tami. Neither Violet nor Mandy laugh—don't have to understand the joke to know they were the brunt of it.

"Don't mind Tung, he thinks making jokes is the cure to all that is awkward," Yi says smacking him in the arm. "We grew up not far from each other." He laughs at this and smacks Masato in the arm as well, like smacking each other makes the moment less uncomfortable. It sort of works. It's a weird moment, but less offensive, I guess.

I'm less obsessed with following around the other exchange students. They do dumb things, like Tung did at lunch, but in a normal teen way. Trying to recover awkward moments with humor is a tricky path for anyone to tread.

Tami remains on my radar though. I can't figure her out. I'm a little worried she simply lacks basic English and I'm misjudging her. Meaning, I'm a terrible-terrible person. I don't want that to be the case. I must find something to proves that theory wrong.

I want to find something morally reprehensible with Tami, if only to prove I'm right to suspect her of being someone I need to spy on. If I can't, I'm the jerk. Yes. I want to find a reason to justify my poor behavior.

11

My remaining classes don't overlap with Sara's or Tami's. Though I have pre-calc with Derrick and Nathaniel, I wish I had a class with Sara. After school, I wait by the doors for Tami. After twenty minutes, I question if I made it clear I'd give her a ride home. Or maybe I didn't tell her where I'd meet her. I can't imagine she could miss me standing right in the main exit. It's been one day and the rust-red lockers are already peppered with paper decorations and stickers.

Derrick and Nathaniel say hi before they go home. Sara, Lacy, and Violet leave together. Sara gives me a shoulder shrug indicating she's not sure if I want her to stay and hang while I wait. "I'm sure she'll be here any second," I assure the three of them. I don't see Max, but I know he's probably doing his second track practice of the day, or something dedicated like that.

After another fifteen minutes go by, I check the office and ask the secretary to try to locate Tami. The office has flowers in vases on every surface, like someone mistook starting the school year with Valentine's Day—or a funeral. It smells like old-lady perfume bomb as well. A person can hide murder in the heavy perfume cloud. It's not long before the phone rings. Mrs. Conklin, one of the three art teachers, informs the secretary that Tami, and the rest of the exchange students have all joined the art club, whose first club meeting is day one—right after school.

Who has a club meeting the first day of school?

"Do I wait?" I ask the secretary.

She turns her back to me to speak into the phone with Mrs. Conklin making it hard to eavesdrop. The best I can make out is, "Are you sure? Just be certain all the kids get home safe."

I can guess what she's about to tell me, but wait for the secretary to speak first. "You're free to go."

"Do I tell my parents who will be bringing Tami home? Or... I mean, what do I do here?"

"I think you've done everything you can."

I take that as permission to leave free and clear. Grabbing my bag and keys, I drive home without Tami. When I walk through the door, the first thing out of Mom's mouth is, "Where's Tami?"

"She's in art club."

"You didn't wait for her?"

"The secretary called the club leader or something—they all said she had a ride."

"Are you sure?"

I shrug. What else could I do? It was awkward enough waiting and the secretary told me I could go. "I asked."

"If she's not here by five, you're grounded."

"More grounded? How much more grounded can I get?" Mom swipes my car keys off the counter. I shouldn't have snarked back, but come on! "You're taking the car?"

"You were responsible for getting her to and from school. Maybe the bus would be a better option for me to rely on for both of you."

"Mom!" I stomp, like Howell, who watches from his chair as I have a fit. "I'm not riding the bus."

"You better hope she gets home before five."

The clock says four-forty already. I have twenty minutes. "How long do clubs meet for anyway?"

"Maybe you should have joined too."

"I'm not artsy or clubby."

"It wouldn't hurt you to get involved."

It's like Mom doesn't even know my friends. Being best buds with Sara and her family is basically the same as agreeing to participate in every charity event, function, and fundraiser from now until the end of time. "Do you want me to drive back?"

"Yes. Yes, I do."

"Fine." I hold my hand out for her to put *my* keys in *my* palm.

She drops the keys so they land on my fingertips and drop to the floor. I bend to pick them up and notice Howell has my favorite eyeliner in his hand, like a twistable Crayola crayon, he's using it to color on construction paper. "He's not supposed to be in my room."

"I guess we've all dropped the ball today."

So far, this exchange student thing really brings our family together. But not in an agreeable fashion. Yes. I'm blaming all of this on Tami. The person I must drive all the way back to high school to pick up, because the secretary told me to go home. I partly blame the secretary.

When I get to school, the parking lot is mostly empty. Luckily the doors are still open. I walk to the office. No secretary. Great. I'm not taking any art classes this semester, but I know where the rooms are located. I assume art club would be held somewhere near the art rooms.

"Do you know where Tami is?" I ask one of the art teachers—not Mrs. Conklin. "She's in the art club, I guess."

"Mrs. Conklin has an exchange student group, is that what you mean? It's not just for art—they're doing a lot of support activities and cultural awareness stuff. I didn't know it was a club though." The teacher says.

It sounds like a smart idea. "Do you know where they are? I'm supposed to give Tami, one of the exchange students, a ride." I know it's wrong to not claim her as 'our houseguest' or 'our student.' I can't make those words come out.

"Well, I think everyone left before the buses departed."

"Not possible. I was in the office after that, the secretary spoke with Mrs. Conklin on the phone and told me they were still meeting."

"Are you sure they were still meeting?"

I'm not sure. The secretary turned her back to me at the time. "She definitely mentioned the club meeting."

"And she said they were all still meeting?"

"Not exactly."

"Have you checked with the office?" The teacher who does things like pottery and other advanced art classes says, carrying a bunch of plastic wrapped clay.

"I have." But the teacher leaves without waiting for me to answer, returning the art supplies to some closet at the back of the room. "And I'll go check again," I say to myself.

Someone's in the office this time, not the same secretary as before. "Can you page Tami for me? I'm her ride."

The person behind the desk sends an intercom announcement without question. "Tami, your ride is waiting for you in the office. Please come to the main office, Tami." She looks at me as if she expects more instruction or some thanks.

"Thanks."

A boy I recognize from English pokes his head in the office, "You the one looking for Tami?"

I nod.

"She's gone. Left around four-fifteen I think."

"That's right before I left the first time." Not that he knows what I'm talking about, evident by his bland expression.

"I saw a group of kids in the back parking lot leave around then, I could have sworn she was with them."

I can't even call Tami to confirm her whereabouts—I never got her cell number. "You've got to be kidding me."

"Sorry. Thought you'd want to know." He lets the door close as he leaves.

I check my phone to see if Mom has texted me that Tami made it home safe already. No messages. "Crud." My car looks lonely in the parking lot. Not that I should worry about that much longer, it's probably the last day my car will have the privilege of sitting in the lot, since I'm going to be a bus-rider starting tomorrow, unless I can find Tami.

I drive home under the speed limit. Best to give as much time as possible for a miracle to happen—like Tami magically appearing. Half a mile before turning off the highway toward my house I see a dark-haired girl walking along the side of the road.

"Tami!" I pull over, scaring her to death. Trying not to laugh—she totally thought I was going to run her over—I roll down the window and shout, "What the heck are you doing on the road?"

"No phone. I have not your address."

"Seriously, where did you learn English? You need to practice big time." I smile feeling chummy relief at finding her, but nothing on Tami's face gives me the impression we're connecting here. Still, I found her, she's not dead—and I can drive her the few blocks to our house. "Get in." I reach across and open the passenger door.

She opens the door to the back seat and slides over—behind me. I roll my eyes and pull the passenger door closed. "Whatever," I say. Happy I haven't totally failed today. "Next time your club meets let me know. I can wait to give you a ride—save us both a lot of trouble."

Tami doesn't answer. I'm in no mood to deal with figuring out what the heck her deal is.

"I thought I saw you with a phone at school—you guys were all entering your contact info or something, right? Did your battery die?"

Again, Tami chooses to be mute. I start the car, happy when the engine hums, finally something responds.

"Well, I'm glad I found you. I was about to be in a lot of trouble. Tomorrow let me know your schedule ahead of time, so this doesn't happen again?" Before I even turn off the car, Tami unbuckles rushes out the car, and through the side door. When I get inside, there's no sign of Tami. Mom and Howie are both in the kitchen.

"Where'd she go?"

"She's probably tired from her first day," Mom says. "Thanks for going back for her."

"You have no idea," I mutter.

"What's that?"

"Nothing. Everything is perfectly normal, no concerns whatsoever."

"Good. Can you help me with dinner?"

Obviously, Mom no longer recognizes sarcasm, which probably works in my favor. Counting my blessings of motherly ignorance, I agree to help make stuffed chicken breast—doing my least favorite part —stuffing the filling into the raw meat. I despise touching raw meat.

"You know Mom, if you let Tami sleep all day, she'll be up all night."

"It's called jetlag when you travel to new time zones. People need to sleep more to get onto a regular schedule."

"I know about jetlag, Mom. I'm trying to tell you, Tami's been staying up at night—lights on, on the phone. Up."

"She goes to bed the same time as you." Mom hands me another sliced chicken breast to stuff.

"Except she's not sleeping at night—she's sleeping all day long, while she hides in her room and doesn't practice speaking English. She's the worst speaker in the group of exchange students."

Mom turns so fast, I jump away from the knife in her hand. "I'm glad she didn't hear you say that."

"Like she'd understand me."

Mom sets the knife on the counter. "I have had enough of your attitude. I know you miss Bevan and Tami is no replacement for your brother."

"I didn't say that at all," I say.

"But, he needs a chance to be independent. Tami needs some support and some understanding—that's your job." It's like Mom has no idea about anything in the world. She's so self-absorbed. I'll give her some insight of what's really going on—that'll bring her out of her delusion that I'm missing Bevan.

"Did you know she won't even sit in the front of the car with me? Like she can't stand to be seen with this." I point to the purple-slash birthmark across my face.

"Give her time."

"She was totally rude to Max the other day." I wasn't supposed to say that.

Mom's shoulders soften, falling an inch. "Is that why you both took off like that?"

I lift one shoulder.

"I'm sorry." She puts a raw-chicken hand on my shoulder. I'm going to have to wash all my clothes immediately. "I know this is hard. It's not what I imagined when we agreed to host, but that doesn't mean we quit on Tami. It means that everything is a little more of a challenge than expected, or anticipated. Right?"

I feel like I'm being brainwashed into kindness. I nod, and help Mom get the rest of the chicken into the oven before escaping to my room. Tami's door gaps open and I can't help but creep down the hall to peek in and see if she's awake or asleep.

Tami's tucked into the farthest corner of the room, sleeping on the floor in a crunched wad. There's no chance she's comfortable. Why not sleep on the bed? She doesn't have any books out, no homework pages, no tablet with school assignments open. Weird. I have enough homework to last me till the weekend already.

I shed my raw-meat-contaminated shirt in my room and throw on an oversized T. From now until dinner I can get some chapters read and a few pages of math done. I end up falling asleep too. A rustling in my room rouses me.

"Howie, don't touch my make-up."

But, it isn't Howell. Tami rushes out of my room without a word, her door closes. I'm wide awake now, scanning the room for what she was looking for. My homework papers are a mess, but I left it that way before dozing off.

My purse spills over the floor. I pick it up and look in my wallet, fifteen dollars in cash still there. That's about the extent of my valuables. "What the heck, dude!" I yell down the hall, not helping anything between Tami and me. Suddenly I want to drive to the hardware store and purchase a lock for my bedroom. My heart pounds so hard I could choke on it. I cough to relieve some pressure, but the blood presses so tight in my veins. It has been since Tami arrived, but today the most.

"Dinner," Mom calls from the top of the stairs.

I wait for Tami to open her door. She stares at me. I stare back. It's intense enough that we could be cast in a music video. Both of us seem to be waiting for the other to speak first, move first, anything first. And neither of us moves.

"Girls, come on," Dad calls. Lumping us both together. I think it's obvious, standing here staring each other down, we are not going to be doing much of anything together by choice.

I concede and move toward the stairs first, making sure to pull my door closed with enough force to express a very clear, 'stay the heck out of my space.' Tami slams her own door closed—same warning. I'd like to tell her that this is my house and I'll go wherever I dang well please, but I really want her to stay out of my room, so I might have to keep my mouth shut for the moment.

"Stop slamming doors, please," Dad says when we arrive at the top of the stairs.

Neither of us says anything.

We each take a seat and eat in silence, though it's hard to believe no one can hear the slam of my heart pumping against my ribs. Has anyone ever broken a rib due to a racing heart?

After dinner, Tami returns downstairs while I help Mom with dishes and clean-up. Tami hasn't once helped around the house since she's been here—like she's at some full-service resort. So far, I've learned jack about other cultures, other than the fact being judgmental isn't a strictly American flaw.

12

By Friday, I'm suffering jetlag. Not from being on a jet—from losing sleep trying to keep tabs on Tami's home habits. She wanders the house after everyone else goes to sleep, but I can't seem to figure out what she's doing.

I sleep through classes at school. Current affairs in social studies melt into history. While English gains more absolutes than Math. *That assignment was absolutely due today.*

"Lowry, you alright? You seem weird lately." Sara asks between classes.

"I'm fine. Has no one ever been tired before? I'm tired." Spending all night trying to catch Tami doing something worthy of alerting my parents exhausts me. Unless I have something unequivocally weird, they will find a way to brush all of Tami's behavior off on cultural differences.

Sara puts her hands up and steps back. "Whoa, dude. Whatever's up with you, don't let it leak out all over the rest of us. You know, Tung thinks you hate him and the rest of the kids because they don't know American norms. I told him you didn't get his humor—granted he has hyperactive humor." Sara chuckles to herself, but I'm barely listening.

I think she said something about the exchange students. I don't have the alert power to spare for whatever Sara's talking about. As far as I can tell, of all the exchange students, Tami stands out as the only one with odd sleep patterns, racial issues, and complete lack of English skills or any prep on how to get along with others.

I see less and less of Sara over the next few days. I think she keeps telling me to 'get out of my head' and 'be more involved with the group,' but how am I supposed to do that when I'm battling that tight feeling of being on edge all the time. Tami went through my things and I still don't know why.

By week two Tami opts to take the bus, which works great for me. If she wants less to do with me, fine. It won't interfere with my spying schedule. Now I'm curious if she knows I'm keeping tabs on her and chooses to ride the bus for some added separation. Lack of sleep kills my reasoning skills! Aside from the moment Mom pulls me aside after breakfast.

"Did you say something to make her not want to ride to school with you?" Mom asks.

"Nothing. She hates me."

"I don't believe that for a second. No one hates you, you're wonderful."

Mom's the best for saying those words—even if it's obligatory because half of me consists of her DNA and to say anything otherwise would be a diss to herself and the man she married. But, she also highlights how much Tami sucks, without even realizing it. I mean, if everyone loves me—what the freak is wrong with Tami? Because she definitely doesn't *love* me. "I'm serious, I didn't do anything."

"How am I supposed to know where she is, if she's okay… I'm responsible for her while she's living with us."

"You didn't choose to send your emotionally-stunted teen half a world away. You're not responsible," I say. Mom's face freezes on a half shocked, half heartbroken expression. What'd I say?

Mom steps back, slides her hands through her hair and completely misses the point. "Is that what you think I did to Bevan? Do you think he isn't ready to be out on his own? Does he need us looking out for him, not some minimum wage compensated work-study helper who gets paid to keep him safe, watch out for him... Do you think I did the wrong thing, even if that's what he said he wanted?"

Whoa—that came out of left field. In no way was I thinking about Bevan, which is a new feeling now that I realize it. This whole 'Tami' thing makes a lot more sense. Mom wants to over-care for Tami so that somehow the universe will balance everything out and someone will watch out for Bevan—at least while Mom can't. "No. I don't think that at all. For one thing, Bevan isn't that far away. He's not in a culture drastically different from his own. Everyone who works with him is aware of his intellectual and emotional needs and concerns. But, we have crap information about—"

Mom cuts me off, unwilling to let me say anything negative about a child in her care, which is mostly awesome, but in this case, super frustrating because there's something seriously abnormal with that chick. "We know she likes noodles."

I can't tell Mom that Tami doesn't love noodles, but she doesn't like any of the other food we have. And I sort of wonder if she's putting on a show called 'what I think this host family wants me to act like.' "You can always text her, if you need to know where she is or who she's with."

"She doesn't have a cell phone plan," Mom says. That's weird. Because I know I've heard Tami talking to someone in a different language at night. I assumed it was people from home on different day schedules. "I can't call her, or text, or get any messages to her. And she can only contact me if someone lets her borrow a phone."

"She has an iPhone," I point out because I've seen it. Hope rises that maybe I've stumbled upon the thing to get Mom on my side about how off Tami is.

"There isn't a cellular plan enabled. It's for hooking up to wifi and games and stuff."

How does Mom know that and not me? Oh wait, I've had no actual conversation with Tami since she arrived. That's how. "Find out her friends' numbers?" I suggest.

"Can you do that for me? I wouldn't know where to start, or who to ask."

Me either. "Sure. I'll see what I can find. Now can I go to school?" As I leave the house, the UPS man pulls into our driveway for the fifth time since Tami arrived. She gets a box every four days filled with things from home: snacks, anime comics, clothing, and feminine hygiene supplies. I tried to explain once that she could purchase sanitary napkins at the local store and save a ton on shipping. Big surprise, Tami shut her door in my face. Let her family waste hundreds of dollars in shipping then, what do I care?

I'm now on a first-name basis with the package driver. "Hey Aaron." It's warm enough in September to drive with the windows down.

"Study hard Low-low, or you'll drive a truck for the rest of your life."

"Doesn't sound so bad."

When Aaron doesn't answer, I move on in my Tami-obsession filled life. I need to find evidence. Like she might be a serial killer, or an identity thief—*oh my laws! She's totally an identity thief!* Demonstrate that it isn't cultural prejudice or misunderstanding causing issues between Tami and me. Besides I'm looking out for Howie, right? Because of that one weird night that no one believed was weird except me. *It totally was the weirdest.*

When I park the car, my enthusiasm wanes. Driving can do that—give me the thought time I need to eliminate a plan I'd been gung-ho about. I've been set on exposing Tami's poor behavior to my parents, but what does that get me? It sort of does make me a monster—waiting in shadows to snap a picture of her being weird.

Max doesn't seem to be having any more issues with Tami, since I never see much of him. He's so busy with sports and clubs, and practice and volunteer work.

I need to be busy. I spin to try to find something to do right this second. Wipe things—even though I have no rag. I use my sleeve and wipe the wall... Because that's normal.

"Need help with your... (what am I going to say? I sound like a lunatic waiting to come up with something) bag?" I ask a freshman girl.

She runs toward the lockers clutching her bag like I'm going to rob her. Maybe startling freshman isn't the solution.

"Find a club, find a club, find a club," I chant all the way into the school, hoping it will distract me from watching which direction Tami turns, who she walks with, judge the weight of her backpack and wonder if she ever takes schoolbooks home or does any assignments... Yeah, it's not working.

"Debate club still has an opening." Sara holds the door open for me. "I could hear you—it's not like you were talking in your head," she says.

I probably could have chanted a little quieter. "Debate?" Posters advertising to join the debate team are plastered along every open space of the hall. Like club matchmakers were waiting for a kid who needed a club at exactly that time. "I'm not so sure." The problem with debate hinges on the fact I have to stand in front of people, judging my words and appearance, and pretty much everything about me. If living with Tami has taught me anything, it's that I don't handle judgementjudgment gracefully.

"You're smart, well spoken, you do your research—" Sara obviously doesn't know how behind I am on my homework. "I think Derrick's considering joining," Sara adds in a slightly higher tone, like this bit of news ices the club cake.

I'd like to tell Sarah that my interest in Derrick has cooled a bit. With Lacy at his side every free hour, and Max confusing the bejeezus out of me, and Tami freaking out whatever remains, I haven't had time to devote to a superficial crush. The problem is, I can't bring up Max. Not with his sister. "No harm in giving it a shot, right?"

"That's the spirit."

I have enough spirit to be on Violet's cheer squad with how great I feel. Until I notice Tami standing to the side of a large indoor pillar—*watching me*!

She doesn't flinch or hide her face to conceal the fact she's staring at me. She holds her gaze. I'll hand it to her, it's ballsy to stare someone down like that. I want to tell Sara to shut up for a second and look over at Tami, my heart drops to my stomach and starts pounding around in there. I might be sick, but can't make my mouth form words beyond, "Spirit." And "Shot."

The exchange group calls for Tami to join them on their way to choir. A few of the girls in the group wave at Sara and me. Sara returns a joyful gesture, and I sort of fight my joints to respond like a well-oiled robot.

Sara turns to me. "I'm so happy you have an exchange student. It's been amazing getting to know other cultures."

"When have you gotten to know other cultures? I've been grounded since the fair."

"I hang out with them all the time. Maybe if you'd stop spacing off you'd get to know them too. We're all planning a big Sadie Hawkins date together. It's going to be awesome."

I'm so confused. Sara's besties with Tami and I didn't know? "It is? We are?"

"Tami didn't tell you?" Sara's arm does an involuntary lift in Tami's direction. I'm pretty sure Tami notices. Why does that please me?

"Was she supposed to?"

"I didn't tell her she had to or anything, I guess I figured, since you live together..."

"I've been grounded a lot."

We walk to the end of the commons area and pause, like we're on the verge of parting, but the bell hasn't called the tides yet. "I noticed. What's up with your parents lately? They never grounded you last year."

"Everyone was so focused on Bevan (I could throw Max's name in there as to why the focus was constantly on Bevan), I don't think my parents would have noticed if I robbed a bank last year. This year, I can't pick my nose without it being a criminal offense."

Sara quiets, because she knows I miss Bevan. People always talk about empty-nesters like only Moms can be affected when a child moves out of the house. But, it's sort of like a piece of my life was ripped away, exposing all the things I don't like about myself that had been covered up by the now absent sibling.

"Don't worry, I'll plan everything and convince your mom to let you come."

With Sara on the case, I'm sure I won't miss out.

"Now we need to get you on that debate team with Derrick, and I can open my business as a matchmaking problem solver." She winks before turning the direction of her first-hour class and leaving me standing in the commons while the rest of the high school population rushes around me.

I should get to class too. And later—debate. A distraction from Tami will be good for me.

13

Debate meets right after school, which isn't a problem, since I drive myself. What surprises me—Max shows for debate. Doesn't he have enough extra-curricular activities? And wouldn't something overlap? But, it's not like I'm going to complain or encourage him to go elsewhere.

I take a seat next to him without saying anything.

"Sara mentioned she encouraged you to join debate," he says.

"She didn't mention you were in the group."

"I wasn't. Didn't want to miss seeing you scold someone to tears over political issues."

"Ugh. Is that what we do here?" Honestly, that sounds awful. I hate arguing. I always lose.

Max covers his mouth to speak unnoticed as our debate coach walks in. "I know. I'm the one who told Bevan how to win arguments against you every time."

The debate coach, a Social Economics and Communications teacher named Mr. Therault, does a perimeter march of the room. Mr. Therault walks backwards when he talks sometimes. I can see why kids say he talks out of his butt most the time. It's not his abrasive nature. I really hope his laugh means he's joking. I sort of imagined debate as some kind of junior law show. Maybe we'd do mock defense or something.

Derrick walks in with both Nathaniel and Lacy. Lacy has become a Derrick-fixture as much as Nathaniel. Though Derrick doesn't appear bothered by his human adornments. Poor Lacy, though, he doesn't seem to distinguish her from Nathaniel's rank either.

Sliding in next to Max, Derrick holds his knuckles in the air waiting for a fist bump. "How cool is this? We could make up a whole team."

Max knocks his fist against Derrick's, then Nathaniel who copies the gesture. Lacy and I join, because who doesn't love a fist bump? Pretty soon it's a confusing mass of knuckle punching.

"We need Violet to be our personal cheerleader, am I right?" Derrick says—deflating Lacy from the spine down. She drops a good four inches in posture.

"If the raucous gang in the back will settle down, we'll get started." Mr. Therault claps his hands together, like we're at some prep-school. BTSH is in no way a prep-school unless what you're prepping for is a life of mediocrity.

Lacy whispers, "He could be teaching drama with all that pomp." When Derrick laughs at her comment she brightens and shifts a little in her seat. It's like she's an attention barometer tuned only to Derrick.

"Out theme this year," Mr. Therault continues speaking with hands clasped, like a big surprise waits for us all. "Is social, cultural, historical, and beyond."

"That's narrow," Max says at my side containing a smirk.

Mr. Therault turns his head in our direction. We're the riff-raff of debate team, which is funny if you think about it. "Our first topic will be 'slavery'."

"What? You can't debate slavery, it's one sided—stupid, inhumane, the end." Max half stands while speaking. Being born in Haiti, Max didn't have a lot of ties to American reparation or its decedents, except for the fact that treating other humans as 'less than' is inherently wrong —he didn't have to be born in America to feel that deeply.

"Max Nelson is the team captain for pro-slavery."

"No way." Max fully stands at that.

"Derrick, would you please choose your team against slavery." Mr. Therault licks his lips like the idea of breaking up our band of fist bumping testosterone tops a major accomplishment in his life. He barely knows us. "Debate is not about believing in the cause you're supporting, but rather convincing others to side with you."

Worse than I feared. I am going to suck eggs at debate.

"Politics," Spencer Tracy comments. Spencer has blond hair, blue eyes, and 'future Senator' etched across his high hairline.

Derrick points to Spencer and announces, "I'll take Future Leader of America for one-hundred."

Lacy droops slightly in her seat. She must have expected Derrick to pick her first, but I doubt he'd choose any woman over Nathaniel—if only for Nathaniel's well-being.

"I call Lowry," Max says right after Derrick's pick, which surprises me.

From his earlier remark about helping Bevan win arguments against me, I'd think he wanted to argue against me, not with me. "Thanks," I say to him. "You know we're screwed, right?"

"Yeah."

"Nathaniel." Derrick picks causing Lacy to look even more crestfallen.

Max, more aware of Lacy's reactions than Derrick, chooses Ben Lowman, a junior with a red nose and sideburns. Leaving Derrick one more chance to choose the poor girl.

"Uhm..." Derrick pans the room, like it's a tough pick between Lacy —someone he knows and trusts and who definitely doesn't want to get stuck arguing *for* slavery, and Janet Voorhees—a girl who both looks and acts like she fell out of a Nicolas Sparks novel, complete with puffy red eyes. "Lacy."

Which means, we get Janet.

Max sucks in a breath, keeps hold of it and calls Janet to his team. Completing our Pro-Slavery group with one girl who looks like she's already crying, the kid who might as well be leading the infantry with a trumpet call, Max—one of the only persons of color at school, and me with a big slash birthmark across my face like I'm calling everything off-limits via mime.

"Oh yeah, this was a good idea," Max says rolling his eyes.

“You’ll have one week to prepare your arguments.” Mr. Therault unclasps his hands finally. “When we meet next week, I expect each side to present their argument without interruption from the other team. We will take turns countering. If we go over time, the debate will continue into the next scheduled meeting. Any questions?”

Spencer’s hand shoots into the air. “What do we get if we win?” He’s obviously already polishing some trophy in his head.

Like its even fair, Spencer has anti-slavery as his platform. Of course they’re going to win. I’d like to throw a trophy at his head right now, get this humiliation over with. Poor Max, he must stand in front of his peers and argue why he believes a group of people should have the right to treat someone like him as less than a person. Mr. Therault might be the devil.

Our team members exchange contact information and phone numbers.

“Do you think it’d be weird if we worked on our arguments together?” Derrick asks. The rest of the room breaks up, Spencer and Ben leave separately, followed by Janet.

“I don’t think that’d be weird,” Lacy says. Bless her heart. It totally would be.

“I have to get a 5K in before dinner,” Max drops a running term like we have any clue what distance a ‘5K’ is. It sounds like a big deal.

“I’m behind on homework as it is,” I say, which earns me puzzled stares. It’s not like me to slouch on schoolwork. The fact that I’ve been grounded for the past ‘every’ week makes it even more confusing for those that know me, but I’ve been devoting so much time to spying that other things have slipped.

“I think we should work in our teams anyway,” Max says.

Lacy perks up again. “That makes sense.” She has a team full of males, of course she’s thrilled about it.

“Text me when your homework’s caught up. We can go over any points—if we can even think of anything.” Max pulls his bag over one shoulder and leaves the room.

"I'm available whenever," Janet pipes up—the last thing anyone in high school wants to admit to is being available whenever. It's much cooler to have unavailable times.

"You guys are so screwed." Derrick puts his knuckles up to his mouth and laughs, like biting them makes more sense than a fist bump right now. I think he's right on all points.

By the time I arrive at home, dinner's on the table. With no time to set my schoolwork aside before sitting, I pile some books next to my placemat and mouth an apology to Mom. Dad's working late, so it's us girls and Howie. When I say 'us girls' I mean Tami too—and I wonder if anything has been rifled through in my room while I was away. Between her and Howie—my room needs its own security camera.

"It's okay, I'm glad you're involved in an activity," she says holding up her phone showing me the text I sent her earlier to let her know why I'd be late—like I don't know I sent it.

"I wouldn't call being assigned to argue in favor of slavery much of a chance for debate."

"You got assigned pro-slavery? Not cool," Mom says sounding so much more not cool than my assignment, simply by her using the term 'not cool'.

I nod, until Tami speaks. "Slave is happy. Not good for mingle between kinds." Her tone slides so even and steady I can't determine if she's asking a question or stating a fact. I suspect the latter, but Mom appears to be worried about the former.

Mom raises one hand, "It's alright, Tami. I don't think you understand. Lowry is not in favor of slavery—she has to argue the point for an assignment."

"Japanese sold as slave to Africa before America has country." Tami speaks in a tone that makes me wonder if she's trying to justify American slavery as some sort of karma against Africa for having slaves of Japanese descent at some point in history. "All thing go around." She draws a circle in the air with one finger.

It's the most I've heard Tami speak since she's arrived. Her words also inform me that she's both educated and opinionated. Some things

I've been skeptical about because Tami never interacts with us. The other thing it tells me—Tami holds a grudge. Even centuries old grudges that don't belong to her. Which might explain her dislike for Max.

"I don't think that justifies it," I say.

"Justice burn America to the ground," she says in response. Her finger once again circles the air—full circle. Little prickles stand up on my arms, and the back of my neck. My appetite flushes away only to be replaced with boiling stomach acid.

No one moves, as if stillness can clarify the very scary statement Tami has made. Howell drops his fork on the floor, making Mom and I jump.

Mom drops below the table top to retrieve the utensil. Being left at head level with Tami and no parent blocker has me sweating. In my discomfort, and to my horror, words come out of my mouth. "Internment camps were terrible, I agree." I'm stabbing at the possibility she's referencing all Japanese maltreatment by her blanket anti-American statement. "But, people today can't be held accountable for the actions of persons from decades ago."

Tami doesn't meet my eyes. "Learn history."

Mom resurfaces. "Yes. We should all learn from history." She hands Howell his fork, contaminated by floor germs. "Treat all people well, no matter their differences. We all deserve a chance to do better than those who came before us."

Howell throws his fork onto the floor again. As if in the face of Mom's statement, Tami, Mom, and me all drop our eyes to stare at the fork, then raise our eyes to meet each other's somber faces. No one bends to retrieve it this time. Howell eats his dinner with his hands—the rest of us eat in silence.

14

I can't sleep. I haven't finished all my homework. How can I be me, if I don't have my homework turned in early with extra embellishments in the margins? It's like I'm missing the substance of a meal that defines me. Lately I'm nothing more than the pudding in my once accomplished life. Assignment backup/overload isn't the only reason I can't sleep. What's up with Tami being chatty and terrifying all at the same time? I now prefer the silent and distant Tami.

When I hear Dad come home I quietly slip out of my room and gently step on the least squeaky stairs—careful not to make a sound and alert Tami. Halfway up the stairs I hear Mom whisper-talking. "I *was* going to ask her to help out around here. I thought it might be nice if she had a night to make dinner or help with dishes, but now I'm worried she'll take it the wrong way."

"Slavery?" Dad asks. They've obviously been discussing the same thing I was hoping to bring up. I choose to remain on the stairs and eavesdrop on their conversation. "She can't honestly think that's still prevalent."

"You weren't here, Hon. It sort of freaked me out."

I nod in the concealment of the stairwell.

"This hasn't been anything like I thought it would be," Mom says.

"We both know that expectations are rarely reality. Let's not judge the whole experience by one odd moment at dinner. Maybe I can talk to her in the morning before she leaves for school."

Mom must nod in agreement, I don't hear her response. Their footsteps move out of the kitchen toward the living room. I remain on the steps for some time thinking. Mom's a little weirded out by Tami. At least I'm not alone in my discomfort with her in the house, but that doesn't put me at ease. Quite the opposite. I'm on higher alert.

Part of me fears to turn around because Tami might be behind me in the dark—just staring at me. I back down three steps, plenty of prior warning which way I'm moving, in case she's acting the lunatic in the shadows behind me.

No stirring, swishing, or skittering sounds behind me so I turn and rush the last few steps to my room without looking around. Shutting the door firmly, with an added push after it latches, I breathe. I've made it to safety.

Just when I finally snuggle down into my covers and close my eyes long enough that they hurt to open, a digital siren forces me awake.

"What the-?" My breathing fast and ragged. I imagine fire alarms and Howell in danger. Jumping out of bed, I race for my door, tap, tap, tapping the knob in quick succession in case it was a fire alarm that woke me. Cold. I turn it to reveal a dark empty hallway, with one exception. A line of light streaming from the crack under Tami's door.

Tiptoeing to her door, my ears take in every sound like a shattering scream all around me. *Step silently feet, dang it.* Less than a foot from her room I pick up the argumentative tones of Tami's native language. Again, it sounds like a two-way conversation, which I'm only hearing one half of.

Why didn't I bring my phone with me? I could have recorded her talking and played it for Masato so he could tell me what Tami's saying. I lean closer, not wanting to touch the door, but still get close enough that I might hear the voice on the other end of whatever device Tami's using to communicate with someone. I know I can't get that close, but lack of sleep has me feeling brash. I must be getting closer because Tami's words get clearer—even though I can't understand a dang thing.

Then a crack of sound and mechanical click of door gears makes me lose my balance—falling against the wall. Her door shuts. I had no idea it wasn't closed entirely, and it shut inches from my snooping face. Dark shadows at the base of the door alert me to the fact Tami stands right on the other side. Why didn't I watch that space before?

How long has she known I was standing out here? What does she think I've heard? I catch myself from falling all the way to the carpet and stumble with my back sliding against the wall—away from Tami's room. I run into the trim around the bathroom door and I push myself off the wall. Not sure if I expect Tami to burst out of her room with a knife or a net to fall over the top of me. I race back to my own room and shut the door—not caring that it slams.

"Stop slamming doors—it's the middle of the night!" Mom hollers from the room above mine. I check my phone for the time. Three in the morning. There's no freaking way I'm getting another wink of sleep tonight. My eyes won't close—not even the itch of dryness can force them shut.

The same siren sound that originally drew me out of my room goes off twice more, at four and five in the morning—on the hour according to my phone. And it's not a fire alarm. It's the chime of a cell phone, which my sleepish brain distorted into sirens in the night. Tami must receive phone calls on the hour.

There's no point in leaving my room to listen in. She only seems to speak Japanese at these unnatural hours of wakefulness. By the time my morning alarm chimes my nerves are shot. My eyes are so scratchy that every blink draws tears. Forget showering or breakfast, I can barely pull on jeans and a clean shirt to make it out the door in time to drive to class before the late bell.

All my intention of listening in to Dad's morning conversation with Tami are wasted on jitters not induced by caffeine. I completely miss loitering in the halls with Violet and Sara before class. I feel cut off from my friends and all forms of calm. Knowing I won't last with my eyes open once I sit down in first period, I take a seat near the back. My eyes close the second I connect with chair.

Dreams don't reach me—I'm that tired. The next thing I know, a freshman I haven't met shakes my shoulder to let me know a different class starts. That's how the entire day goes. I sleep through one class and then another. I have no idea what assignments I'm supposed to get done, reading pages, reports, tests to prep for... Not a clue.

Thank goodness debate doesn't meet tonight. I'm going straight to bed once I get home.

I must not get woken up right away after last period, which is embarrassing because that's the one I have with Derrick. I'll have to text him later, to get our assignment. The parking lot's half-clear when I pull out. With all the micro-naps I've slipped in all day, I'd think I'd be fully rested, but all I can think about is my bed.

Until I arrive at home to see Tami playing with Howell on the front lawn.

Panic floods my chest—Howell's too close to the road. *Doesn't she know how many pets are lost to this road?* It's supposed to be residential speeds, but no one pays attention to that. Cars zoom past way too fast for three-year-olds to play in any unfenced portion of the yard. At least that's how us Dodds have always conducted front-yard life—danger danger, no fence, danger.

I stop my car barely inside the driveway and fling my door open. "Howell can't be out here unattended." I know, I know, technically Tami tends him, but it's Tami! Like anyone would believe she's actually tending him? "Howie, come here."

Howell throws a foam football toward Tami, who doesn't catch it. My baby brother runs right to the edge of the grass, next to the road where two cars zip past.

"Howie!" I race over and lift him in my arms. "Tami, what's wrong with you?"In all fairness, Howell looks fine. He's happy and enjoying the attention from Tami, which makes it so much worse.

Howell likes her. Tami doesn't smile, thank goodness. I'd totally smack any smirk off her perfectly unbirthmarked face if she dared taunt me like that right now. Sleep deprived as I am, there's no telling how many inhibitions are compromised.

"They're fine, Low-low." Mom's head pops out from the front door. "I've been keeping an eye on them from inside while I make dinner."

Keeping an eye on them? What does she expect to use the supernatural-space-geek-force to prevent Howie from running out in the road at a split-second's notice? Mom's words don't console me.

"Tami volunteered to watch him so I could get some work done," Mom goes on.

"Did she? Without charging you for her services?" I snap.

Mom lowers her brow. She knows I'm referencing Tami's comments from yesterday's dinner. "That's uncalled for."

I'm on the edge of being grounded again... Or still...

I should write a book and call it, 'My Junior Year Spent Grounded.'

Tami watches the exchange between Mom and me. I wish I could read her. There's no telling if she's enjoying the chaos she's orchestrated, or if she simply can't follow the English. Or maybe the whole, no-English thing is a ruse. Nothing would surprise me right now.

"You know what would be nice?" Mom's setting me up, I can feel it. No way am I answering this question. "If you helped Tami with her English homework."

My jaw falls a few inches. I'm a tutor now? Next to me, Tami remains stoic. I close my mouth and try to picture what I am supposed to look like—the composed version of how that's the stupidest thing ever.

On a full night's sleep, I could consider the possibility that Tami's family and friends all live on the opposite side of the world, and two am here is probably lunch time there. But, I haven't slept a full night in weeks. And now Mom's suggesting I spend my homework catch-up time helping someone who refers to me as 'monster' and recently said Americans should all burn, or something like that—no... Screw it. I don't know what she said. Sleep takes a toll on precise memory.

"Yeah, sure," I say after enough time has gone by that I'm certain everyone knows what I really think.

"Fantastic. Howie, you come inside too—or play in the backyard."

Tami counts her steps (at least I think the foreign words she says are numbers) as she walks inside. As if she's remembering some buried treasure she's hidden in the yard.

Howie bolts for the backyard, reminding me that it's a nice time to be outside. He's happy to play when it's not too hot outside. Which is precisely why Max runs at the cooler hours of early morning and later evening. Why am I thinking of Max? Not helpful stupid brain.

Tami unloads her laptop on the table, ready to work.

"Don't you have textbooks, or assignment pages?" It'd be awesome if our high school was completely digital, but it's not yet. I've heard lots of districts have gone that way, but we still have physical books and paper assignments sent home.

Tami responds with a slow blink, which I take to mean she's either annoyed or not following a word I'm saying. My bottom lip protrudes in a pout, not a sad one, but a frustrated lip thrust. Except Mom sees me and points a finger at my face. I can't tell what words she mouths at me.

I'm certain it's something like, 'put that thing (my lip) back where it goes and don't let that girl feel unwelcome—she's likely to burn us all to the ground.' And I suck my lip back in. Because, if that's not the best point ever, though unspoken—technically I came up with it myself, I don't know what is.

"Show me what you need help with," I say.

Tami points to her computer screen. This is not going to be easy. I bend down to read if an assignment shows via email, and discover everything written in a language I can't read. Even if I could read it, I have no idea what any of it means. There's certain symbols I recognize from items Tami gets from the UPS guy. A subject line shows:

.

It stands out because this one looks a little different than some of the other writing. I've seen something similar on food items and feminine supplies Tami gets from Japan. Tami notices me staring at the subject line I recognize and turns the computer screen away from my view.

"This is in Japanese."

"It's not supposed to be," Mom says. "Part of the program is immersing oneself in the new language and culture." A snort escapes my mouth and I slap a hand over my face. Mom startles like I've detonated a bomb she must defuse. Her recovery defaults, as always, to 'give the total stranger the benefit of the doubt' while casting blame on her own kid. "I'm sure it's an internet page. Go to word documents."

"I'm in word." I tip the screen so Mom can view it.

"How do you turn in homework if it's not done in English?" Mom directs her question to Tami while keeping a watchful eye on me. Most likely, trying to make sure my mouth doesn't open, letting wild thoughts fly. "I better call your placement coordinator, to make sure."

Tami pulls her phone from her pocket before Mom has a chance to reach her cell resting on the countertop.

"Are you calling?" Mom asks, and then pauses to wait for an answer from Tami. Tami glances toward Mom, thumbs flying across the keypad. Obviously, she's texting someone at frantic speed.

"I'm calling," Mom announced and enters the number from a magnet on the fridge. The line picks up after only a few rings. "Yes, this is Abbie Dodds. I need to clarify about home and school requirements for Tami." A brief pause. "No. Not at all, she's a sweet girl."

Tami's eyes move above the line of her phone a second time. Still composing messages to the unknown source, obviously not the person Mom's currently speaking to on the phone. I feel like a ghostly witness, like they've forgotten about me in the room. However, if I try to exit I might draw too much attention to myself. Not to mention it'd be more difficult to glean information outside of the room. At least I can read facial expressions from Mom—Tami seriously has no range of expression so there's no point trying to read her.

"Whose responsibility is it to follow up with school assignments? I was under the impression the program was monitoring school performance and we were to help provide a safe and enriching home environment, filled with the same expectations we give our own kids."

Mom's totally trying to weasel in Tami helping around the house. Though, maybe if she got involved a little more I wouldn't find her so terrifyingly unibomber-ish.

"That's what I figured. Yes... Absolutely we can. We were trying to help with tutoring homework today—just now to be honest, but we can't understand any of the language settings... Is that something we should worry about, or ... Right, right. Yeah, thanks. I mean, I figured, but wanted to make certain... There is sort of... The light on all night long—all night. Yes. And napping most of the days." Holy Hannah! I can't believe Mom ratted Tami out right in front of Tami. I could hug her right now, she's the coolest Mom ever. "Sure. She's right here. I'll let you speak with her."

Mom hands the phone to Tami, who sets down her own phone. I see the name 'Mindy Boston' above the text message before the screen goes dark. I think Mindy is the Eastern office coordinator in charge of all Asian nation placements. I could be wrong. Though, I could have sworn Aiko, Jin, and Masato were all talking about Mindy from Boston. If I'm right, that means Tami has contacted someone with authority over the local coordinator. She's already going over Mom and the contacts available to her here.

Tami accepts the phone and leaves the room with it. I half expect Mom to follow her. Why does Tami have the right to a private phone conversation? With weird behavior should come a mandatory wire tap. I stand, like I'm going to follow. Mom snaps her fingers and motions me to sit my butt back down.

Several minutes later, Tami comes back from the basement and returns the phone to Mom, who holds the receiver to her ear. "Still there?" After a nod, I assume the answer was 'yes' and the person on the other end won't shut up.

Across the table from me, Tami pulls her laptop away and walks down the stairs with all her things, not bothering to wait to find out how the conversation goes with Mom and the person on the phone. That could mean a couple of things, such as, Tami pulled all the strings, runs the show and doesn't need to hang around to watch Mom crumble. Or, Tami didn't get her way and doesn't want to hang around while we gloat about our victory over her having to reign in the creepy-weird flag she's flying.

"I hadn't thought of that," Mom says into the phone, drawing my attention back to her end of events. What hadn't she thought of? I thought Mom covered every scenario always. She's a worrier, that's what we do. "Absolutely we can enforce some ground rules. I'm sure it won't hurt Lowry to have to comply with them as well."

What now? Comply how? In what way? Why is my name being mentioned at all?

"We'll touch base in a few days then? That sounds perfect, thanks, bye."

Before Mom can push the 'end call' button I'm seeking clarification... "Ground rules? And what am I complying with exactly?"

"To curb some of the late-night activities taking place in the house, we're instilling a 'no electronics after ten pm' rule. No phones, tablets, computers, anything. At ten-o-clock everyone will deposit all electronics into a lockbox that will only be opened at six am the following morning."

Worst idea ever. "I use my phone as an alarm clock. How is that going to work?"

"We'll get you an actual alarm clock, if we have to." Mom grabs her purse and keys off the counter. "Actually, I need to go pick up a few things for this to work, can you watch Howie while I'm out?" I nod. "And finish making dinner—all that's left, remove the foil when the timer goes off, let it brown five more minutes after that. I'll be home in time to help set the table."

"I can do that too—it's not that big of a deal."

"Dad'll be home in time for dinner today."

Dad's going to hate this no-electronics all night thing as much as I do. "I'll set a place."

Mom calls Howie in from the backyard and puts on a show that emphasizes word use for toddlers, like that will encourage him to speak on his own. From Mom's over-nurturing gesture-rich speaking he's placed in front of a high-volume television to keep him occupied while she's gone. I listen to the television ask the kids to name things, count items, jump, clap, and shout their favorite part. Howie kicks his feet on the edge of the couch without verbally interacting.

It makes sense that he would like Tami—she never asks him to speak.

15

By the time Mom returns I have the table set. She drops three plastic bags next to the trivet with the oven-fresh casserole dish on it.

"Mom." A hole melts into the bag instantly. The plastic prefers to stay with the glass dish when I pull it away, what was inside spills out onto the table.

A fabric tote tips on its side, toppling a small digital alarm clock, a Hawaiian flower night light, and a baby monitor. Mom sweeps the items back into the tote with one hand like she's brushing crumbs off the table—chunky electronic crumbs.

"What's with the baby gear?" I include the nightlight and the monitor together in my gesture.

"Tami never told me that she's afraid of the dark," Mom says. "Honestly, I wouldn't have made a big deal about it, had I known."

"You bought her a night light? Aren't those for six-year-olds?"

"They have some decorative ones. Showier. For adult spaces."

I pick the baby monitor out of her tote. "And this? Very singles loft chic. You know, for independent international travelers and all."

Mom grabs the listening device from me and returns it to the tote. "Solutions don't have age limits."

"You know digital alarms are basically the same thing as using a phone."

Mom does take the alarm clock from the tote, takes my hand in hers, turns my palm right side up, and places the box, highlighting 'cordless' in big block letters, in my hand. "No internet, text, or wifi though."

"Wifi and internet are the same thing."

"Are they really?"

I don't know for sure. "Basically." They're both used in reference to surfing the web, or being online, I think. "They're synonyms."

Mom shrugs and stows her store goods on top of an upper cabinet. "Call everyone in for dinner. We have to discuss some new family rules tonight."

Normally I hate additional family rules. In the past, they were always because Bevan had an unexpected seizure without wearing his foam helmet, or the time Max snuck Bevan out of the house to climb a cliff by moonlight without ropes. It was the 'without ropes' part that lead to new family rules.

Tonight, I'm looking forward to what will come. Maybe Tami won't be up all night freaking me out in her fully lighted room having heated conversations over her 'no text or talk plan enabled' phone.

I haven't even checked what's in the other two bags. While Mom's busy stashing the tote out of sight I take a peek. I can see through enough to know it's a brightly colored game. "Candyland? Chutes and Ladders? Monopoly Jr?" I let go of the plastic handle. "You're on a toddler kick—are you trying to hint at something?" I pat my stomach.

"No," Mom says.

I call the rest of the family in for dinner. Mom starts talking about 'new rules' before anyone's finished dishing their plates with mystery casserole. "There will no longer be any personal electronics after ten pm."

"Abbie, I'm not sure that's going to work," Dad says. His hand clenches the phone he brought to the table.

"It goes for everyone," Mom replies in a firm tone.

Dad reacts worse than I do. He rolls his eyes and slumps his shoulders.

“At ten, all personal devices go in the tote. They can be collected the next morning at six.”

“You’ve got to be kidding me,” Dad says.

“I’m not.” Mom grabs the tote from above the cabinet. I notice the baby monitor isn’t in it. “I have digital alarm clocks for anyone who needs one. Lowry has hers. Tami?” Mom holds an identical cheap alarm in the air for Tami to claim. She accepts it, but doesn’t seem entirely aware of what’s being said. “James, you too.”

Dad takes it with the same enthusiasm as any teenager—none.

“Next, the rule that we will play a board game together once every week. Since Howell can’t read and still needs to be included, I picked some kids games to start with. Maybe we’ll like it so much we’ll buy some more complicated games later.” Mom sounds excited about this rule. “Everyone will have a night to cook and do dishes. So, if you make a royal mess with the pots and pans, you’re on deck to clean it up.”

“And if we don’t make a mess?” I ask. “Does someone else have to clean then?”

“No. But, you’ll appreciate yourself for not making a mess when dinner’s over.” Mom holds up a third finger even though she hasn’t been counting on her fingers until this exact second. “Weekly schedules will be posted—you girls have to fill in your activities and assignments. I have to know if you’re turning in your work.”

Suddenly I feel like this one aims at me. Does Mom know I’m behind in homework?

“If you leave with friends,” Mom goes on. “I expect you to write down who you’re with and how I can contact you, if I need to.”

Pretty sure that one’s aimed at me again. These rules are beginning to feel like previous ‘new family rule’ dinners. Blanket rules targeting me.

“Are there any questions?” she asks.

Tami’s alarm clock sets to the side of her plate, as if touching it contaminates her food. She hardly eats any of the meal, normal for her at family dinners. She has tons of food stashed in her room—shipped from her overseas family at weekly intervals.

“Good. Since there are no questions, game night starts tonight.”

"But... Homework," I say.

"How long do you think it takes to play one round of Candyland?" Is this a trick question? How should I know? "No time at all."

As it turns out, the answer to that question should have been, 'a gazillion million reshuffles,' thanks to GumbaGumbie, Peppermint Pete, and the rest of the candy characters that send each of us to early sticky sections on the board right when we think someone might win.

"I hate this game." I sigh after drawing the peanut brittle dude for the third time since we started.

"Someone has to win eventually," Dad says. He's totally into it—probably because, at the moment, he's the closest to the finish.

Howell plays on Mom's team. There are only four character pieces, but he'd probably be on her team even if there were more. He doesn't seem to care about the game at all. Mom holds his hand on the token to move it for their turn. He tries to pull away the whole time, but still refuses to say 'no' or 'stop' or 'why did you buy this horrible game?'

"Low-low, can you watch him while I use the bathroom?" Mom asks.

"Sure." By watch him, I assume she means—look at Howell while he jumps on the couch in every attempt to avoid the game playing area, which I'm good at. Mom goes through the kitchen to the downstairs bathroom, which is weird, because she's verbalized several times how much she prefers the upstairs bathroom to the downstairs one. No one's using either bathroom, so there shouldn't be a conflict for her to use the one she likes.

I don't say anything. Mom's had a day already. "Hurry, Dad, move your character to finish." I nudge him.

"Mom'll know."

"No, she won't. Besides, I really should finish my homework, before the calendar becomes nothing more than a grocery list of late assignments."

"You're that behind? Why did you join debate, if you're already behind in your work?"

"I'll catch up, I promise." Why am I trying to remain in debate? I have the worst topic. It'd be nice to have an out that wasn't me quitting. I imagine how good it would feel to explain that my dad *made me quit.*

"Fine, fine." Dad picks a card, like that makes the fact he's cheating any easier to swallow. He then moves his character into the finish rainbow, and does a little open mouthed 'whoo' in addition to a seated dance. Howell gets in on it, even though he has no idea we're celebrating how we talked Dad into cheating so the game could end. I'm a terrible influence. "You girls go get your homework done. Parent teacher conferences are next month. I want to hear glowing reports from all your teachers."

I like how Dad includes Tami in his fatherly spiel. If I lived in someone else's house for a year, I'd want the father figure to include me like that. Like Tami's one of his own kids, and he has expectations that we all do and try our best.

Mom passes us on our way downstairs.

"Over already?" she asks.

"Dad won. We have to do homework."

"Excellent, way to be productive." Mom must be feeling proud of herself for our good choices. I love it when she does that too—it's cute of her to take credit. For some reason, she rarely takes credit for her own true efforts, but this type of situation she'll claim.

At ten pm on the dot, according to my satellite linked phone, Mom knocks on the door to collect all my 'personal electronic devices.'

"You're serious about this?" I complain because it's expected of me, more than because I mean it. I'm relieved Tami will be without a means of overseas communication all night. I can finally get some sleep.

I shut the door and return to my homework. I'm up till eleven and then retreat to bed. It's not until two-thirty that I'm awakened by a cold breeze. I pull my covers tighter. Chilled air freezes my nose. New Mexico isn't known for frigid fall weather, but we're not immune to cold fronts. Already sleep deprived, I get out of bed to check my window. Closed. I walk toward the door—open?

I'm awake now.

I walk into the hall and notice Tami's light on again—her door closed, but light flooding the space between the carpet and the bottom of her door. Also, a steady breeze whistles under her door. I fold my arms tight over my chest—no idea what I'm supposed to do. Why does she open my door at night? Just—why?

Mom's been working hard to include Tami. When Tami chooses involvement with the family she's less terrifying, but nights completely throw me off. Even a nightlight hasn't dented her use of overhead lighting after midnight. And what is with the windows? Whatever I do, will most likely be the wrong choice. I step toward Tami's door, then pivot, take three steps toward my door. Stop. Go back toward Tami's door. Stop. Put my head down, turn back, enter my room, close the door—making no effort to soften the closure, and wedge my vanity bench seat against the door. It doesn't have a seat back to jamb under the knob. There is literally no way the bench seat can prevent someone from opening my door, but I feel better knowing it's there.

I'm too tired to stay awake all night keeping a vigilant watch for strange activity. I assume there will be strange activity—it's Tami for crying out loud—the girl screams sociopath or something that might be crazy-smart or crazy-crazy. Heck she probably discovered new ways to torture me with that Candyland game—*go back to peanut brittle, brittle, brittle.* With all her run-around behavior, I do feel like I'm stuck in a psychopath loop filled with gummy nightmares of Tami opening my bedroom at night dropping peppermint oil in my eyes. At least it feels like that kind of torture by morning—followed by licked lollipops of homework due dates being flung at my hair all day.

Or, maybe she's none of those things. Maybe she's just—not smart. That's not a nice thing for me to assume. But it's also not the worst thing I've come up with. It's not like every American achieves the same level of intelligence, I assume that not all Japanese teens are math and science geniuses... right? Maybe Tami is simply below average?

I bury myself in covers—warm, padded, safer the deeper I go, except I hate breathing through blanket layers. I make myself a tunnel for cool air to reach my mouth and nose so I can breathe easy—and fall back to sleep. The heavy kind that a dump truck and wrecking ball invading my room couldn't disturb.

A cordless alarm clock, also no match. I sleep past seven.

Yellow light with tiny little dust particles, dancing in morning rays of sun, greet me awake. I yawn and stretch, thinking it must be Saturday. The terrible pit in my stomach remains from one of those horrible dreams where I miss class or show up without my pants on. Except I'm wearing pants and it's not Saturday.

"Shit." Of course, Howell's standing at the side of my bed, my favorite lipstick in hand. "I mean..." I can't think of any replacement words for my curse snafu. "Shit. I'm so late."

I grab the lipstick tube, making Howie cry, snag a clean shirt, change in the bathroom, loop an arm through my bag, and run for the front door.

"Low-low, why is your brother crying?" Mom asks when I reach the top of the stairs.

"I took my lipstick out of his hand."

"Did you say sorry?"

I have to apologize for that? "It's my lipstick."

"He's three."

It occurs to me that both Mom and I say that to people a lot. *"But, Howell is three..."*

"I'm late." Lucky for me, Mom has bananas ready for a 'grab and go' meal.

"You slept in, you're not late."

I don't have time to listen.

"Your hair?"

"Late," I shout over one shoulder—not stopping to pull the door closed behind me.

"Your phone?" Mom stands in the still open doorway with the tote in hand. "Too late for that?"

Never too late to collect my phone. But, I want to play it cool. I open the door to my car, chuck my bags inside, then rush up the steps to the tote to retrieve my precious—my phone.

"Hug for a phone." Mom extends her arms for a hug. "I love you, Sweetie."

Weird. "Are you okay?"

"Can't I hug my daughter without having some ulterior motive?" I really don't know if I'm supposed to answer that. Can she? Then she adds, "And try to include Tami. You know, when you can." And there's the ulterior motive. At least my mind can be at ease regarding Mom's health.

"I do." Sara does anyway. Since Sara's my best friend, by default I too include Tami whenever I can. "We eat lunch together and everything." One time, but it counts.

Mom pulls me in for a second hug—totally disregarding how late I am.

"I love you too, but I have to go."

Somehow I'm on time to school. Waking late does that to me—leave the house earlier than normal and still feel like I'm going to get in trouble for sleeping in. Sara waves me over to where she's sitting. Derrick, Nathaniel, Lacy, Aiko, and Violet are there too.

I pick a spot next to Derrick and set my stuff on the floor. On his other side Aiko looks very demure and yet, the way her eyes shine, she has the appearance of a tigress on the hunt. Derrick doesn't seem concerned about being her prey. I've never seen him look unsure about himself, except in front of Aiko. The way he doesn't know where to put his hands, in his pockets, on his knees, at his side... He likes her, no doubt. At least he's too self-conscious to notice the spit puddle on my book.

"We're planning on going to the Sadie Hawkins dance as a whole group," Derrick talks to me with his eyes on Aiko. Her head bent low, like she's being shy, yet her eyes still blaze like there are completely opposite thoughts inside her head. "It's all planned out."

"What's happening?" I hear Derrick, but don't absorb any of his words. Other than the fact Aiko eats him with her eyes, I can't concentrate. Until I notice Lacy. Sitting cross-legged on the floor, her head low like Aiko, except that instead of playing at shy, Lacy's hiding the fact her eyes are red and wet. Her hair falls forward to help obstruct her face. I sit up, much more awake. Lacy's not the sad type. I didn't think she had anything other than happy in her DNA.

"It's going to be so fun," Sara says. "We're all going to the Hawkins dance together—well we still have to figure out who is going with whom." Sara looks at me and Lacy. Are we the only ones without dates?

"It's girl's choice, right?" I ask.

Sara nods. "But, to help with those who don't really know anyone, we're doing a set-up, kind of."

If there's one thing Sara loves more than goodwill, its set-ups. Maybe she's learned her lesson with her friends since Lacy and I are obviously not on the list. Though Lacy doesn't look too thrilled about it. Maybe she's one of those rare ducks who likes them. "We'll find dates, right Lace?"

She wipes under her eyes—eye liner and mascara can give away even the most discrete tears. "I have someone in mind actually."

"Who?" I'm going to be the only person without a date.

"I was thinking of asking Spencer."

"From debate?" Derrick takes notice.

Lacy bites her bottom lip before answering. Very 'now I've got his attention' esque with the added drama of shaded lower lids from smeared makeup. "Why not? All the guys I regularly know are taken,"

"They are?" I was sort of hoping Max was still available. I really am going to be the only stag. I rub my eyes and sit up straighter. "Who planned this?"

"All of us," Sara says. Which means she did.

Something I remind myself at this moment, Sara has the best of intentions, and she sees the need to include the foreign kids and make new friends. She's not seeing Lacy's raw eyes or my concern of being left out. Or worse, ending up paired with someone who can't see past my birthmark.

Just then, the last bell sounds. Everyone in the group gets to their feet, grabbing their bags. Conversations end, not 'get back to you later on that.' I don't know when the trend to stop talking and leave things unresolved became popular, but it's definitely a 'thing.'

All I can think about the rest of the day is, *Who's Max going with?* If every guy in our friend group is already spoken for—that includes Max. Maybe it's a good sign. I'm obviously less worried about Tami. Maybe I have a longer than average adjustment period to people living in my home. It's important to learn that now, before I leave home and have roommates and worry they're all serial killers.

17

I don't see Max the rest of the week due to his busy schedule, not my lack of trying. Spying on Tami turns out to be eaiser than tailing Max. Also, I might have an issue with stalking—ew. I better knock it off. Also, Mom packed me a lunch along with one for Tami. A dry ham and cheese sandwich (because mayo might go bad before its time to eat lunch according to Mom), grapes on the stem in a baggie, and an honest to goodness cheese stick. At the bottom of the bag there are saniwipes. I'm guessing those are for pre-sanitation because there isn't anything particularly saucy or stainy. Count on Mom to sanitize the world.

Mom can't pre-sanitize Tami out of my worries though. She's everywhere now, since Sara befriended the exchange group Tami hangs with. As it turns out there are exchange subcultures. The Asian kids all found each other and pivot around Sara's social magnetism. The kids from Europe, which there totally are it turns out, tend to hang with the skater crowd. I wish there were statistics I could look up to see how the social dynamics of exchange students this year compares to prior years. There's probably a record of students in yearbooks past, but whoever looks at the years they're not in? Especially where it comes to Tami. She confuses the bejeezus out of me.

At school, she has a bounce in her step, a smile on her face—the fact her eyes are always flat... irrelevant—she's smiling. I've seen her leave cute little packages on teachers' desks too—I know this because I'm the world's worst host sibling who spies on international house guests.

Just the other day, she left a box in the choir room. It was small, and undecorated. She didn't leave it by the choir teacher's desk or anything, but it's a choir room. The teacher doesn't have a desk. There's a music stand and a podium thing. Tami left the box in the pulpit thing. When I snuck in to check it out—it was a box. Nothing sinister about it. It didn't even rattle when I shook it.

She also laughs when other people laugh and raises her eyebrows when spoken to, indicating a level of investment in what the other person's saying. Dare I say, understanding English.

At home, she goes out of her way to avoid looking at my face. Like she's going to catch a birthmark. On the night I make dinner, I choose homemade macaroni with a garlic cheese sauce I look up on allrecipes. To get the sauce right I'm supposed to heat it low and add the grated cheese slowly. It turns out gritty and feels squeaky on my teeth. I might have rushed it.

Tami scoops the same portion size to her plate that Howell gets—maybe five regular bites worth of food. It's not perfect, but it's not that bad. She also covers her mouth when she chews each bite. Given, she does that every night, but tonight it bothers me.

To get my irritation across, I make sure to chew with my mouth open, and lean into the table—getting my whole head closer to Tami. (I would do the same thing to Bevan if he were here annoying me). Not like she ever looks at me anyway.

"Low-low, chew with your mouth closed." Mom says.

Tami pushes her chair back—not once making eye contact with anyone except Howie. She leaves her plate at the table, even though one of Mom's new family rules includes clearing your place to make it easier on the person doing dishes, and goes to her room. I close my mouth and chew the rest of my dinner.

After everyone eats, I take my station at the sink. Thank goodness for dishwashers. Apparently, no one started the dang thing for the last —forever. I can only fit three plates, two cups, and the utensils in it. I'm stuck hand washing everything else. I want to blame Tami, or Mom. But I'm pretty sure Mom told me I needed to start the dishwasher as I ran out of the house this morning—thinking I was late, which technically puts the blame on me.

Hard labor—dishes one night a week—brings me back to debate. I have to come up with some way to argue pro-slavery in less than five days. I look out the window in time to see Max run past our house. Does his practice run always pass our house? I've never noticed before. Now, instead of the debate topic, all I can think about is Max. *I'm definitely pro-Max.*

Mom squeezes behind me, stands at the top of the stairs and calls down, "Homework," without specifying if she expects it to be finished already, worked on, or turned in tomorrow.

"Did you hear anything last night?" I ask her when she passes behind me again.

"Hear what?"

"Like, I don't know—what that baby monitor was for? Howie already has three in his room."

Mom purses her lips like she's bugged with some FBI listening device as well as the rest of the house. "You think it's an invasion of privacy?" She pinches the bridge of her nose. "I did not think of that."

I roll my eyes and continue washing, because Mom has lost it worse than I ever did. "I'm sure Tami's just weird." It's like she caught my paranoia and took it five notches higher. "While you're here," I try to change the subject before Mom comes up with a dumber solution than a baby monitor. "I have debate next week after school, and Tami and I are both going to the Sadie Hawkins dance."

"Put it on the chart."

I hold up dripping wet hands. Mom pens in the events. "I hope you're keeping up with your schoolwork. Only four weeks to parent-teacher conference."

"You've got to be kidding me, that soon?" I'm mocking, but Mom doesn't notice the joking tone.

"Mid semester happens fast."

I finish my dishes and decide I need to take my grades seriously, mostly because grades matter to Mom and I don't want to be left behind when her 'serious train' comes into the station to find me lighting my future on fire. Getting serious means no more distractions.

Starting tomorrow.

Tonight, I'm too tired to do homework.

I shove my vanity bench in front of the door before I go to sleep, knowing it only functions as peace of mind. It hasn't grown magical door-locking powers overnight. For good measure, I place several bottles of nail polish on top of it. If the bench gets knocked over, the bottles will fall making a tinkling of noise.

I spend the next day awake enough to hear all my teachers talk about stuff I've never even heard of, demonstrating how behind I am. With several tests on the horizon for stuff I haven't studied, I skip social hour at lunch—to study. After school, I miss the debate team meeting so I can finish reading for lit class. I have no ideas about pro-inhumanity anyway. It's not like I'd be any help.

It's Tami's night to cook and clean, which means I can get more homework done before dinner. I expect exotic scents to draw me in before Mom knocks on my door.

"Dinner's ready." She stays in the doorway like she thinks that's going to speed me along. "And be nice, maybe even have seconds."

Now I'm worried.

At the table are mugs—the ones we use for hot cocoa maybe twice a year. We're not a huge hot beverage family. We live in New Mexico, who needs hot beverages? In the center of the table are brightly colored packages exploding with symbols, lettering, and tons of different fonts in all colors. My head hurts trying to figure out where to start reading, or which way is up. Maybe if I could read any of it, it wouldn't be so overwhelming. What does American packaging look like to Tami? Boring? Confusing?

There isn't a single odor in the air either. Nothing to tantalize my taste buds or warn me regarding what I should expect.

"Pick." Tami points to the packages.

This counts for cooking? She didn't do anything. I had to follow a recipe and use two pots and everything. I've seen Tami do more than this with lame old ramen noodle soup. I try to brush my judgment aside. The packages have pictures of pink bears and exuberant floating cartoon faces along with a small icon that looks like jelly or a dollop of beans.

"I don't know what any of it is," I say.

Howell grabs a package from the table. "Not safe for small young." Tami snatches the package out of his hand and puts it back on the table. She opens a shipping box set on top of the counter and retrieves a different package to hand Howell.

"Not safe for kids? What's in this stuff?" I put the item I'm holding back on the table.

"Kids don't eat." Tami again points to the assortment of mystery food items on the table.

If this turns out to be my last meal, due to poisoning or something, I'm going to be really pissed off. At my side, Mom looks equally skeptical about picking a dinner option. Dad on the other hand settles for the yellow, pink, orange and blue wording with the picture of a glob of bean goo in the corner.

Tami cuts the top open, dumps the contents into a mug and pours hot water from a kettle over the top. She hands it to Dad alone with a stirring spoon. Steam and an ocean mire scent rise in the air. The little sizzling sound that accompanies the mix connecting with water satisfies too.

Dad wastes no time sipping—probably burning his tongue on the steam, which isn't the worst idea come to think of it. It smells like stagnant tide pool aroma. Burning my tongue might help me get down whatever I'm about to consume.

Dad doesn't convulse or pass out within thirty seconds, so I reach out and pick something that looks like a shrimp party blew up all over plastic wrap. Mom too, grabs a package. Tami cuts both our items open and dumps the powder and freeze-dried veggies and what I think are tofu bits into a cup. Howie gets the shrimp-slposion package as well—with no safety warning, which comforts me.

Steaming water ignites the scents of both cups. Mine smells like a brine pool full or floating green strips—seaweed. Mom has a yellowish-orange broth in her cup and a warm spice scent. I sort of wish I picked the one she has. I prefer the color and aroma, like a chicken curry almost.

Tami goes back to the box and pulls out a package of flower shaped colored marshmallows. Dessert? She cuts the bag open and hands one to Howell.

"Kids under four can't have marshmallows," Mom puts her hand under Howells mouth for him to spit it out. He left it fall from his mouth into her palm.

"Not marshmallow." Tami dumps half of a small handful into Dad's cup, then slips the rest from her hand into my drink before I can pull away.

Five fluffy flowers soak up the broth. They expand like sponges until they double in size. "Is it sweet?"

Tami looks confused by my question. I fish one out with my spoon. Dad copies me. Where I'm finding this dinner experience underwhelming, Dad beams with excitement. He loves new things. I imagine the level of unexpectedness of this meal has him dancing on the inside. No one saw this coming. We're not even sitting at the table for crying out loud, and no one has given Howell anything to eat besides a soup sponge flower thing.

I pop the pink flower thing into my mouth, expecting it to taste like seaweed, or bread, or even marshmallow. It has no flavor. Literally a soggy sponge. It's not even easy to chew. I wish Mom would put her hand under my chin so I can spit this thing out.

"What flavor is this?" Dad asks. He's subtle that way.

"Flavor?" Tami scrunches her forehead. "Is for soup."

"I'm having a hard time knowing what flavor it is though," Dad says.

Ha! Even he wants to spit it out. The texture stays off. It's like Mom cut her cleaning sponge into squares, let it dry out, and then dropped the hard-dry pieces into our dinner.

"Taste of soup," she says. "Soft flavor. Japan." She puts a hand on her chest to demonstrate that it's the flavors of where she comes from.

"We do like big and bold, don't we?" I say. American flavors are known for kicking teeth in for all the flavor punching we enjoy. This food might be better if we were starving, or only ate rice, so our tongues weren't flavor blocked by actual yummy things. I still have a taste memory of the cool ranch Doritos I ate for lunch.

Tami opens Howell's food. Inside are crackers with cream filling. I wonder if he'd trade dinners with me? It's like Tami didn't want to make anything for all of us, so she brought up a box of hodgepodge from her weekly mail deliveries to get this task over with. Or maybe, these really are her favorite foods and she wants us to appreciate the flavor of air croutons and salt water.

Before I return to my homework cave—my room—Mom reminds everyone, "I'm collecting board games for our family nights. If anyone has suggestions or knows anyone who plays board games and can ask for recommendations, I'm taking suggestions."

Mental note: Ask Sara if they play games, and which ones end the fastest. Except I see the pile of homework I still have left to do and forget to even look at my phone. By the time Mom comes to put all electronics in the tote, I haven't even checked it. I put up one finger to buy a minute of time.

"Now, Low-low. Family rule."

Max texted me. Twice. *Missed you in debate. Do you already have a date for Hawkins?*

"I have to answer this," I say.

"It will be there to answer in the morning."

"No. But, Mom—"

This time her finger goes up. When Mom's finger goes up, I stop talking. Because Mom doesn't bluff about grounding or revoking privileges. I haven't even earned all mine back from my earlier groundings. Like Fridays with friends, or allowance. No way do I want to lose my phone completely—she'd do it too.

"Put it in the tote. You can reply in the morning." Her fingers open and close like she's grabbing for my phone.

I grumble the whole way over, "Stupidest rule ever."

I worry Max thinks I saw the text and never answered. Or maybe he thinks I'm avoiding him. I wasn't at debate, I didn't respond to his texts, but I'm not avoiding him. Worst feeling ever. I wanted to send one text—one. That's all. To let Max know I got his text. Mom doesn't understand anything.

I follow my new sleeping ritual of setting a booby trap against my door. From the moment I climb into bed until I fall asleep, thinking of what I should have texted to Max in the three seconds my phone was in my hand. I could have sent something—a smiley face—anything.

18

In order to avoid any miscommunication, I try to find Max the next morning so I can explain the whole 'new family rules' thing in person. The dance isn't for a few more weeks. It should be plenty of time to figure stuff out. I realize with Halloween the following week, that Sadie Hawkins will be themed and everyone's planning early so that they can coordinate costumes, but I mean who needs a month to come up with a matchy-matchy costume idea?

I don't see Max before school. Lunch promises my chance to apologize—and I really need to now. By not texting back at this point, I've crossed that line of 'trying to do the in-person conversation' with being a socially inept weirdo. At least for today's social standards and how media plays into communication norms. Why didn't I simply text him first thing in the morning? What was I thinking? In person isn't better —it's worse. Made worse still as hopes of an 'in-person convo' dissolve. I haven't seen Max. I bet it totally looks like I'm ghosting because I've liked seven things on social media and reposted another two. It's obvious I have my tech back, and still haven't contacted Max.

In the lunch room, the exchange kids in Tami's friend group sit near, but not with, Sara and all the people that orbit her world. Like two galaxies that have learned to meet in the stardust between them. And I'm Pluto—barely claimed by Sara's gravity anymore, even though I want to be one of the big players. They're all still chatting back and forth, it requires leaning and raised voices, but everyone seems fine with this arrangement.

Max sits next to Violet. I pause. How awkward to 'talk; with Vi listening. Would it be the worst if I run to the bathroom and try talking to him again later without an audience? It's difficult to ask out a person in my friend circle, because if something doesn't go well, I'm still friends with everyone they know.

No. I need to talk to Max. Now. I push down anxiety over having waited so long and stride forward. That's when I notice the commotion. A rotund student stands in front of the exchange table near Tami, grasping his throat, eyes wide and bulging. No one on Sara's table seems to notice because the student isn't making a single sound, but looks to be in very real distress.

Tami and several of the kids at the exchange table look the other student in the face, watching him point to his throat, retch forward like gagging or vomiting soundlessly. Aiko looks concerned, but confused. Tung on the other hand laughs like the whole thing's a gag. Maybe it is. I squint a little to get a better read of the kid's face. I recognize him from gym. His name is Neil and he's the 'practical-joker' sort. He once slicked the pull-up bar during timed trials and one kid almost punched himself in the face when his hands slipped off.

Tung's also in my gym class. He's familiar with Neil the prankster. Except, Neil doesn't appear to be in on the gag part of it, the 'hey, I'm going to die' end of things.

Tami, as usual, remains stone-faced.

Max has noticed me standing in the center of the room at this point. The expression on his face tells me he's read into my text silence, like I'd hoped he hadn't. I look from him, to Neil who is either an excellent mime or in real danger, back to Max, Neil... Tung.

I rush to Neil. "Do you need help?" Probably making things even worse between me and Max. The student continues to grab his neck. The skin of his lips and edge of his nose turn a purplish-blue color. He's not joking, which makes Tung a world-class ass with all his laughing and pointing. Or he's *dangerously* uncomfortable in awkward social settings.

"He's choking!" I shout over the spectacle that is Tung.

Sara stands to see over seated students, then everyone stands.

"Get the nurse," Derrick directs a student near the doors."Go!" He then rushes to the student, "Why are you all standing there, doing nothing? Do something!"

None of us knows what to do. I shuffle in a circle, because it's something.

Derrick clears a path between kids who've gathered around the drama. Standing behind Neil, he grips his hands together in front and thrusts a fist up into Neil's stomach below the ribcage and thrusting in and up, so that it almost looks like Derrick buries his hands in Neil's fleshy tummy.

Before the nurse arrives, Neil's arms go limp. Derrick thrusts one more time, a huge chunk of bread roll, soggy but compacted into a tight ball, launches from Neil's mouth. His arms don't raise in celebration though. His eyes remain closed as well. He's passed out.

Derrick lays him on the floor as the nurse takes over. It's not long until EMTs are on the scene. No administrator wants to get sued for pinching pennies when a student's life is at risk. Neil's rushed out of school. I hear rumors an ambulance hauled him to the hospital.

I'm too shaken to even think about the dumb 'no electronics after ten' thing to Max. That's small potatoes compared to what Neil went through.

Sara's having some intense conversation with Derrick—along with every female in a fifty-mile radius. He'll probably be interviewed for the local paper, not the school news. Lunch ends anyway. Tung also has a crowd around him—he's no longer laughing. Tears roll down his cheeks. I wedge my way through the hero worship crowd to get a better idea what's going on with Tung.

"It's not your fault man, there's no way you could have known he was serious," someone says.

Tung appears genuinely shaken now that the spectacle ends. "We all make jokes when we're nervous—it's okay. Don't be so hard on yourself," another kid comforts Tung.

Aside from Derrick the hero, Neil stars as the talk of the school for the rest of the day. Tung's part in the drama drops away from retellings. Some rumors go as far as to say Neil died for a whole minute, but the principal announces that the student from lunch recovers well at the hospital and to please not play chubby monkey with bread rolls during school hours or on school grounds.

The next time I could possibly see Max is during debate group meeting. Where yesterday the teams met individually to discuss argument points and strategy, today includes both teams. Seems I can't avoid an audience if I hope to grace Max's presence.

I practice what I might say to Max the rest of the day. Looking over my shoulder to check no one watches me in the bathroom, I face the row of mirrors and rehearse. "Have *you* got a date?" I lower one shoulder—the casual slouch look. "Have you got a *date?*" Straight backed, head tipped forward so my hair covers part of my stained face. A demure look. "Have you got a date..."

"What are you doing?" Mandy asks. The same Mandy on varsity cheer with Violet. She's chewing gum, never chomping the same side twice in a row, like some volleyball double touch rule, but for gum.

"Me?" I twist on the water and shove my hands under the stream. "Just washing my hands." I don't presume Mandy dumb enough to buy that lie, I assume she's kind enough to let it slide.

"You're friends with Derrick, aren't you?"

"Derrick? Yeah." Mandy's the best—totally throwing me a change-of-subject bone.

"Are he and Violet, like... A thing?" She walks to the small high window and lifts the pane so a breeze enters the space. I sniff like I've missed a bad odor—I don't notice anything.

Violet? I thought Violet was into Max. It's so hard to keep track of who my friends are interested in, even within the same friend group. I keep flipping between Derrick and Max myself, so how can I expect to know where everyone else's romantic compass points at any given time? "I don't think so."

"Cool." Mandy doesn't leave. Instead she pulls a cigarette pack from her jacket and draws a small white stick from inside it. "You'd be more subtle if you practiced your line without actually speaking. Like say it in your head, and move your lips and all, but don't actually speak out loud."

The parts of my face that aren't always discolored, turn pink.

She nods toward the door. "Everyone can hear you in the hall. It's sort of a big joke right now."

I'm fifty shades redder than pink now.

"You might want to stay in here for a few minutes, so it dies down a bit before you show your face." Mandy lights her cigarette and pulls on the end in her mouth so that the glowing embers fight to destroy the clean white wrapping.

"Are you serious?"

Mandy nods, waves the smoke toward the open window, wets the butt in the sink and washes her hands before walking out like she's done some civic good deed and will now receive a 'get out of jail free' card.

I'm never leaving the bathroom. Except, it really stinks in here now and I have to talk to Max. Maybe I won't bring up the date question. Then anyone who might have heard me in the hall won't know who I'm talking about.

I face my reflection again. The red color of my normally pale skin drains to white. I want to match the tan colored tiles like a chameleon and blend into the background for my escape. Instead I exit the bathroom, head down, turn right, and go straight to the fine arts pod where debate meets.

"Sorry, got a date," some jerkwad says as I rush past—forcing myself not to make eye contact with him.

I even pass Tami with one of her non-decoratively wrapped boxes she's been leaving in teachers' rooms and don't say anything, or try to spy—or anything. Even though she tries to hide the box, and now I suspect she's bribing teachers to raise her grades before parent teacher conferences. Like that would ever work anyway. Not a chance.

I'm last to arrive for the group. "Wasn't sure you decided to be an official member of the team." Mr. Therault says when I enter the room. "Take a seat with your captain."

I sit next to Max. "I need to talk to you."

"Can it wait?" he asks. His shoulders are rigid and his head bends over his phone like the president waves on the screen or something else super epic. More important than talking to me.

"Not really. You see, my mom made all these new rules, so we can't have our phone after ten pm and I tri—"

"I messaged you before ten pm."

He's totally mad! Guys are exactly like girls! Everyone is drama. "Yes, but I didn't have my phone at the time, and when I did check it—I noticed the text, but then my Mom came to collect the phone and she wouldn't let me send a single response until the morning—she has these lame rules now."

"And it stopped working the rest of the day?"

Max turns much less attractive when he's upset. "No. I wanted to talk to you in person. I don't have a date, but right now I'm not sure I care about ever having a date."

"Good to know," he says. "Because I'm going with Yi."

"That was fast."

Mr. Therault whines on about argument techniques to help "...get one's point across without belittling the judges' intelligence or our opponents." I'm barely listening. All my energy expends trying to read Max's body language. It's not good.

"It didn't happen right this minute," Max whispers—not even facing me. He can't even look at me? He's that upset?

"Ben?" I shout, even though he's sitting right next to me.

He jumps. "What?" Janet and Spencer notice too. I officially have the attention of everyone in the entire room. Including Mr. Therrault, who I'm pretty sure doesn't like me at this point.

"Will you go with me to Sadie Hawkins, unless you already have a date?"

"Not a very romantic way to ask someone," Max whispers hoarsely. "Besides, I thought you didn't want a date—ever."

"I changed my mind." I don't whisper.

"Sure." Both Max and I startle when Ben responds. "I'd love to go to the dance, and yeah—" He shakes his head like he woke up from a nap. "No one's asked me yet."

My voice cracks. "Okay then. I have a date."

"If we can get back to debate, then?" Mr. Therault crosses his arms while staring me down. I nod. A lot of seat shuffling goes on behind me.

Derrick, Nathaniel, and Lacy all wiggle in closer.

"You guys okay?" Lacy whispers. Mr. Therault hears anyway—giving us the hush-glance. The man has sonar hearing.

"Fine." I hate it when people ask that question, when it's obvious by the red-rimmed eyes that people are not okay. But again, Janet's sitting with us—red rimmed glistening eyes and she seems fine—other than the 'I'm about to cry' expression.

Lacy doesn't hush. She leans in closer and whispers toward Max. "You've been weird since Lowry used you to get out of being grounded by going to Silver City. You've got to forgive her for any trouble you got into—she was having a hard time. Her parents like grounded her for weeks."

"She what?" Max turns in his seat so he's looking right at Lacy. "Lowry didn't hijack my car or force me to go to Silver City." Mr. Therault walks over to stand by us while he discusses picking at your opponent's cracks in reason. Total teacher move.

Lacy looks from Max to me and back to Max. She even looks at Mr. Therault, like he has the answers. The confusion on her face accusatory at the same time. She continues to bounce glances off each of us, like that will somehow clear everything up. "That's what Lowry told us. I thought that's why you guys are so mad at each other."

Max lets out a pent-up breath, which smells strongly of sweat. Runners must sweat through their mouths as well as everywhere else. Weirdly, I don't mind the scent of Max's sweat. Is that gross?

"I'm not mad," I say, putting an end to 'tennis-match-eye' the term I'm using to describe the constant back and forth glances they are all coordinating between Max and me. Everyone lands on me. "I needed a date for our group thing, and the dance. Ben stepped up though." At that Lacy switches her focus back to Max. No one else does. Her eyes narrow. Lacy isn't known for being discerning. If she's picked up on anything neither Max or I are ready to reveal about what's going on between us, we're in trouble. Anyone could be next to catch the signs. Signs regarding how 'in-like' someone is, have a viral effect.

"You know you girls can come with the group, even if you don't have dates," Derrick says. It's the 'you girls' blanket statement that bothers me more than 'even if you don't' part of his remark.

"Is that invitation open to anyone who doesn't have a date?" Janet asks. "I mean, I have a date. I have a serious boyfriend, anyway. But, I don't think he wants to go to the dance. He's like twenty." *Maybe she did step out of a Nicolas Sparks novel?* Awkward silence provides the pause Lacy needs to form a bad idea.

Lacy's face brightens the littlest bit. None of the guys seem to notice. "Spencer," she calls across the room to where Spencer studies debate footage, having lost interest in whatever I'm talking about, like its football reels for training purposes. When he looks up, in a daze of arguments, Lacy says, "Will you be my date for Hawkins? We're going with a whole group, so no pressure one-on-one or anything."

"Same." I shout to Ben. Even though, he's still—right next to me. And, he already said yes. He flinches back like I'm damaging his ears. There's a good chance I'm damaging everyone's ears. "No pressure. One-on-one stuff. It's a group. A whole group." I don't want him to think I'm into him or anything. I don't want anyone thinking that ever —how embarrassing.

Spencer waits for me to finish speaking. "Sure. Sounds..." Whether it's the debate footage or the lame stuff I said, he seems lost for words to describe how flattered (or unflattered) he is. "Big groups are cool."

Ouch. But, Lacy is all smiles, not because of anything Spencer said. She's smirking at the way Derrick sizes up Spencer. Doing the whole, arms across the chest, leaning back a bit thing. What Lacy doesn't realize is that Derrick's doing the exact thing Bevan used to do for me. It's a protective big-brother pose, not a 'that's my girl not yours' sort of thing.

Derrick I can read. Max on the other hand, escapes me, total jerk. Because I missed one text? I'm glad he already has a date. Like I'd want to go with him—and his dumb hot face and his defined forearms around me, swaying to slow music... I need to force myself to think about him less. That might help me curb the way my fingertips go numb whenever my hands get too close to his.

We don't spend any of our club time working on debate topics.

19

The rest of the week consists of me battling not thinking about Max with not being creeped out by Tami. It's one or the other, which makes nighttime go something like, "don't think about Max... Max is the person I am not thinking about. I am absolutely not thinking about how Max looks when he is sprinting to a finish line... I bet Tami would trip him before he reached the finish line. What if Max got hurt? Is Max okay right now? Max!" I mean. "I am not thinking about Max."

I'm either wide awake because of unidentified noises outside my personal room barricade, or obsessing over possibly getting a text that I can't answer because my phone gets jailed in the family-electronic-overnight-tote and social-life-death-row.

I've accomplished close to two hours sleep per night by the time I realize our first real debate comes due, and I have nothing. I haven't prepared a single counterpoint. Or—point-point. Is forfeiting legal? And won't Max think I'm the worst by leaving him hanging on a topic he despises? Or maybe he'd find it more offensive if I came fully prepared to advocate for slavery.

There's no winning.

I need a nap. And, my phone is dead. MOM! She didn't plug it in to charge overnight, a lot like how I feel at the moment. It weighs more in my pocket once I realize how useless it is.

Lacy, Derrick, Nathaniel, and Spencer all exchange strategy texts during lunch, so I can't eavesdrop on their plans for the debate. Max is nowhere to be seen. Avoiding me much? I slide my phone out of my pocket, look at the black screen, sigh, then stash it back where it was. It's not like I have Ben or Janet's numbers anyway.

On a happy note, Neil (who tried to fit three entire potato rolls into his mouth at lunch last week) returns to school. I'd consider pulling a similar stunt to miss three days of school, if I could guarantee someone would save me before I accidentally asphyxiate myself. With my luck, the only witnesses would think I was joking and laugh the whole time I suffocate to death. I'd probably get a Darwin award—dumbest excuse to avoid debate. It'd be my first award of my high school career.

When I walk into the room where debate meets I immediately regret it. Derrick dresses as Abraham Lincoln. So is Nathaniel. And Spencer. And not to be left out, Lacy, too, sports a Presidential top hat and stick-on beard.

Panic turns my stomach. I rush to Mr. Therault. "I didn't think this was a period debate. I mean, I thought we could draw from examples in present social media or current events."

"You know of supportive pro-slavery points in current events?" he asks.

I stammer. There's not a whole lot on my reaction scale for this situation. "Well... No. But, I didn't think we had to dress up."

He puts a hand on my shoulder, which doesn't help at all. It's making it way worse. Grody teacher hand on my shoulder sucks all my focus—big red-knuckled hand—get off. "You don't have to dress up, but there's no rule against it either." He takes his hand away. Now I can look at his face and maybe listen to whatever he's still saying. "If a team feels they gain an advantage by dressing as a character, time period, or other gimmick, they're free to do so."

My team looks benched already. The debate hasn't even started. They sit, no one facing each other, on a red painted bench. Max doubles over with his head between his legs, Ben rocks in his seat, like he's been traumatized by the Lincolns. His lips move and he glances at index cards. Where did he find something to memorize that could possibly help us? And will he split the cards with me?

Janet's eyes are more puffy and red than usual. Ten bucks says she cries when it's her turn to counter argue. That or she's hit the first third of her tragic-romance life story and the hero will soon grace her life, but she won't know it's the hero for another seven years or something agonizing like that.

Mr. Therault stands behind a mobile wooden pulpit. Spencer/ Lincoln eyes the thing like he'd like to give a campaign speech right about now. Mr. Therault leans so close to the mic I think he might try to bite it. "Because I'm such a nice guy, I'd like to open the debate with the team against slavery." He leans toward our sorry corner of self-pity. "This way you won't feel so attacked after you deliver your points. You'll have a better idea of what's coming at you."

The old 'beat them down before they're hit' teaching method.

Derrick and Spencer both move toward the speaking platform. Noticing each other, neither immediately concedes the path. Testosterone electrifies the air, even dragging Ben's rocking to a halt. We stare to see who will claim the platform first. Derrick surveys the room briefly—all our eyes are on the two of them. He smiles at Spencer. I can't tell if he's trying to defuse the tension between them, or if he's worked out the 'gentlemen' loophole in this situation. Derrick gestures the way forward, Spencer being the future senator that he is, takes that to mean 'you first.'

From her seat, Lacy adjusts her stick-on beard, to hide a smile.

The first point covers all things horrific about slavery. Breaking family units apart, cruelty, inhumane living conditions, false beliefs of superiority from owners, abuse, and all kinds of despicable treatments. Spencer tips his Lincoln hat toward us when he finishes. Like he's opened and shut this case. I sort of agree. This whole thing is stupid.

"Counter debate?" Mr.Therault looks at our group. "Is someone prepared with a point specifically addressing some of the concerns brought up by Mr. Tracy?"

Concerns? He listed a number of serious felonies.

"I'll go," Ben says. His shoulders remain rolled and his head hangs as he drags his feet against the scratchy carpet. "Slavery enabled wealthy land owners to establish a thriving economic system upon which capitalism was founded—"

"False!" Spencer shouts from the Lincoln gallery.

"Let Ben make his point, and someone from your team will have the opportunity to counter," Mr. Therault says.

Spencer immediately leans in to coach the rest of the team members on how false Ben's statement is.

Ben scratches his head. "Do I keep going, or...?"

"Keep going," Mr. Therault says.

"Capitalism helped America to establish itself as a dominant world power. So, one might say the practice of slavery was a catalyst for an independent nation."

Spencer scoffs from the Lincoln corner—so does Max in our corner. Ben walks away from the speaking area.

"Lacy, you're up," Derrick says.

"Independence established by the misuse of another person, is not true independence," she begins. Lacy has an entire list of reasons capitalism and independence can't claim slavery as a stepping stool to success. I start to wonder if our nation ever established true independence.

Spencer brightens like he's proud of his future Hawkins date. Derrick steps in front of Spencer and claps for Lacy. At the front of the room, Lacy glows. Hot overhead lights both create sweat, and reflect it like stardust across Lacy's skin, or at least the parts not obstructed by a top hat and fake facial hair.

Janet stands behind the pulpit from our side next. She stands there. Several minutes tick by. Her eyes become more and more puffy. Her breathing increases. Janet looks at us, like we can save her. Reality is, I'm getting a glimpse into my near future. The humiliation of failure and a topic I abhor.

"It's the worst," she finally says—throwing her cards. "I'm sorry, I can't argue this." Max gives her a tiny smile of gratitude. Janet runs from the room. No doubt headed straight for the security of a girl's bathroom stall.

I don't get this. We've been set up to fail. And our team leader is either supposed to humiliate himself, or debase himself. In debate, we should find some aspect to argue in our favor. It's not supposed to matter what the topic, but Mr. Therault deliberately gave us the worst topic ever.

Nathaniel takes the stand next. I see the opposing team's confidence grow in equal measure to ours tanking. Nathaniel has several highly detailed firsthand accounts of severe grievances against slaves by slave owners. He also points out that animals were protected by law before fellow human beings—slaves—where awarded any security. People couldn't abuse their animals, but they could their slaves.

Max has his arms wrapped over his ears. He crunches further into himself with each of Nathaniel's detailed accounts. True to his nature, Nathaniel has facts in spades. There seems to be no end to the gruesome historical records he somehow found. When he finishes, I see Max make an effort to uncurl. I know he doesn't want to go up there, none of us do.

So, I go.

"Slavery was not started in the United States." Everyone looks at me. "America is a young nation, which took economic and political cues from other countries." Max sits up a little. A spark of possibility buoys me on, about having decent points the second I remember some of the things Tami mentioned. "As a matter of fact, and unrelated to the establishment of slavery in America, African nations used to kidnap and transport Japanese slaves. And though slavery has abundant negative aspects, it also introduces cross cultural interactions, which opens doors down the road for healthy relations based on equality and trade." I can tell I'm losing them again.

Don't use the word equality in conjunction with pro-slavery arguments—like ever. Never. I continue minus that taboo word. "Also, the majority of stories that gained attention are those that are the most dramatic. Like in the movie Apollo thirteen when the television networks didn't want to broadcast the astronaut flight when everything was going well, but it was the only thing anyone wanted covered the second something went wrong. Human nature craves hearing the worst news. We sit on the edge of our seats and point fingers. I suggest the same can be true of historical accounts of slavery. Consider the vast number of people that owned slaves, and though there are substantial accounts of mistreatment, it doesn't compare to the number of owned slaves."

I look at the Lincolns and something else comes to mind. War. "Not only has slavery been historically misrepresented by media coverage." I'm overstepping and I see it on their faces, but I'm not done. I have one more point before they take me out to the firing squad. "Slavery was a front for the real motivations behind the civil war. Lincoln wanted to prevent the southern states from succeeding and starting their own nation. He knew that would create a weakened condition for the young country that we might never recover from. His only legitimate platform to roster support around was the slavery cause, because of course the North had heard the sensationalized accounts from the most atrocious experiences of former slaves. Like in politics today the slavery issue was attached to the union cause like true lobbyists, win one, win 'em all. And our nation remained intact with freedoms for all. I would put money on the notion that slavery might never have been abolished, or at least not addressed nationally, had it not been timed in conjunction with the threat to the nation dividing."

When I finish Mr. Therault's mouth opens as he stares at me. Max too has his mouth open, but he doesn't look impressed by my government knowledge or ability to argue a point. He looks very much betrayed.

"Well done, Ms. Dobbs. But, you still haven't convinced me to own slaves." He looks at his bare wrist, a habit from a time he must have worn a watch. "We're out of time today. You all did wonderfully. We can continue this debate next session or start to discuss possible championship topics and prepare for competition."

"Competition." Spencer echoes as if seconding the notion, practically bounces in his seat.

"In that case, I declare anti-slavery the winners, despite Ms. Dobbs impressive preparation in support." At that, Mr. Therault claps his hands, grabs his bag and leaves the room.

Max grabs his bag too.

"Max," I say.

"Good job."

"Are you mad at me?" I ask. "I don't condone slavery. I didn't even prepare."

"How is that supposed to make me feel better? Where did you get all those facts then?" He slings his bag over his shoulder. "You don't show up to practice, you steal my argument and my spot in the line-up, and you ask Ben to Hawkins. What am I supposed to do? Send you flowers?"

It's my turn for my jaw to drop. I have no idea where to start with all of that. "I didn't steal your counter points—I didn't even know you were prepared."

"Wow, that was awesome." Derrick walks up and fist bumps my clenched hand—held straight down at my side. He bends to hit it just right. Derrick doesn't seem to notice anything weird between Max and me, either. That's part of the reason I like him so much. No drama, because he doesn't notice a damn thing. "Way to government bill the slave issue, I guess last year's government class wasn't wasted on one of us."

Spencer comes along, like a newly adopted pet in our group. "Government is never a waste. We need highly educated youth to fix the wrongs of those before us. No more uneducated voters," he says like he's rehearsed it.

"I've got practice." Max weaves his way out of the room.

Derrick blocks his path and I almost think there will be a new and very tiny civil war right here in this room when I see the look on Max's face. "I almost thought you guys were going to win for a minute. How sick would that be?" He holds his fist in the air for Max to pound before he passes.

Max licks his lips, apparently deep in a debate of his own, before deciding to lightly brush his knuckles against Derrick's. Then he leaves.

And we all leave.

20

No matter what I do, things keep getting worse between Max and me. It's weird because I thought something was maybe developing, but it's taken this weird ugly turn. I imagine all Max sees now… my red slashed face and how much it looks like a 'do not cross' sign.

I'm the last one to arrive home, even Dad gets there before me today. I should feel accomplished for not bombing debate, but I feel like a failure. The table's already set for dinner with steaming rice and vegetables at the center.

"I'm not hungry," I lie. The truth is I could eat everything in the house right now. But it wouldn't fill the emptiness that's plaguing me and I know it. So why even bother with eating?

"If you don't join us for dinner, you'll have to do the dishes." I don't know how that's remotely fair, but I don't argue with Mom.

I sit at the table, gazing out the window at my side. While Howell pushes rice mounds to the floor, I notice Max jogging past our house. He has his head turned toward our windows as he runs at a slow pace. When he sees me through the glass he startles and increases his speed.

I don't get him.

My appetite roars under my frustration with what I did to make him so mad, why's he still jogging past our house? I'm sure there are a million options for getting a three to six-mile run in each night that don't include our road. I shove the rice and veg in my mouth and swallow without tasting anything. Like there's any flavor in rice and veg anyway.

When I finally make it downstairs I notice a draft coming from Tami's room. First priority, charge my phone—then I'm dealing with that stupid indoor breeze. The only moving air indoors should be mechanical. I am too overwhelmed by all the weird relationship crap in my life to worry about offending Tami right now. I stomp to her door, thrust it open so it bounces off the door stop, practically hitting me in the face on its return. "Why is your window always open?" I demand to know.

Tami isn't in the room. She must still be enjoying dinner. Flavorless seems to be her most preferred food. Why would someone have their window open all the time? Mandy lighting up in the bathroom comes to mind. I bet Mom would send Tami home if she found out Tami was smoking under Howell's bedroom.

The search is on. I bet my driving privileges Tami's hiding something that will send her butt back to Japan. That would be one less headache in my school year. I want to feel relaxed in my homeand all I am is twitchy.

If Tami's hiding something, I'll find it. If not, no harm done. Invasion of privacy and loss of trust never hurt anyone, right? Right?

Nothing under the bed. It's not even dusty under there. The closet has several stacks of books. I look over, under, between, aside—nothing. I open every drawer, shift every item of clothing, upturn every shoe... I even check to see if the electric socket screws look loosened (I saw it in a movie once—great hiding place for small items). Nope.

If I were going to hide something, I might tape it to the window ledge outside the room so long as it's weather proof. The last place I look, outside the open window. There's no screen. Does Mom know that? But, nothing hidden.

I take a second to consider the space, standing roughly center of the room. Tami doesn't own much, and what she does own I've invaded thoroughly. Pretty much everything's visible from where I stand. Including the fact there's no baby monitor in this room. Unless Mom's better at hiding things than I am, which I doubt. But, she would still have to plug it in—unless it used batteries. Maybe that's it. Mom removed the monitor to replace the batteries and hasn't had the chance to return it yet.

How can I check without drawing Tami's attention? Listen to the receiving end. Mom's room. I run up the stairs where the rest of the family watches TV. Even Tami—news declares tensions are rising in countries I've never learned about in high school. The names are common on news channels, but aren't part of the curriculum, not that our school has a world relations curriculum (outside debate, which seems to have the policy that everything's horrible all the time and arguments are the solution). Howie leans against Tami's side cuddled up the way he used to sit with Bevan.

It should make me like her more, but instead I feel like she's stealing something from Bevan without him even knowing. And the television isn't helping with that blasted nasal anchorwoman nosing information to us through a funnel of doomsday still images and yellow *caution* type-font headlines captioning video footage. The need to find a reason for Tami to go increases tenfold.

"What're you doing? I thought you didn't feel well." Leave it to Mom to ruin my plans.

"I don't."

"Then.What.Are.You. Doing?"

"Getting your heat pad."

Mom purses her lips. Somehow, she knows I'm lying. I take her silence as permission to continue to her room. Then I realize the big flaw in my plan. Nothing's noisey currently in Tami's room—so I can't test if the device is in there at all.

Except for one thing. My phone chimes. I check my pocket to see if I forgot to plug it in and happen to have it on me. Except it was totally dead. It would have to be plugged in to chime. So, the monitor must still be downstairs. The chime rings again, loudly.

"That's weird."

I lean closer to listen better. Sounds chimes right here in the room with me, that's how close it is to the monitor. Like... As if the monitor was in my room—not Tami's. But, that doesn't make any sense.

I run out of the room to check the location of my phone.

"Did you forget something?" Mom asks.

I ignore her. I know I didn't back up my cover story by hauling the heat pad with me. Who has time to find that when I'm being bugged by my own mother? I arrive at my door and stop to listen. The phone doesn't ring. Maybe it was Tami's phone I was hearing... But, I know it wasn't. I have a customized chime from a popular comedy show opening. The rings I've heard come from Tami's devices are standard. Pre-programmed.

I rush to my room. Next to my phone charger plugs another device, leading behind my vanity mirror. Why didn't I pay attention before? Wedged between the wall and mirror I find the baby monitor. Plugged in, so it won't run out of batteries.

Mom comes down the stairs. She doesn't soften the crushing weight of her feet against the carpeted stairs, obviously she's not happy with me. When she gets to my door she lets out a huff. In her hand, the heat pad. "You forgot this."

"Did you put this in here?" I ask, pointing to where the hidden monitor.

"No." She hands the heating pad to me and crouches to get a better look. "How did that..?" Mom stands straight. Her eyes widen, she whispers to me, like someone's listening in on the other end, which at this point—I can't rule out. "Did Tami do this?"

I shrug, my jaw gaping because Mom's been spying on me the whole time she thought she was listening in on Tami. And I've been under the impression Mom had this thing handled—that I didn't need to be as diligent. Tami could have been getting away with anything during the night.

"Where do you keep the cell phone tote?" I whisper.

"In the kitchen."

I slap my forehead—loudly. "Mom." Scream whispering sort of defeats whispering, but I'm so mad right now. Mom and I are supposed to be the most expert helicopter family members of all time and we're sucking at it. "Couldn't you tell it was me on the other end?"

"You must not make a lot of noise." She gestures with her whisper to emphasize without yelling.

It's true. I'm not known for being loud in my room. I don't understand the need for volume when I'm by myself.

"You're sure you didn't do this?" Mom asks.

I almost break from my whisper. "Why would I invade my personal space to allow you to spy on me all the time?"

"Oh my gosh, is that what this is? Am I spying?"

Seriously, she didn't realize that? "What do you call it?" And that's the moment I realize my snark loses any ground I might have had to convince Mom to force Tami out of our house. Mom has guilt. It's all over her face. She's practically sweating the stuff. When Mom suffers this type of guilt, she goes out of her way to make up for the error. The fact Tami discovered the listening device, snuck into my room, and replanted it out of earshot from whatever the heck she's doing all night—even the fact she's probably using her phone since it's not actually out of accessibility range, doesn't compare to the fact Mom feels bad about 'spying' on our guest.

She has committed an oversight now blown out of proportion in her head and she will forgive Tami any weirdness for at least a month. Which means, I have one month to build a solid case before Mom's ready to hear it and do something about it.

"I don't want this in my room," I tell Mom.

"Should I apologize to Tami?" she asks me, like I'm the best person to offer advice here. I guarantee I'm not. Mom and I are not on the same page on this issue.

"I think you should keep the electronics overnight tote locked in your room at night, that's what I think."

Mom's forehead scrunches. I'm not sure if she hears me, or if she's thinking how to broach the subject of being discovered bugging an international guest. She's probably worried it's a national security issue. She's likely to call the Boston office and make sure she hasn't broken trade relations and peace treaties with Japan by her breach of trust. Seriously, Mom totally overreacts when she has guilt. I'm not going to lie, it's great when it's in my favor, but this is so the opposite.

Then I remember my phone chimed. "I've got homework." I shoo Mom out of the room. In case the message comes from Max, I don't want an audience. Not like he's going to send me anything confidential...

Once Mom exits the room I check my phone.

Turning Sadie Hawkins into a Girls weekend. You in? It's from Sara.

My shoulders drop. I'm not sure what I hope Max might text me. I never actually responded to his last text. Maybe I should text him.

I'll check to make sure I can go. Probably have to include Tami.

Of course, Tami's a given. She texts back.

Tami's a given? Since when? I remind myself to let it go. I'll solve this in a month. I can last that long, and I'm sure to have enough evidence to evict her by then.

I text back a smiley face to confirm I received the message. Then I open the thread from Max. I chew on my bottom lip trying to figure out what I should type. I'm kind of proud of my debate performance today, but I know it upset Max.

Sorry about debate.

I read it twice to make sure there isn't room to misinterpret anything. I think it's good and hit send.

21

Max doesn't text back. I know because I keep checking my phone to see if the ringer accidentally got switched off until Mom comes to collect electronics. I view the screen one last time before dropping it in the tote. Now I wonder if he's ghosting me—just to get back at me.

Sleep doesn't come easy, and doesn't last long. I'm back to restless paranoia with Tami down the hall. I hear her rummaging around in her room. I wake with a racing heart too early for it to be considered morning. Thinking a jiggling doorknob woke me, I listen as intently as I can over the pounding inside my chest. Nothing. My nail polish booby trap still stands. I must have dreamed the doorknob thing.

I'll never sleep soundly with nightlife-Tami around. Why doesn't she sleep at night?

When morning finally arrives, I'm beat. Retrieving my phone, I see Max didn't text me back. Now I'm embarrassed. I wish I hadn't sent that message. He's pretty involved with track and other school events. Maybe I won't see him today... If I'm lucky.

So of course, he's with Sara when I get to school. There's nowhere to hide since they're standing at the front doors like greeters at an eighth-grade dance. "Hey guys."

Max sort of smiles. I think it's a smile. It looks a little like he's trying to read my mind at the same time. Panicked I block all thoughts of him and return a smile, like he maybe really can read my mind and I don't want him knowing I lost sleep over the text I sent him—well not only that, but still.

"Oh my heck, we have so much to plan before the dance." She looks at Max like he's invading the girl's locker room. "And I'm sure the guys have plans to make too, right?"

Max rolls his eyes. "Sure, dinner and flowers take weeks of planning."

Sara puts her hands on her hips. "I hope that's not all you guys are working on."

"We're not working on anything. We're dudes. We hope to smell good and not step on toes if we actually dance. Besides, it's Sadie Hawkins—the girls are in charge. If we plan anything its kind of anti-feminist of us, isn't it?"

Sara thinks about this for a minute. When she doesn't speak for a while Max speaks again. "Don't worry. Derrick has a whole thing planned."

Meanwhile, I'm standing there trying not to steal glances at Max, but failing miserably. I'm pretty sure he catches me at least twice—or maybe he's doing the same thing I'm doing.

Sara brightens. "Great. The girls are going to talk dresses, shoes, and hair."

"I'm leaving." Max meets my eyes and we both jerk our heads to the side like we were looking somewhere else, before he backs a few steps, scratches his close shaved head, and walks down the hall.

The rest of the week goes the same way. I never speak directly to Max, he doesn't address me either, but our eyes keep stumbling upon each other like we're having a visual affair. It's a totally different story with Tami. I keep looking for her to keep tabs, but never actually see her at school. Either she's a whole lot better at going unseen than Max, or I have a serious problem with my attention dial. Namely, it's set to Max.

I do keep seeing those bribery packages Tami keeps leaving for teachers. I even see one in the office. "What's that about?" I ask the secretary.

"It's a gift from Japan, from one of the exchange students. Isn't that thoughtful?" the secretary says.

"But, what is it?" And why hasn't Tami given our family a thoughtful gift? Am I being selfish? I feel like I'm being a little defensive and change my wording. "Like an air freshener or something?"

"Some art piece, I guess," the secretary says. "There's a few of them—like an installation or something. Kind of cool, right? Exchange students really deepen connections with other countries." She says. "Like I didn't even know about abstract Japanese art installments until recently."

Neither did I. Because Tami doesn't share anything about her cool culture with me. I'm interested. I'd actually love to learn about Japan and its art. "Connections—totally," I say.

Days pass this way. No sign of Tami at school even though I know she gets on the bus that stops in front of our house every morning. Way too much eye contact with Max to be normal. Then home, where Howell follows Tami around like a puppy, unless she's in her room. She's in her room all the time during the day, which means Howell stands in the hall, waiting to play on Tami's wifi phone.

At night its creaky noises, hushed whispers, and nerves—all the creeped out nerves my body can spare on so little sleep. I expect to lose my conscious mind any day now—go completely off-the-rails insane from lack of uninterrupted sleep.

"Are you alright? You don't look so good," Sara asks three days before the dance. "I don't want you to be out sick for the dance."

If it were anyone else—and mostly due to my deranged mental state, I might suspect them of not wanting odd numbers for the group activity, but it's Sara.

"Not sleeping well."

"What can I do to help?"

I should be careful. If I suggest Sara sing me lullabies all night, she would. I don't really know how anyone can aid in my sleep unless they take Tami away for a few days. Or, and much more feasible, I get away from the house for a few days. "Can I crash at your place this weekend?"

"Trouble at home?"

Dang it. What can I say? "No trouble. I'm not even grounded for once."

"Should we invite Tami?"

I want to slap my forehead, because the whole point is to get away from Tami and her odd nighttime behavior for one stinking night. Then it occurs to me, if Sara sees Tami doing weird stuff all night, she might be on my side and help me. "Good idea."

"We can have a sleepover before the dance—like a whole girl's night —all night."

I'm never going to get sleep. Never.

22

The night before the dance, I drive to Sara's house with Tami in the back seat. Everyone brings their dress, shoes, and makeup bags. It's basically a massive makeover party that's going to last thirty-seven hours straight.

I forgot to prep Tami on what to expect when she sees Sara's house. It looks like a shipping box has been stretched to house size. Yes, it's brown, but it's also very straight and has sharp corners and a flat roof with solar panels attached to it. Sara's family defines massive, I've always thought saving money on heating and electric was what spurred them toward the whole 'off the grid' lifestyle. But, I don't really know. They're sort of known, by the judgier folks in the town, as the weird family who adopted lots of kids and live in a box, like the little old lady who starved her children in a shoe. But, maybe they'd be the weird family who live in a box and eat organic non-GMO everything (except Max who goes out of his way to find the junkiest foods) if they didn't have adopted kids.

Tami has the look of a deer in the headlights when the front door opens. The split-level entry contains generalized chaos. One kid hangs from the upper stair rails and another bounces from the couch to the oversized ottoman and back in the sitting room.

"Hey, come on in." Sara calls from downstairs. "We get the whole basement to ourselves." When Sara says the whole basement, she means a large room with a wood stove and one of those massive, outdated boxed televisions that always have a dark corner so a quarter of the screen is indiscernible. If I had to guess, I'd say it's battery operated and running low on power. The unfinished walls are framed, but not insulated, with a concrete floor. But, it's set up as a functioning living space.

"No," Tami says planting her feet on the welcome mat.

"Don't worry. Your friends are here too," I say, assuming Tami feels uncomfortable with all the American kids.

I don't know. Maybe that's not the only thing. Partly I feel bad because I've gone my whole life being judged by the way I look, and I've judged Tami by her attempts to adjust to my cultural expectations.

But, what are my expectations of her cultural differences based on? Stereotypes? Movies? I have no idea what's normal for her and what isn't. Sure, she has a limited range of facial expressions. I have a big red slash across my face. She's awake all night, but lately—so am I.

Maybe we're both terrified of each other, staying awake because every noise we hear we assume means the other person does something weird. I mean, Mom did bug her room...

"I not want," she says, not moving. Her knuckles are white from gripping her overnight bag so tightly.

I follow Tami's gaze to the younger Nelsons, now wrestling over the remote control in the room slightly to the left of our heads. "Is it the kids? They're loud, but I promise they won't be downstairs where we are."

"Not want."

Sara reappears at the base of the lower half of stairs like she expected us to have followed her already. We're not even on the indoor landing yet. "What's the holdup? Is everything okay?"

"It's cool. We need a minute," I say.

Yi appears behind Sara. She rolls her eyes toward Tami and saunters back into the basement great room. Maybe I'm not the only one who doesn't know how to take Tami. I'm not sure if I feel comforted or concerned thinking about that.

"I car." Tami pivots toward the driveway.

"I don't know what you're struggling with. If you could tell me, explain to me what the problem is, maybe then I could help."

Tami stares. I've probably used too many words.

"What don't you want?" More staring in return. "Not want?"

"Not want sleep. This." She circles her hand indicating the entire Nelson house.

"This what?" I ask. "The whole house? You were fine ten minutes ago when we left."

Tami circles the air again. Not helping clarify anything.

"What, Tami, what? I don't know what this," I circle the air like she does, "means."

"Dirty. I not want."

My jaw drops. I look at the kids wrestling on the floor. Like Max the two of them were adopted from an orphanage in Haiti when they were very small. I'm so used to them I think of them as Nelsons, like they're not afraid of my face—it's me.

All those warm feelings of misjudgment plow into the front lines of feeling wronged. "You can't catch a skin color," I say. "Surely you know that."

"Mom say, people hate Japan." She indicates the entire house again —like her mom told her that the entire Nelson family in Nowhere, New Mexico is known throughout Japan for hating all these Japanese. "I not want sleep where hate Japan."

"That makes no sense," I say. "If you've spent any time with Sara, you know that she loves everybody. She wants to be friends with every single person on the whole planet. And her family raised her to be that way—they are the most accepting people you'll ever meet. Their family demonstrates that by how they treat people every day."

"Is Korea and China. Mom say all hate Japan. All same room—night. Dark. Scary. Cannot be safe place. Too many. No hide. Not want."

"I thought Yi and Aiko were your friends."

"All hate Japan. No place hide."

"No one hates Japan!" It's possible I'm losing my patience, and the night air gets colder by the second with no cloud cover to hold the heat in.

"Pearl harbor."

I didn't even know she knew those words. "That was decades ago. Water under the bridge." I could have chosen a metaphor using something other than water.

"Slave."

"History," I say. "Ever heard of progress? Or Forgiveness? Or the fact that none of us has a perfectly untarnished national heritage?" I feel like I'm back in debate, except this time I'm arguing the good side.

Tami shakes her head no.

I realize I'm not going to win by using a bunch of English arguments that she can probably understand less than half of, so I grab her overnight bag and pull her toward the door. "You're coming with me."

Tami pulls toward the driveway. "Not want."

"You need to learn that not everyone holds a grudge." Says the girl who's been holding a grudge for Tami calling me a monster on day one. "Get in here and have *fun*."

I manage to pull Tami through the front door and onto the landing between the split floors. I'm a little concerned about dragging her down the minor flight of stairs to the basement. If she falls while I drag her in, does that qualify as some kind of abuse? "Flora, can you come shut this door?" I holler up the stairs to the two kids still fighting over the TV, which shows one of those boring kitchen goods infomercials.

Sara hears me and sticks her head out from behind the wall. "Does she not want to be here?"

"Still adjusting to American norms. They watch a lot of Gossip Girl reruns in Japan—sleepovers are sort of bully central on that show—even for the kids you think are nice." I'm totally making this up. But, I've seen the show, years ago when it was cool and I had to watch it without Mom knowing. Mom hates shows about mean kids immortalized, basically the whole point of the series.

Sara puts her hands over her mouth in shock. "Oh my heck, no kidding. That'd be terrifying." She then addresses Tami, in slow, downpitch words. "No one here is mean. We are aaall nice."

I want to smack Sara. Tami's not slow, she's Japanese. At least I think the two aren't mutually exclusive in this case. It's impossible to not make a political correctness error, cultural error, racial error, intelligence error... Error, error, error. When anyone mentions exchange relations that's all I'm going to think from now on. Error.

By this time, Flora has closed the door. I stop pulling on Tami's bag and rush around behind her to start pushing before she has a chance to try to grab the door handle. I shove her toward the basement stairs. She moves—decides to go for it, and causes me to almost fly down to the bottom landing.

Tami finds the farthest corner and hugs her bag tight to her chest with both elbows resting protectively over the top.

"Is she going to be okay?" Sara asks me.

"Oh yeah. She's going to have a blast," I say. "I think she's warming up already." Absolutely nothing has changed from her cornered huddled.

Sara smiles—not at all detecting my sarcasm.

The basement room is huge, like half a football field huge—all cement and supporting structure. It's completely taken over with tulle sparkles, ruffles, satin, puffy slips and honest to goodness buttresses. I mean, who even uses buttresses these days. It's like a Texas toddler pageant threw up all over Sara's basement. "What happened in here?"

"We decided to use 'Disney Princess' as the theme—you know since it's Halloween on Tuesday and everything—basically a Halloween dance," Violet says from where she's adjusting a buttress in front of three long mirrors set up in a corner.

"Okay... But, what's with the—that?" I point to the wiry undergarment.

"Lacy and I are dressing as the ugly stepsisters, isn't that awesome?"

Not the word I would have used, or the Disney inspiration I would want to be associated with. Lacy and Violet couldn't look ugly no matter how hard they tried—both not being born with a 'do not' stamp across their faces like my slashy birthmark, No one will ever guess they're the ugly stepsisters though. Not in a million years.

Sara texted earlier informing me that she had dresses for me and Tami. We brought our own Sunday wear with us, in case nothing fit right. There's a decent chance I'll be wearing my flowered shift. Now I'm a little afraid of what my options are. They're obviously not going for typical princess tropes.

"Okay, so you're Maid Marian," she tells me, handing me a fox-eared hat with tulle streaming from the ear points She wasn't joking about Disney versions—cartoon ones at that. "And Tami..."

Don't say Mulan, don't say Mulan... I'm not certain, but I think that could be taken the wrong way.

"Your dress is Snow White," Sara says.

Not a dwarf, or the evil queen. That's great. I think. Tami doesn't move from her bag-guarding position.

Yi puts on a Native American looking outfit complete with turquoise accents. I'm guessing Pocahontas. Aiko shines in full rainbow sequins that hug her entire stick-thin body. Little Mermaid for sure. Sara isn't dressed.

"So, what princess are you going with?" I ask.

"Princess Leia," she jumps up and down with excitement, then shows me a headband with hair buns attached where ear warmers would go.

"That's awesome!" I'm so glad she didn't give me that one. Guys everywhere only care about Princess Leia in the gold bikini. Not exactly the dance attire I want—and the ultra-thin fabric, white dress with no-bra-support, look—isn't much better.

"We're doing a fashion show in one hour, so get ready," Lacy announces.

Everyone appears relaxed and like they're having fun, even Yi and Aiko laugh and help the other girls with make-up. Tami stands out as the only one not participating. "Hey, Sara?'

"Yeah?"

"I'm going to go hang out with Tami for a bit. Maybe I can take pictures for the fashion show, instead of be in it?" I say.

She looks a little sad that I'm basically saying I don't want to play dress-up. When she glances stiff-backed Tami she gives me a side smile. "Okay. That's probably a good idea. Maybe Tami wants to take pictures too?"

I'm pretty sure that's a stereotype, but I'm not going to say anything. And I'm definitely not mentioning it to Tami. "Cool. Thanks."

Sitting by Tami's super boring. No matter what I try to get her talking, it's me talking to myself. I eventually give up, and we sit in silence. Both of us overtired from two months of not sleeping because we don't trust each other.

The other girls take so long to get ready for the show... I don't know at what point I fall asleep.

Gray light annoys me first thing. Yi takes second slot. I'm not sure if I've mentioned her nasal way of speaking, but Yi sounds in person the way 'Yeeee" sounds pronounced. A very fitting name.

"Oh my gosh, you guys," she says. "You must like be so Cinderella at your house. Both of you, like, totally fell asleep before anyone else."

"Cinderella?" I rub my eyes, hoping I'm dreaming this.

"Yeah. Like slaves or shit."

Kids who learn English second to any other language, learn all the curse words first. Mostly kids in school teach them that the word for football is asshole or something, and they believe it and start screaming that word at public events.

I remind myself that I'm in public and censor my own word choices. It's alarming to wake up in a foreign room—not that Sara's house is all that foreign to me, but I completely forget where I am when Yi wakes me all gangstralia style and my curse-in-response-to-curse inhibitors require several undisturbed minutes to fire up.

"What's wrong with you?" I ask. This question regards the fact that Yi brought up the word 'slaves' in front of Tami—in Max's house because, even though Yi has no idea, that's a huge trigger word right now. *Thanks a lot Yi.*

"Who is grumpy in the morning?" Yi points both of her index fingers at me—not Tami or anyone else—me alone. "I hope I'm not in the same car as you today." Yi gets out of my face.

This reveals Sara behind Yi, with a not so impressed with my 'morning-game' demeanor. "You sure you're up for today?"

I continue to rub my neck. If Sara can read non-verbals she would know that I'm signaling her 'I know I'm not up for today. I have no interest in spending the next sixteen hours with Ben when I've never spent sixteen straight hours with any non-familial boy, and am likely to kill him so I can find a comfy bed and sleep for three more days so long as Tami isn't around.'

Sara cannot read non-verbals.

"We have one hour to eat breakfast and get ready for the morning hike," she says, beaming. Puffy red eyes clue me in that she hasn't slept a wink. A family of empty Red Bull cans lines the windowsill. Sara doesn't drink caffeine. I can't imagine what a Red Bull would do to her insides. She's wired. She has no idea her body is trying to punch her in the eyeballs for missing sleep.

"How does that fit in the Disney theme?" I ask, hoping to out of the hike on a technicality.

"Every Disney movie has nature in it," Sara says.

"Do we have to dress up?"

"Not till later. We'll come home for lunch, and then get ready for dinner and the dance."

It's obvious Sara put a lot of thought and hard work into this day going well. I don't want to be the reason it doesn't. "That sounds awesome. Let me splash some water on my face and I'll meet you guys for breakfast."

Next to me, Tami's curled into a tight ball surrounding her overnight bag. She must have the most valuable face cream on the planet for this kind of devotion to her things. I shake her shoulder. "Tami."

She doesn't open her eyes, but her arms pull in tighter.

"Tami, you're going to miss breakfast. Come on." I shake her vigorously. "If you don't come with me, I'm sending the little kids down here to tickle you awake."

At that Tami sits as tall as her short spine permits.

"Bevan taught me that trick." I pat her on the shoulder and offer a hand up. Of course, she doesn't take it. "You're going to adore Bevan when he visits for Thanksgiving."

Tami's forward progress toward breakfast stops. She takes a step back toward her nesting location. "No."

Holy shenanigans. I can't take any more vague 'no's. "What the heck is it this time?"

"Brother no allowed come home."

"Bevan is definitely allowed home. There's no way anyone can prevent him from coming home."

"Old brother. No allow in home." Tami sits like she's cemented herself to her statement and neither she nor it have any intention of budging unless I agree, which is stupid as hell.

"You've never even met Bevan. You can't make that kind of judgment call." She might have seen pictures around the house. His portwine stain much more severe than mine, with rough bubbling looking skin that spreads onto his scalp affecting his hair growth. With one exception. It's not on his face.

"I have brother. He go against his family. Is shame on family." Tami's English stands out so badly. I'm trying not to hold it against her, but none of the other exchange kids sound like they could be in Howell's playdate group.

"Let me get this straight." I feel like I'm playing twenty-one questions with a toddler. "You have a brother?"

She nods once, sharply.

"Your brother's older than you?"

Again, she nods.

"He's not allowed in your house?"

Tami nods two times.

"Like. Ever."

Nod.

"Why?"

Her face, the statue version of Tami. Cold, distant, and without any effort toward communication. She probably couldn't tell me why if she tried. It's obvious she's not trying anyway. I wait a few beats to try to figure out what I should say here. It's not normal, is it? For Japanese older siblings to be banned from their homes? Maybe it is.

"Is that common?" I ask.

Tami statue doesn't even blink. She's really selling the stone-cold bitch look.

"Are you afraid of your brother?"

A flinch. I totally see it. She almost looks at me, her eyes twitch my direction before she catches herself and resumes ignoring.

"You are..."

Her face sours. I hit a nerve.

"There is nothing to be afraid of with Bevan." Tami makes no effort to appear as though she's getting a dang thing I'm saying. "He's like Howell." *Only scarier to look at than I am, if the top of his head is exposed,* which I leave out.

Tami clings to her bag.

"Can't you be normal for one day?" I think my question's directed at Tami, but there's a mirror at the far end of the room, in which I catch my reflection, and wonder how much of that quandary is for me. Dumb question. "I'll make you a deal."

Tami breaks her mold to look at me. I suspect she thinks I'm going to say Bevan won't come for Thanksgiving if... But, that's not happening.

"Stick by me today. You don't have to worry about anyone else, and I'll take your making-dinner night at home for a—" I don't want to be too generous. She might be able to handle this challenge and then I'd be stuck with a month of twice a week dinner duty. "For two weeks."

Tami rolls her eyes, pulls her bag to her side farthest from me—as if I'm the one she's keeping it from, and walks ahead of me toward the upstairs. Not the reaction I anticipate.

"So, we're on?" Kind of hard to read her. I follow upstairs for breakfast.

At the table, Tami chooses a seat between Yi and Aiko. Her comfort zone, I suppose. So, I guess all deals are off.

"I'm so glad you gals made it," Sara says. She brings two plates of fruit covered pancakes and points to bottles of whip cream on the table before licking her fingers. "We're going to have so much fun today, but first eat up. You're gonna need energy if we're going to out-hike the guys."

Most of the girls giggle, whisper to one another, or continue eating. Tami has no reaction. I want to bury my face in the whip cream now covering my plate. Instead, I spray more white lardy-sugar on top. I'm going to need it. I'm the least athletic of the bunch. I have visions of Violet tumbling cheer-style to the top of the mountain, Sara sprinting it, and Lacy leapfrogging from one hot boy's back to the other. I have no doubt she won't be able to accomplish the task without touching each and every dude there. Good thing I'm not into my date. Every guy likes Violet and/or Lacy.

After breakfast, we pile into Sara's thirteen-passenger van, which won't fit the whole group for once. "The plan is to stop by Derrick's house, where the guys will meet us. We'll split into date pairs and drive to the trail in two cars."

"Can't they meet us at the trailhead?" Maybe she can't hear me, because instead of answering she keeps talking.

"We have a bet going," Sara announces. "If we beat the guys to the top of the trail, they buy us ice cream, and vice versa."

"It should have been steak," I say. Yi and Aiko both 'ew' me. Like steak tastes gross. It's awesome—and way more expensive than ice cream. If someone wants to motivate me to work hard, promise me steak. I stay quiet the rest of the drive, even though I really want to point out how dumb it is to meet up, divide into dates, then race non-dates (guys vs girls) to the top of the trail.. Even after we pair up. I get to stay in Sara's car with Tami, Ben, Nathaniel—who's not happy that Derrick isn't in the same car as him—Violet, Quon, Ishii, Masato, and Tung. Tung and Quon are grade A smart mouths. But, they appear to think they're talking to entertain the rest of the car. It's annoyingly endearing.

Derrick's car holds Aiko, Yi, Max, Spencer, and Lacy. No one sits next to their assigned date except Quon and Ishii, Tung and Violet.

Ben's way in the front, next to Nathaniel. Neither of them says anything. Ben doesn't even turn around. I can't blame him. I haven't really spoken to him since debate. Even then, it isn't like we're chatty.

"Are the guys also dressing Disney style?" I shout over the benches.

"Unfortunately. What a lame theme," Quon says. He laughs after, like everyone will appreciate his insight. Tung laughs. So does Ishi, but it's a nervous laugh like she's only laughing so Quon doesn't feel bad.

How can I save this? "Nathaniel, you're going to make a perfect Prince Charming."

"I am going as Thor, who is both a prince and a God. Not to mention a far better role model for any young man or woman than any Disney prince."

That didn't save anything. "Thor. Great. Good choice." I stop trying. If it were me driving, having a bad day, Sara would save me. I have no doubt she'd find seven different ways to make me feel better. I tried one and have no clue what else I can possibly do.

Sara pulls into the trailhead without a cheerful, "We're here."

As people pile out of the car they migrate to their designated dates. I stand next to Ben, who smiles at me, then throws his eyebrows halfway up his forehead while simultaneously plunging his hands deep into his pockets, like he's worried I might want to hold his hand or something. Not even. I feel like I'm waiting for an elevator to arrive. I return the greeting anyway, complete with pocket hands, because what else can I do?

Tami hovers at the fringe of the group. Nathaniel tries to stand near her and she moves away another foot.

"Here's a scavenger list." Sara passes out half page sized maps with items listed on the reverse side. "Mark on the map if and where you find any of the items listed on the reverse side." That's the end of her presentation. Not very Sara-like at all.

"Aaaaand, go!" Lacy steps in with her never failing enthusiasm, earning herself a half smile of appreciation from Sara. I feel like I'm losing my best friend status this year.

Worse, Max hasn't looked my way once. I drop my head so all I can see are my Chuck Taylors. I gesture Tami and Nathaniel to walk ahead of Ben and me, mostly so Tami doesn't bolt without me knowing—she looks spring loaded to get out of here. In front of them are Derrick, Aiko, and Lacy in one line, with Spencer in front of them. It's a weird progression up the mountain.

The hike has so many switchbacks. It's like nature itself is trying to pit my insides against all relationships—shifting direction and elevation at the exact moment.

I haven't looked at our items to hunt, much less at the landscape. To make matters worse, about half a mile in Tami starts chanting "I hate hike," over and over.

"This sucks," Ben admits at my side.

"Sorry," I say. "I didn't mean to invite you. I bet you wish you could be home right now."

"Didn't mean to?" He's quiet for a minute then very quietly says, "I wanted to go with you."

Past tense. Ouch. "And now?"

"Let's say I'd prefer the company of just the two of us to this whole group thing."

I can't help but laugh a little. Also, Ben's smiling now, which really helps with tolerating Tami's constant "I hate hike."

"Find anything on the list?" I ask reaching over to Ben's personal space to snag the map.

"Hey, watch it—I'm a certified boy scout after all, qualifying me for map-duty."

"You're holding it upside down, Mr. Scout." We both laugh, and the day feels like it's not going to be the worst thing in history. Until I notice Max, who definitely looks at me now. He looks like he's having the worst day in history. I shouldn't gloat on the inside, but I do. As a result, I play in a little too well with the chemistry slowly building between Ben and me, 'accidentally' bumping into him as we climb over a boulder.

"Whoa there. Good thing I'm here to catch you," Ben says.

"Because no one else has arms," Max says—then covers his mouth and pays lots of hands-on attention to Yi... "Let me help you over this trickling stream." His hands go to her toned waist. He lifts her three feet higher than he needs to, demonstrating either his strength or her lightness, before gently setting her down on dry gravel.

Not cool.

"Want to see if we can beat everyone up this mountain?" I snag the map and as quickly let it go, so it flutters down the hillside. "Forget about the hunt?"

"You're on." Ben's hand wraps around my fingers as he guides both of us to the front of the line. Abandoning my Tami-watch duties in favor of living my life.

I try not to look back. I tell myself it'll be a mistake to make eye contact with Max at this point, but can't prevent my head from swiveling in his direction. I immediately regret my action. His eyebrows knit tightly into a line and his jaw sets. He tries nudging Yi into taking the same challenge, but she shows no interest in sweating. Ben and I put more and more distance between us and Max.

Things between Ben and me are awesome the rest of the day. I make a point to stop looking to see if Max notices how many times I say something and Ben laughs.

Just to be clear, Max notices each time.

The rest of the hike turns out uneventful, unless the fact that I'm now possibly crushing on Ben is considered an event. With Max, I figured we'd bonded over the fact we both love food. But now with Ben, it's really a mix of sweat stink, hand holding, and the hope of inducing jealousy in Max that has me all butterfly-tummied.

By the time the boys pull together dinner, my stomach twists with crush confusion, I can barely eat. I also happen to be sitting between Ben and Max, with Derrick on the other side of the table from me. It's like every guy I ever so much as pretended to like falls under magnetic karma. My head hurts, I'm so unsure about who I like and why. Or if there's even a remote chance any one of them likes me for real, despite my face stamp—or if I'm simply misinterpreting their kindness.

There's no room in my head to dedicate to how Tami's handling her date. Though I do glance her way now and then. Nathaniel stands stiff-backed with his jaw slightly risen. He would make an excellent British nobleman. Tami looks equally stiff. Perfect match.

Derrick stands up to pour every female a glassful of homemade lemonade. Given dinner is at his house, I can see how he'd take it upon himself, but Derrick does this sort of thing no matter where we are. I rule his interest out as nothing more than innate gentlemanliness. He doesn't even see Lacy as 'one of the hottest girls in school' which she is according to last year's yearbook.

Max has me stumped too, except in a completely different way. I don't know if we're even friends anymore. I bump him for the third when I try to cut my chicken parm. I stop cutting pieces off and decide to push the slab around my plate instead. I'm not terribly hungry with all the fluttering confusion in my guts.

Ben. He's not what I'd call a catch, but if I'm being honest, neither am I. We probably make the most sense out of all the guys I've liked before, with his red nose and my stained face... That should be a country song.

"You're not eating." Max startles me by speaking low, out of the side of his mouth, in my direction. "Everything okay?"

"My stomach is being weird," I say.

Max quiets. I wonder if he even heard me, since I do try to keep my response away from Ben noticing. I don't want my date thinking I'm flirting with someone else's date. *Am I doing that?*

"Just don't be someone you're not, to impress anyone," Max says.

Where does he get off? I drop my fork. It clatters on the plate. As if to draw as much attention as possible, the fork falls from the plate to the table where it connects with a loud spoon. I turn toward Max, mouth open and brain loaded with plenty to say in response to his remark, when I feel Ben staring at the back of my head.

I close my mouth, collect my fork, and bow my head to give myself time to think of how to make that whole reaction come off normal. Normal has never been my strong point. "Etiquette lessons really failed me, didn't they?"

Ben laughs. Sara chortles, as if she's unsure what on earth I'm talking about, nor why I was about to, what I imagine looked like 'chicken peck,' her brother for a split second. I set my fork gently to the side of my plate away from the troublesome spoon.

Tami stares at me too. It's not like she's eating anything either. I swear, she's only had saltine crackers at breakfast for the last three weeks, and she has the nerve to give me a judgey look. I'm not starving myself. I'm nervous. It's different. Still, I skip dessert along with everyone who has a fitted dress to force themselves into after dinner. Tami included.

Nathaniel continues to recite mountain-trail facts as a carryover from our excursion. For instance, "Did you know that in two thousand four a scout group built all the bridge crossings we passed over today? Before that, hikers had to get their feet wet." Riveting stuff .I'd rather be seated next to Nathaniel. Tami won't look at him, which apparently makes him talk even more than normal.

When I finally start paying attention to dynamics other than my own, it occurs to me that Tami's exceptionally uncomfortable. Her shoulders are pulled in tight, and her head crouches enough to be noticeable. She has the appearance she's seated at the plague-carriers' table, with a dread-fear of touching anything. She shifts herself away from movement on her right and movement on her left. Neither Max or I sit near her, which makes her behavior oddly comforting—like 'it's not just me—yay.'

She's wedged between Nathaniel and Derrick—not a bad placement. Max sits across from Tami, making her adjacent to my left. I've never known someone with such high anxiety around run of the mill American high schoolers. I feel bad for her having come to a strange country with her head full of 'everyone will hate you' social-prep. Then, I notice the muttering.

Her mouth moves very slowly, almost like she's casting a spell under her breath. Her eyes flick toward Max while her lips twitch together and apart soundlessly. He's not the only visual target though. Tami shifts away from Nathaniel, she jerks her vision in his direction while her body moves away, still muttering. I get a few glances with inaudible mouth service as well. She makes it so hard to appreciate her plight. My sympathy toward Tami gets used up for the night by the whole chanting while flashing people the death-eye thing.

Once dinner ends, the girls return to Sara's house to prep for the dance. We don't eat in our dresses, mostly because we rented some of them from costume shops. That's the way it goes when the group embraces a theme.

While everyone changes into mostly flattering dresses—the ugly stepsisters' outfits aren't exactly ugly so much as over-the-top. I have a sheet with arm holes and a belt crisscrossed over my chest. I regret falling asleep before getting a good grasp on what Sara expected me to wear. It's toga-esque. I feel like I'm in nothing more than a slip. To be fair, Sara's sporting the Princess Leah in white tent, free-boobing-it style, leaving me no room to complain.

"Can you see my underwear?" I ask the group.

"I brought a spare slip, you can borrow it, if you're worried." Lacy to the rescue. I'm sure Sara would have offered me one of hers, but she needs all the slips she can get—her white dress is totally see-through, which makes me question my own get-up in the first place.

Even with the slip addition, my entire outfit airs sparse. It takes me a total of seven minutes to de-frock, add the slip and reassemble myself. The other girls go in phases, underthing supports and lace for reasons I can't figure out—no one will ever see that layer, slips and shifts layer, dress, bodice and other adornments to complete the final layer. I'm basically parading around in what everyone else wears as underwear.

"I can't wear this," I announce after noticing my polka-dot unders managing to shine through all the sheer layers.

Lacy takes one look at me and sucks in the biggest breath. "Oh my heck, I have the best idea. Give me ten minutes." She grabs her car keys and leaves the basement. Fifteen minutes later Lacy returns with black spandex pants. Awesome. And what I'm guessing labels a 'sexy maid' costume. Less awesome.

"I can't wear that," I say.

"It'll be fine, with the leggings and a little shawl, you'll be the Maid Marion no one saw coming." Lacy glows with excitement in contrast to the sinking discomfort growing inside me. "We can even give you a nametag that says 'Marion' in case no one gets it." Then Lacy does something worse. Without asking me she dabs a huge glob of concealer on my face—to hide my birthmark. "No harm in covering this up for one night."

I hate hiding my birthmark. Not because I love the splotchy stain I was born with, but because it feels like a lie about myself to conceal it. It's who I am.

Tami applauds Lacy, making it worse. I know Lacy means well, so I don't say anything. But, I sort of want to cry.

The guys come by Sara's house to collect us. Max has an eye-mask all Zorro style, well-fitted slacks, and a black hoodie, totally the Jamie Fox version of James Bond meets Spanish-vigilante hot. I shake my head to unfocus my thoughts surrounding Max. Ben is... He looks alright. He's wearing a green blazer, a snap front shirt, and has a bowtie on. It's not exactly the look Max has going on.

Before we leave, Sara's mom snaps pictures of everyone paparazzi style. It's fun. She even holds her camera around a corner and snaps a million shots of the doorframe, unaware that she didn't extend far enough. I love Sara's mom. She takes some formal shots too.

The high school looks normal from the outside. With all the enthusiasm of the decorations before the gym, the night promises no memories of magic tonight—nothing more than having a date during parent-teacher conferences. Once inside however, it's like a glitter bomb went off. Sparkles cover the floor. Lights string from one raised basketball hoop to the next. Streamers are pulled from the twinkle lights to the sides of the room so that the ceiling hovers lower, closer, more intimate. The lights are blue and strobe-like throughout the whole space. However, no degree of decent decorations can take away from the awkwardness of an empty dance floor.

The dance brings out the twelve-year-old in all of us. No one wants to be the first couple on the dance floor. The lighting's dim, but not low enough to hide how awkward the whole thing is. Ben keeps rubbing his palms against his thighs. I hope it's because he can't seem to remember he doesn't have pockets, and not that he's sweating that badly.

My sexy Maid Marion outfit draws far more eyes than I'm comfortable with. Most of the looks I get start below my face and travel up until the leerer notices the strike of red missing, when without fail, their eyebrows go up in shock. I can't tell if they're surprised there's something beyond a birthmark to notice about me, or if it's something else to their surprise.

Ben clears his throat. "Thanks for inviting me."

"Yeah, no problem." I shout as the music rises with a fast song. "Thanks for coming."

Ben licks his lips. It's as awkward as it sounds. "Want to dance?"

There are literally no couples on the floor other than long established daters. And those couples aren't making the dance floor look all that safe with way too familiar grinding and bumping to the rapid beat. "It's a fast song."

"It'll be fun." Ben extends a hand. I take it, noting how my stomach flips faster than the music rages.

"Let's do this, Yi." Max pumps his hands like he's about to 'break it down'? (if that's a thing), beating Ben and me to the center of the dance floor. Yi joins him, every bit a perfect fit for his enthusiasm. Her sharp elbows and toothpick frame slice angles through the air as she punctuates the space around Max, who breakdances. Breakdances!

When did Max learn how to do that? And he's good. Like really good. He spins on his shoulder blades, kicks his legs out so that he's suddenly standing, and all in time to the music, jumps so that he lands with only one palm supporting his weight.

Ben's sweaty palm slips from my hand before I realize he's dancing. Am I supposed to be dancing too? I reference Yi for what on earth I'm supposed to do with my body to music like this. There's no way I look as cool as her when I bend my arms and sway my head. I definitely don't have the right lip pucker down. Yi looks like a princess about to bust a cap in someone's knee if they don't 'respect.' I feel like a skank-maid.

Without warning the music changes. I'm mid hop when Ben slides an arm behind my back to draw me in for a slow dance. Butterflies dominate my insides again. Seriously, my internal workings are set to 'like everyone who gives you attention' mode.

I try not to stare into Ben's eyes. For one thing, I have no idea how long the song will last, and it would be weird to stare at each other while swaying side to side for five minutes—no matter how much you like them. This is only our first date—the pressure of this slow music kills me. His eyes are boring a hole into the side of my head. Ben's obviously immune to when things are awkward. Does that make me like him more?

"You look good. Nice, I mean." I can't tell if Ben's filling the slower pace of the song with words, or if he's serious.

I make the mistake of meeting his eyes because I'm curious which it is. He scans the length of where my birthmark hides and I wonder if sweat has revealed it again.

"You can't even tell it's there," he says. "Why don't you wear make-up more often? It suits you, you know." His words come out soft and sincere, like it's meant to be a compliment, but all I hear is, 'good job hiding the grotesque reality of your monster face.'

I stop swaying. "I have to pee." My brain can only conjure the verbiage I'd use with Howie. 'Pee'? Did I really say that in front of my date?

"What?" Ben stops moving too. We're the only people not dancing in the middle of the room. "Right now?"

Two couples away Max looks my direction. His mask makes it impossible to know what thoughts race behind his dark eyes, but I think he squints discerningly at Ben, like he knows I'm fighting back tears.

Without more explanation, I race to the girls' bathroom. Waving my hand under the motion activated faucet, I cup and splash water all over my face, until I'm a mascara-smeared mess, and my birthmark is no longer covered. Tears mix with the water, until it doesn't matter what I look like.

"Lowry?" Max stands in the doorway. "Is it okay for me to come in?"

I nod. Because, it's Max. I've convinced myself that I imagined his interest in me to be anything more than friendly. Friends don't judge mascara streaks and stupid insecurities.

He sits on the edge of one sink without asking what happened. I grab a paper towel and start clearing what's left of the make-up off my face. "What kind of prince Eric are you?"

"I'm not." He takes the towel from my hand, dabs it with more water and gently rubs the gunk away. "Some robins are all black," he says.

Then I see it. He's dressed like a robin-bird, but like from the hood. *He's dressed to match me.* "I look ridiculous." I say of my own outfit, which I didn't get to pick out.

Max laughs. "A little."

"So do you," I tease even though I think he looks awesome. "I could have used this tonight." I snap the front of his mask and then cringe because it makes a much more painful sound than I anticipate. "Sorry."

He takes the mask off, lowering his hood at the same time. "I think you look best without a mask." He stops dabbing my face with the paper towel and looks at me—really looks at me.

My stomach has lost all control. It's like a butterfly breeding ground on my insides. My heart races like I've challenged Max to a long-distance sprint. The damp paper towel falls away, replaced by the closeness of Max. Heat from his skin dries any lingering sadness. Is he going to kiss me? Why else would he be this close? And then his lips touch mine.

I've never kissed anyone other than pecks from my family. I have no idea what I'm doing and can barely process the fact it's happening at all. Thank goodness Max keeps it simple, no open mouth or wondering hands—he holds my face and breathes me in while our lips meet.

"Lowry? Everything okay?" Ben asks from outside the girls' bathroom.

Max pulls away when I look toward the door. I don't know what do. I feel like I've done something wrong. I came here with Ben. I'm not the kind of girl who finds herself in this type of situation.

"You've been in the bathroom a while," Ben says knocking two times. "Can I come in?"

I look at Max with my eyebrows high and my jaw low. I have no idea what to do. Squeaks come out of my mouth when I try to make words.

"I'm sorry. I shouldn't have done that." Max apologizes for kissing me? That was the best part of the whole night.

"Lowry?" Ben must have heard Max's voice.

"Max." It's all I manage to say. I want to follow it with, 'don't apologize' but before I can say anything Max walks toward the door without looking back at me, and leaves as Ben pushes in.

"Hey," Ben says when Max passes—none too friendly. He watches Max until he's practically on the dance floor—like there's not enough distance.

Normally I'd laugh at how ridiculous it is to think Ben has anything to worry about when it comes to competition for my affection, but life proves weird, and he doesn't stand a chance compared to Max.

"What was that about?" Ben asks, apparently not aware what he interrupted. "Your make-up." Ben notices my face. "You took it off? Why?"

I walk toward where Max left.

"I said something wrong, didn't I?" Ben puts both hands on his head. "That's why you took it off, and Max was in here making you feel better." Ben reaches for my hand, snagging me before I'm out of reach. "I'm so sorry. I never meant to... I'm not very good at this stuff, I say dumb things—it doesn't mean anything. I mean, I don't mean anything." Ben practically falls over himself to take back his comments. "I'm so, so sorry."

Guilt fights against confusion and anger inside my head. What happened?

Ben touches my hand tentatively. "Will you dance with me?" The butterflies return like baby things. But, it's the same intensity that feeling has always been with Ben. A twinge and nothing more. When Max touched my hand, it was a frenzy—an explosion of super butterflies. I could have liked Ben. I could have been perfectly content dancing with him the rest of the night, except I have something to compare it to now.

Comparisons ruin everything.

Ben isn't Max. No matter how great he could be, he can never be Max. But, Max didn't stay, he left without taking me with him. He left me behind like a crime scene.

"Sure. Let's dance."

The rest of the night, I spend trying to crane my neck far enough to get glimpses of Max in his hoodie, dancing with the Native American Princess version of Yi. Once or twice I notice Tami sitting against a far wall, always a great distance from Nathaniel, her date.

For once I want to sit next to her, if only so my head will stop spinning with boy-related confusion. It's so much worse watching Max hold Yi in his arms after he kissed me. It's like reverse Cinderella, where the clock chiming turns out to be Ben entering the room and there's no shoe to lose, just Max not looking for me.

25

The dance dies down as groups filter off to late parties, midnight dinners at twenty-four hour diners, and who knows what else.

"You guys want to eat at JC's?" Sara asks.

"I'm game," Ben says. He's holding my hand between songs like this night adds up to more than a marathon date.

"I'm pretty spent," I say.

"I'll drive Lowry home." Max volunteers before I realize he's behind me, startling me and Ben. "I have morning practice and need to get to bed anyway, so it's no big deal to drop her by."

"Is it cool if I stay? I want to keep partying," Yi asks.

"Yeah, that's no big deal, so long as Sara makes sure you get home alright."

Yi jumps around giddily. My mouth lolls, like an idiot. I close it. Then realize I meant to speak and have to open it again—*like an idiot.* "What about Tami?"

"I'll bring Tami home." Sara says. "We've been dancing all night, we need calories right now." The boys in the group nod vigorously.

"Are you sure?" Ben asks Max.

"Really, it's not a problem," Max says.

"And you're sure you don't want to come eat with everyone?" Ben asks me.

"Too tired to eat."

"But, you'll miss all the fun," Ben says. I shrug and yawn to demonstrate how terribly I need to get home to bed. "You're sure it's okay if I go without you?"

"We're not dating." It comes out before I can rephrase my thoughts. "I mean..." Ben's face goes from excited to crushed in zero seconds flat. "You don't have to check with me. You can go have fun and everything's cool between us."

His hand slips from mine, which only reminds me how awkwardly long he's been holding it. I feel a little bad that my insensitive remark made the difference, but also, his hand super sweats so it's nice to get some air to my palm. Ben nods and walks with the rest of the group toward Sara's car.

"What about the ride situation?" I ask. "We all came in only two cars."

Max manages to talk Sara into dropping us by Max's car before everyone else goes to eat. I don't bother explaining to Tami, assuming she knows to stay with the group. She's still clinging her purse so closely—like even after an entire day with these people, she thinks they're going to rob her. I shake my head and let her figure out the rest of her night.

"I'll collect our overnight things later," I inform Sara.

Max turns silent once it's the two of us in his car. I expect him to say something—anything. Especially since he's the one who volunteered to take me home.

"Are we going to talk about what happened?" I ask after letting enough time pass to realize he's not starting the conversation.

"You tell me."

"What's that supposed to mean?" I turn to face him while he drives. He keeps his eyes on the road. "You practically ran out of there when Ben showed up, what was I supposed to think?"

"Maybe you could have told Ben."

"Told him what?"

"Something. Anything. Not holding his hand in my face, the rest of the night would have been a start."

"You're one to talk—the way you were dancing with Yi. Besides, you could have stayed by my side."

His eyes leave the road. "And said what? *Hey, I kissed your date, we cool for debate practice on Tuesday?*"

"Why'd you offer to drive me, if that's how you feel?"

"I wanted to hear your take on things."

"My take?" I fold my arms. This fails how I saw it in my head. For some reason I thought we'd end up making out overlooking the town lights or something romantic. Totally not happening. "I'll tell you my take. You kiss me, and then spend the rest of the night trying to make me jealous—"

"Jealous?"

"Don't cut me off."

"I wasn't trying to make you jealous. I was trying to not be the loser when you chose Ben over me."

"I did what?" My voice shoots to the super-sonic shock range, as it keeps climbing higher with every back and forth pass of our argument. "I didn't do that at all."

"You walked out holding hands, like kissing me was the tipping point regarding who you really wanted to be with."

He's right. Except, he has it completely backwards on which way things tipped. I don't want to admit this and clamp my mouth closed, like this fact will change things in such a permanent way, I might not be ready for the results and I don't know what else to do.

"So that's it? You're not going to say anything?"

"What can I say to go back to Silver City?" I ask.

"You want to drive to the city?"

"No. I want us to be back to normal."

"Seriously? That's all you want?" The hurt in Max's voice crushes me.

Of course I want more than that. I want his hand to reach out and wrap around mine. I want his face close enough that I can feel the heat from his skin. I want him to stay by my side when someone else walks into the room. I want him to not run away as if he's ashamed that he kissed me.

We pull into my driveway. The car idles but I don't go for the door latch.

I want to not think of Max every spare second of the day and night. I focus on my hands in my lap and breathing normally. "Are we okay?" I can't put any other words together.

"I shouldn't have kissed you."

That's when I know it's not okay. It's really not okay. My insides crumble and I want to run in the house, find my bed, and bury myself in blankets for the next three days without seeing anyone.

"We're cool, me and you. We're like always," Max says, rubbing salt deeper into my aching insides. He might as well be pouring lemon on top of a papercut. It hurts like all my heart nerves are on fire. "Ben's an alright guy."

I look up. Is he pushing Ben on me now? Not brushing me off, but pushing me away? He kissed me. I didn't make that up, did I?

So now, Max not only apologized for kissing me, he's also not fighting for me. And tries to brush me off. But mostly, all I can think about is how badly I want him to kiss me again and how stupid I was to imagine him offering to drive me home might end up with Max and I being a couple or some idiotic notion.

I open the passenger door, realizing Max isn't getting out to do it. "You should have kissed me," I say without knowing what I'm trying to say. "You should have asked me to the dance, or not asked Yi—whatever..." I'm not making a lot of sense. "You should have asked me on a date, a real date—maybe it's because of my face, I don't know." Max opens his mouth to say something, but I stop him by continuing to speak. "I know Ben didn't let go of my hand tonight and you did."

I shut the door and walk inside the house. Right now I want nothing more than to be left alone and maybe cry in my room. Instead Mom and Dad are in a frenzy.

"You left Tami by herself?" Mom accuses.

"What? No, I didn't."

"Tami called from Sara's phone." Dad steps between Mom and me, like that's going to prevent me from getting grounded again. "She said you left her there without a ride home. One of us has to drive in to pick her up."

"She stayed with the whole group to go for a late-night meal. I wasn't hungry."

"Did you even offer for her to go home with you?" Mom jumps several times so she can see me over Dad's shoulder while she chews me out.

"No, but she didn't look interested in spending time with me either."

"If you didn't offer, then how would you know what she was interested in?" Mom says, now standing still on her tip toes.

"She's on a date. Shouldn't she work that out with the dude she went with? How rude to leave him there." I hear my mistake before Dad points it out.

"There's another thing, Sara said you left your date behind too. I thought we taught you better manners than that." Does Dad even know what happens after high school dances? He's lucky he has the world's least sexually curious daughter.

"I wasn't hungry. I was tired, and I wanted to go home." I stomp my foot, once again putting myself on the same level as Howell in the maturity department. "Do you have any idea how exhausting a marathon group date can be?"

"Not a problem, because you aren't permitted to go next time," Mom says.

So yep, I'm grounded again. "I'll drive in to pick up Tami, okay?" I'm hoping they'll take this as a peace offering, but that will require overlooking the smart-aleck tone I'm using, which Mom isn't likely to accept.

"Take your phone and be sure to call home as soon as you have her." Dad doesn't offer to come with me, neither does Mom. "She chose to stay behind from going to eat with the group. She's at the dance all alone—waiting for a ride."

"Sara would have taken her," I say.

"She refused to ride with anyone else," Mom says this with the force of it being my fault. Before I'm out the door all the way, Mom adds, "Don't text and drive."

"I know."

I drive myself all the way back to the dumb dance in Mom's beater car, because my car's parked at Sara's house. At least neither Ben nor Max will be there this time.

Unfortunately, Tami isn't either. The dance is officially over, with chaperones waiting for stragglers to disperse or their rides to arrive. The only kids left look tired, in no mood to talk.

"Have you seen Tami?" I ask.

"Who?"

"The exchange student..." I think of saying she lives with me, but how would that help them help me find her? More likely they'd say, why don't you know where she is then? "She's from Japan."

"Haven't noticed."

Great. I have to approach an adult. One of the teachers I'm not familiar with too. Feeling stupid I ask, "Did you happen to see where Tami went—our family's Japanese exchange student?"

"These were the only kids in the building when the dance ended. I'm here to make sure they're all accounted for before I can go home. I'm sorry. I didn't see any exchange students when I left, and we did a full sweep of the building."

Now what? "Okay, well, if you see her, can you tell her to call home?" Tami doesn't have a voice plan with her phone. "Or let her use your phone to call?"

"Sure."

I text Sara. *Did you end up taking Tami home?*

No. Her text comes back immediately. *She wouldn't come with anyone, not even the other foreign kids. What's up?*

Can't find her.

The message dots wiggle an extra-long moment, as if Sara taps and erases message option after message option. Finally, she sends. *That's weird.*

If you hear anything let me know. I have no idea what I expect Sara to know. She didn't take Tami home, and it's not likely Tami would contact her after refusing a ride. Maybe I secretly hope good Samaritan Sara will help me find Tami this late at night, which would probably require ditching the food outing they're all probably still at.

Will do.

I dial home. "Mom? Tami's not here."

"Look again."

"They did a whole sweep. She's not here. Everything's closed down."

"Call Sara, double check—"

"I did. She's not with Sara."

"Call again!" Mom yells in my ear so I pull the receiver away from my head.

"How is that going to help? You think she's going to magically appear at Sara's side? She's gone. She doesn't have a working phone, she can't speak freaking English, she's a spoiled selfish judgmental brat afraid of ,and rude to, anyone and anything different than her, and she freaking left where she said to pick her up, which makes her unreliable and untrustworthy on top of all the other crap!" I might have spoken too bluntly. Everyone in a hundred-foot radius has wide eyes trained on me.

"Call someone else then," Mom orders.

"Everyone I know is with Sara."

"Who dropped you off?"

"Max."

"So not everyone you know is with Sara?"

"Mom!"

"We need to find Tami."

"I know," I say.

"Find her."

"How?" This useless argument looped a few more, 'call everyone you know' 'but, everyone I know is together and Tami isn't with them,' rounds before Mom gave up the thought that I could produce Tami with my phone contacts.

"You're right." Mom lets out a long stretch of breathing out into the phone, which creates a whistling windy rustle on my end. "Come home. It's best we only have to worry about one of our girls."

The way Mom lumps Tami and me in a group, *her girls*, it strikes me that I've kept the idea of Tami distant, not something I've accepted into my life. In my mind, she's not a part—not part of anything I'm a part of. Suddenly I want to find her. Because I realize she belongs in our family, and I can't believe it's taken me this long to accept her weirdness. I'm a unique brand of weird. Why haven't I been able to let Tami be her own kind of weird?

I swallow the guilt building in my throat for all the times I've held Tami's oddness against her. So she's strange, a little creepy, socially bizarre, and a terrible date—it's not like she's the first person in existence to suffer those personality flaws. The whole dislike for anyone different than her still bothers me a little bit, but maybe that's all she's ever known. She deserves a window of adjustment and opportunity to broaden her narrow view of acceptable humanity. I haven't given her an inch of growing room, holding every glance she makes against her.

I drive home five miles under the speed limit to find a car parked in my spot. Tami gets out, so does the art teacher. It crosses my mind to keep driving and come back when the driveway clears. Instead I pull over, kill the engine, and follow the pair into the house. Ms. Conklin gives me a dirty look as I trail behind them. Not a good sign.

Mom opens the door before any of us reach it. The teacher speaks first.

"After your daughter ditched Tami at the dance and she contacted you to pick her up, you refused? I consider than unacceptable and think you should consider the way you treat international guests before volunteering to host students from overseas." Ms. Judgmental-art-teacher turns to Tami. "Now you message me if you need anything—*anything*."

"Excuse me?" Mom says after recovering her dropped jaw.

My face still sags in shock and an attempt to remember my devotion to give Tami some space to be abnormal. Right now, I'd like the space to punch her lights out. What the heck did she say to the art teacher? "Several people offered Tami a ride," I say. "Tami turned them all down."

"I think I know the truth. Tami keeps in regular contact with me about the real state of affairs," Ms. Conklin says.

"How?" I ask, cutting Mom off and making her words come out in a squeak.

"The real state of affairs?" Mom squeaks.

The teacher nods to Tami, like she's abandoning her to Mrs. Hannagan's orphanage for less-fortunate slaves, and wants to make sure Tami will be okay until Monday. "I look forward to seeing you all at parent-teacher conferences next week."

Her words punch. I hear, 'you're all going to get a well edited reaming in three days' time' and pretty sure Mom does too. Why does Tami have to make it so hard to excuse her odd behavior? She must have said something to make Mom look bad. I mean, I haven't been the best host sister, but Mom... Granted Mom did bug Tami's room with a baby monitor.

But then, Sara tried to offer Tami a ride, and Mom made me drive out there, and... Ugh! Tami created this mess! I hate her all over again.

Trying to figure out what is wrong with Tami, I conclude her beef with me and my beef with her aren't centered around cultural misunderstandings. It's difficult to believe anyone can still have diversity hang-ups after living together for three months. Isn't knowledge and exposure the first step to understanding? Tami and I have knowledge and exposure to one another's presence down, but understanding isn't a part of our equation.

I'm not the only person who gets on Tami's nerves. As far as I can tell, she only responds to her art teacher, Howie, and maybe Dad. Not that stalking her has solved the mystery. I tried that when I thought she was a terrorist or something and got squat.

Lucky for me, parent-teacher-conferences are sort of a family event. Held in the cafeteria, the teachers sit at tables while the parents wait in line and slide in for a quick chat before searching out the next almost available teacher on your schedule. It should be easy enough to linger while Tami and Ms. Nosey-Art meet with Mom and Dad.

Except Tami's been giving bribes out to teachers all over the school. They're probably going to dismiss all the assignments she hasn't turned in saying things like, *"She's so thoughtful. No thoughtful person deserves a failing grade."* Why didn't I think of bribing teachers? I'm thoughtful.

#

The cafeteria hums at a low growl, and that's the parent reactions to learning where GPA's really are. Like my parents who find it irritating that, though I have turned in assignments, they've almost all been late. Worse than my lazy assignment return habit, Tami's lack of returning any assignment—the whole year. Somehow Mom and Dad had no idea she wasn't doing a dang thing. So much for teacher bribes. A bunch of zeros decorate Tami's progress report. In comparison, my B average (an all-time low for my schooling history) qualifies for the national honor society. (No one said this, I'm feeling good in comparison).

"The exchange contract includes a C grade average as a condition of staying," Dad whispers to Mom in earshot of Ms. Conklin (who seems to be following us around as if trying to catch us mistreating Tami—or maybe I'm being paranoid). He's pointing to a page full of D's and F's with lots of notes about non-participation in class. That sounds like the Tami I know. Art must be the only class she mentally shows up to.

"The school can mediate the situation with the exchange offices," Ms. Conklin noses in. It's unclear whether she offers because she thinks Dad's saying *"Yeah, now we have grounds to get this kid out of our house?"*Honestly, that's what I hope he means. "I'm sure there's a grace period where Tami's schedule can be remedied to meet her educational needs and abilities without having to send her home early."

I look at Mom, waiting for some kind of, *"Mind your own business Ms. Judgey-pants."*Instead Mom says, "Of course we're going to look into doing everything we can to help Tami be successful." She adds a huff at the end of her sentence—That'll show the art teacher... Also, it doesn't sound like Tami's going anywhere anytime soon. Danger.

Mom gently reaffirms Tami that everything will be okay. She'll contact the exchange offices and *'don't worry dear'* a number of times—all witnessed by the art teacher. And I get a load of, "What's wrong with you? What are you spending your time on? If you can't get your schoolwork done and turned in on time, you don't need any additional distractions."

So basically I'm grounded still—and I'm the one who actually turned in my work. I have a solid B average, but nothing ever goes how I hope it will. I don't know what my parents do to contact people who work with the exchange program, but they do something that gets quick results. Boston acts fast.

Tami has a test FedExed to our house within twenty-four hours. Mom has to drive her to the library on Friday in order for someone to proctor the standardized English test, which happens to be a non-school day after parent-teacher conferences. I don't go with them. I'm on 'stay home with Howie' duty, so I have no idea regarding Tami's test protocols or stop, go, turn pages.... I imagine fill in the blanks "Dick and Jane ____" a) run b) walk c) fight d) potato. Obviously, I need some second language learning experience.

When Mom returns, she looks deflated. Tami, on the other hand, looks the same as ever—no expression. Mom throws her purse and keys on the table, which she usually yells at us for. It's not that much more effort to hang the keys where they go—or put her bag in the closet. "How did this happen?" she asks no one in particular.

Dad's at work because his schedule doesn't revolve around high school like the rest of us.

"What happened?" I ask. Tami walks downstairs—right past Mom's frustrations and my curiosity like it's not a big deal. If Tami isn't worried to the same degree as Mom, then maybe Mom isn't talking about the test. "Is it Dad? Is he okay?

"The test results are electronically scored and Tami," Mom lowers her voice like whatever she says next qualifies under sensitive material. "She doesn't even score high enough to qualify for the program."

"I don't understand."

Mom picks up her purse and drops it again, as if she needs to make noise. "I don't either—I don't understand."

I can't read the situation. Do I ask her to explain it to me? "Howie, go play blocks." Maybe with the two of us, I'll get some adult-level explanation. Not that Howie's going to understand any of it.

Mom leans in as Howie leaves—very confidentially, "Someone forged her qualification papers."

"What? That doesn't make sense."

"I know. It makes no sense. I was on the phone with the Boston office for quite some time—no one's sure yet." She lowers her voice again, because this must be the super-secret part of the story. "It looks like someone forged test scores for Tami to qualify for study abroad."

"Why would anyone do that? It sets Tami up to fail if she doesn't have the foundation of the language to succeed in her exchange country."

Mom walks to the fridge, perhaps in hopes of something stronger than flat ginger ale to greet her. Sadly, we're not much on keeping fancy beverages. She grabs the half-empty two-liter bottle and chugs for half a minute straight. "Ugh, that's bad."

"Seriously. Are you okay?"

As an answer, Mom returns to chugging the rest of the nasty soda.

"Tami mentioned that her older brother wasn't allowed home. Maybe someone forged her papers to get her out of a worse situation?"

Mom draws the bottle away from her mouth. "You never told me that."

"She was freaking out about the idea of Bevan being home for Thanksgiving. All I really reacted to was how she seems to treat people with discolored skin."

Mom doesn't seem to hear the stuff about how Tami poises to freak out at Bevan when he shows up in a few weeks. Her posture switches from drunk deflation to some kind of rigid. She sets the empty ginger ale back in the fridge—something she usually yells at Dad about. "That's something."

Why did I open my mouth? Mom looks like she watched a 'rescue the ASPCA puppies to end animal cruelty' commercial and has the one-eight-hundred number dialed in. "But, doesn't that information mean she has to go home anyway? I mean, she's been here for months and still can't pass the minimum? She's been surrounded by English all day every day."

"That's exactly what that smug teacher wants me to do. I'll show her." I'm starting to wonder if that ginger ale somehow fermented from being in the fridge too long. Mom definitely sounds drunk. "I'll save the crap out of Tami—even if it takes specialized instruction." Mom looks at me. “We’ll get her on a learning program that guarantees success because it’s all individualized?”

“An IEP, like Bevan had?” Pretty sure it’s not a guarantee to success, Bevan’s a hardworking kid when he has attainable goals. “Doesn’t she have to be tested for that?”

“I’ll talk to the counselor, I’m sure there are exceptions for special circumstances like this. It’s not like she has to have special services, specialized classes. And if they don’t listen to that, I’ll 504 their asses.” Don’t mess with a Sped mom who knows the system.

“Pretty sure you still need documentation.”

“I’ve got it.” Mom holds up the progress report along with the computer printout of Tami’s English proficiency test. She keeps hard copies of everything. Bevan practically has an airtight vault of all his IEP’s and medical reports. “I’m going to IEP the hell out of her education.”

“Mom!” As her child it’s my solemn duty to react as though I never hear such lurid language.

“Sorry.”

“Yeah. That’ll show the art teacher,” I say. Mom doesn’t hear me. She’s busy making a list of who to call, email, request documentation from, in order to customize ‘Tami’s American Experience’ as Mom now calls it. She calls teachers and administrators even though it’s technically a non-school day.

By Monday morning, Mom has squared herself with pride and managed to arrange a day full of meetings with counselors, special education teachers, English language learning instructors and every extra-curricular teacher available. When the last bell rings, Tami has a schedule consisting of basic language classes, art, choir, drama, and home ec. With the caveat of being involved in some social activity at least once a week. I kind of wish I failed more effectively on my first quarter. Tami’s schedule rocks.

27

It turns out, I have no 'social involvement' leeway. My only chance to hang with anyone after school hours comes during debate. Spencer takes debate to a whole new level of lame. For him, it's more than a club, it's a lifestyle. His dedication to winning arguments drives me nuts. The debate team's now my only exposure to life outside my house, I lose all confidence I can win any arguments. I even start losing arguments with myself.

I stand outside the classroom ten minutes late contemplating how to not act weird in front of Max. I haven't seen him since the night we kissed. He was away for track meets last week during debate meeting. I can't come up with a good reason to go in, or not go in. Both actions have negative repercussions. If I go in, it'll be weird. If I don't, it'll put more meaning on the situation—making it too heavy.

"Oh hey." Ben clears his throat behind me. "You're late too, then?"

"Ben." I haven't even thought about how to act in front of Ben—not once has he crossed my mind, which I should probably feel bad about because I pretty much ditched him to drive home with Max. I should've at least texted to let him know I had fun. "Was your food cooked through the other night?" Because that's the weirdest thing I could possibly ask—it's the first thing that comes to mind.

"I ordered ice cream."

Not knowing what to say next, I rock on my toes and lift my eye brows as if we're both waiting for elevator doors to open—we tend to have that effect on each other. Ben nods at me, like an acknowledgment that there's no recovery for us. At that moment Max appears around a corner with his hands behind his head and his elbows sticking out as if he came from a hard run. When he sees Ben and me, his hands jolt to his sides like an allergic side-stitch attacked him at the sight of us.

"Look at that, we're all late." Ben states the obvious, getting on my nerves. "You guys hear about Lacy and Derrick?'

When I don't answer, Ben decides to tell us anyway. "They're officially dating. I'm not sure when it happened exactly, except that it was sometime after the dance."

Max continues to look everywhere but at me. "Good for them." But, we all know this already. Because it's high school. News travels.

"I bet they're in there." Ben indicates the classroom like the ability to view Lacy and Derrick holding hands might brighten the setting.

Not seeing a way out of the overwhelming awkwardness, my head nods for Ben to go first. "Lead the way."

Ben holds the door for me.

Mr. Therault smile grows sinisterly as we enter. I swear he tries to devise topics to make his teams uncomfortable."New topic."

Everyone in the sparse room groans, except Spencer who readjusts his butt in his seat—gearing up for a chance to argue something new.

"Terrorism," Mr. Therault announces. Like that's enough for us to understand how we're supposed to argue that. "What it accomplishes for those who employ it, as well as what is accomplished by opposing terrorists. Is it possible to fight back?"

Spencer opens his mouth like he's prepared to engage right now. Mr. Therault puts his hand in the air to silence Spencer. "Everyone has to research the pro side as well as the opposed. Pro side of terrorism, and the pro side of how fighting terrorism helps those they're fighting against."

Spencer's mouth closes.

"This is the stupidest club in the whole school," Max says. "I need more academic involvement." Max looks behind himself as if plotting a path with least resistance. "I swear he's intentionally messing with us."

The same thought crosses my mind. Like our debate coach knows exactly what social situations I'm dealing with in my house. It's like he's mocking my concerns—is he? Has the whole *'someone forged Tami's international papers'* rumor mill reached teachers already? He hints for me to not stop being suspicious of my non-English speaking houseguest? He didn't mention international relations or tensions worldwide, so maybe it has nothing to do with me. It feels like another topic in the bunch that hits one of us too close to home.

Thinking of how Mr. Therault targeted Max's discomfort with slavery for our first group topic, I get thinking about Max more than the new assignment. There's some kind of draw he has on me—I feel when he moves in the room without having to look up and see that he's changed his seat. He moved closer to me—not farther away, but not in the open seat right next to me. Everything inside me sizzles in his direction. Does Max know this is a hard topic for me? Does that explain why he moved slightly closer?

"Class adjourned—use the rest of your time to solidify your arguments with research—read books and interview people. Don't watch movies and call it research, please," Mr. Therault says.

I stand and walk to the door—not paying attention to Ben, who'd been sitting on my non-Max side...

"Want to study together?" Ben asks before I'm in the hallway. "To prep for next time?"

I'm looking where Max sits and don't really hear what Ben says.

Ben still holds the door.

"Are you going to move?" Nathaniel asks behind me. "There are more people waiting to get to the library before all the good resources are gone."

I genuinely doubt that. I move out the door into the hallway followed by Ben.

"So you want to?" Ben asks me something again.

"Yeah, sure." I finally answer, not totally sure what I'm agreeing to.

Derrick and Lacy exit as a unit—knocking shoulders against the doorframe, they laugh and start chatting about all the other times they've made each other laugh.

Ben reaches for my hand, which I'm not expecting "Whoa—" I pull my hand tight to my side. Ben doesn't know how to take my reaction and takes several steps back distancing himself from any misunderstanding between us—neither of us really know what's going on between us, but maybe Ben's more confused than I am. At least, he is now. Ben accidentally steps on Max's shoe, as Max leaves the classroom.

"Not a problem, man," Max slides his shoe out from under Ben's boot and continues his journey away from us.

"At least we have a lighter topic this week, am I right?" Spencer says to those still hovering around outside debate club.

"Lighter?" I ask. "Terrorism isn't a light topic."

"It's bad," Nathaniel adds scrolling his phone newsfeed. "Terrorism equals bad." Nathaniel ticks time with the blade of his hand, like he's cutting the fact terrorism loses into bite sized pieces. "Every account of a terrorist attack includes evidence to support this. Thus, it's an easy topic."

Mr. Therault interrupts our spontaneous hallway research meeting. "But, would those orchestrating the attacks agree? Is it successful to them? Look at both sides? What does it accomplish?"

"So, 'bad' isn't going to be an acceptable argument?" I ask. Dang. I was basing a lot on that point.

"Okay, good." Mr. Therault clasps his arms behind his back and steps around us so that his Old Spice scent crisscrosses between us. "We can all agree terrorism is bad, am I right?"

We nod like we know we're headed for a trap, but can't pull ourselves away.

"But it serves a purpose."

"No," I say before anyone else has a chance. "It serves nothing."

"Then it wouldn't exist." Mr. Therault already debates us. I hate how he does this—like we're in some kind of philosophy class. This is debate. No—it's hallway debate—which doesn't qualify as anything.

It's supposed to be black and white and right and wrong and the end. He makes it gray and murky and sometimes I feel like I'm the bad guy. "But it does exist."

"It's without purpose." Ben says.

"That's your stance?" Mr. Therault challenges.

"Yes," Ben replies.

"Lowry." Mr. Therault calls me out.

"What?" I've been trying to keep my head low since last speaking. Because Mr. Therault argues better than me. And terrorism does exist. So it must serve some purpose. But, it shouldn't. Because we all agree it's bad.

"Your stance is:..." Oh no. I don't want this topic. "It serves a purpose." He slices his hand through the air. As if he's flagged us to begin a debate drag race.

"I'm pro? Again?" I'm being singled out, I swear it. "Shouldn't I get a chance to argue the right side for once?"

"Whose side is right?" Mr. Therault asks.

"The—not." I sound like an idiot. "The no terror side." I point to Ben.

"You might want to work on your argument a little. Word choice, my dear. Word choice." With that Mr. Therault dismisses our hallway meeting, releasing us to do research.

"Library?" Ben asks, not going for my hand this time.

"I'm grounded. I have to go home as soon as debate lets out." Mom didn't actually tell me I'm officially grounded again, but she did tell me I'm on thin ice since my grades had some footnotes explaining my late assignments. I leave before Ben has a chance to say anything else like "I can study at your house."

#

Sara stops me in the hall after debate. I want to find Tami and drive us both home. "We need to hang out. It's like I never see you anymore."

"I'm supposed to drive Tami home." Before the art teacher calls my parents and says I intentionally ditched Tami. I don't understand

Tami's need to make me look bad—along with my whole family. "But, yeah. We should hang out."

Sara gives me a weak half smile, and nods. "Tung, Ishii, Masato, Quon, Aiko, and Yi are really fun to hang out with. You should gather Tami and we could all go to a movie or something."

"Yeah." That sounds awful. I've never understood 'hanging out' at a dark movie theater. You can't even talk to your friends. It's sitting near each other. "Sounds awesome."

Sara smiles and runs off to make arrangements probably. If I were the one planning a get together, we'd be playing board games or having an exotic food tasting challenge. But, I have no energy to try to get people together for that sort of stuff.

This morning Mom discussed Tami and me meeting at the office so I can drive Tami home—*'that'll show Ms. Conklin,"* spilled out under Mom's breath after she told us our to and from schedules. Tami better be there. It means a lot to Mom.

The only person in the office, a receptionist three steps from locking up. "Have you seen Tami?"

"Is she the one hosted by the Dodds?"

Does she not know I'm one of the Dodds? "Yeah, that one."

"She had some paperwork to complete for her program. They faxed it over an hour ago. She should be done soon."

"Am I supposed to wait and drive her home?"

The receptionist lifts her shoulders.

"What's going on?" Mom enters the main office, Howie in tow.

"Who are you?" The receptionist can't recognize anyone. She's crap at her job.

"What're you doing here?" I lift Howie so he can snatch a peppermint from the dusty bowl on the counter.

"Tami has some new conditions to her education plan that I didn't hear about until now. If she doesn't raise her grade in a month they're sending her home."

Tami's a human paper weight at school. There are exchange students on the honor roll, yet Tami requires an Individualized Education

Program for People Who Don't Want to do Any Work Damnit. Or an IEPPWDWAWD—an 'eye-pip-wid-wad' if I read the letters across like a word.

"I think you have to go to the counselor's office for that information." The receptionist points down a hall, like we already forgot where the student services are.

Mom walks out of the main office before I know she's gone. Here I am waiting for her to sling some comeback at the receptionist like, 'Counsel this'. I put Howie down to chase after her.

"What's up with today?"

"Not sure. The last thing I need is that art teacher on my case." Mom stops walking to face me. I almost ram her with my nose. "Like I'm some sort of cut-rate foster parent running a crack house."

"I don't think that's what she was implying."

"I know what she was implying." Mom's finger waggles so close to my eyes I have to lean away. "That somehow, if I'd have paid more attention while I was pregnant I could have eaten the proper nutrients to not pass this condition on to my kids." She motions her face, even though she's portwine-stain free, "and that the same level of neglect is manifest in my ability to parent, or host-parent."

I stop leaning. Mom thinks it's her fault that her children have Sturge-Weber? How did I not know that? "Mom." She puts her finger away. "It's not your fault."

Mom rolls her eyes, pivots one foot, and continues walking toward the counselor office.

"It's not humanly possible to give a person enough attention to overcome heredity, genes, DNA. You can't celery root and quinoa this condition away, and you can't force Tami to be normal." That sounds wrong, like I'm accusing Tami of not being normal simply because she's not like me, or Sara, or the other exchange students. "Not like that, I don't mean," I use air quotes "normal, but, you know. Weird." Same thing. "Creepy." Should have stopped with weird.

"Distant. That's all. Not weird." Mom says.

"A little weird." I jog to catch up only to remember I'm supposed to lug Howie with me.

Mom and one of the school counselor's step out of eavesdropping range and speak in hushed tones. Tami sits in a cushionless chair staring intently on the carpet pattern at her feet. She doesn't look like a failure. She looks like a lost child. It's not a flat expressionless face I see now—it's lost and afraid to show it. Her eyes are strained like she's been holding in tears too long and the juices have swollen her sinuses. Why do I keep misjudging her? And why did Mr. Therault give us such a dumb debate topic right now? I need to think of Tami in a more empathetic frame.

Howie climbs in the seat next to her. I almost think he's going to give her a hug, when he slips a phone from her bag.

"Howie. No." I take the phone to replace it in the bag before noticing I've never seen that phone before. The lock screen shows a symbol I recognize from some of Tami's other belongings. Probably a word in Japanese. I should really work harder at showing interest in Tami's language. She hasn't demonstrated any interest in sharing her culture with us, but maybe if I tried harder.

I make a mental note of the symbol.

I'll look it up when I get home, maybe she'll feel better if she sees me trying to learn more about her, instead of constantly trying to get rid of her. It's the least I can do to let Tami know I care, especially while she's dealing with this testing nightmare.

28

"We're going to the lake this weekend," Mom announces as soon as we walk in the door.

"It's twenty-nine degrees." I try to figure out how to type the symbol into my phone's safari app. I'll need to snap a picture and then do an image ID search. If I knew how to do that.

"It's fifty-nine." Mom corrects me even though I was exaggerating and fifty-nine isn't much better. "And no one said you had to swim in the lake." Mom waits until Tami's in the house before continuing arguing with me. "She needs family time."

I wait for Tami to let go of her bag so I can sneak a picture of the symbol on her phone. She'll be so impressed I figured it out. But, Tami never lets go of her bag—like ever.

"She's under a lot of pressure from her program." Under her breath Mom adds, "And that horrible art teacher's taking it upon herself to mentor Tami against us."

Luckily my phone rings before I say anything to Mom. "Hello."

"Hey, uh, is Lowry around?" Has to be Ben—aside from the fact that no one I know would actually call. Text much, Ben?

"It's me, Ben." Don't engage in a conversation you're not prepared to be honest about, don't engage. "What's up?" Stupid.

"Is that Ben?" Mom asks. Like she didn't hear me say *Ben.* I nod and roll my eyes. I really need to work on my attitude.

"Are you busy this weekend?"

My brain goes blank. Please have an excuse. It's like Ben thinks we're a thing, which is not the case. I know we're going to the lake on the weekend. I couldn't be happier to remember that horrible family outing idea.

"Is he asking you out?" Mom asks loud enough that Ben could probably totally hear her.

I cover the end of my cell. "Mom!"

"Invite him to come to the lake with us," Mom says.

"I'd love to," Ben says over the phone the same second Mom pauses for breath.

"What?" I forget I'm holding the speaking end, take my hand off, which didn't block any sound anyway, since Ben obviously heard my Mom who was talking so loud her voice penetrated my clenched fingers over the receiver

"I'd love to come. What time are you guys leaving? And should I bring anything? Like soda or chips?"

I stare at Mom, searching for how to get out of this mess. Mom doesn't help at all. She nods toward my phone, waiting for me to formally invite Ben. Opening my eyes as wide as they can possibly go, I bite my bottom lip and slowly let it go before speaking again. "Sure. Soda sounds great." What is happening? "We're leaving at eight in the morning."

The lake promises to be the worst.

29

Another parcel delivery waits on our doorstep when I open the door Saturday morning. UPS doesn't usually make weekend deliveries. Yesterday's drama must have muted the doorbell when the delivery man came at his usual hour.

"More maxi pads?" I ask Tami. There must be some black market for Japanese maxi pads—like there's a secret anti-aging formula in the super absorbent stuffing or something. I mean who goes through a case of pads a week? That or Tami works as some sort of international drug mule disguised as an exchange student. Hold up...Mom takes the package from me, as if she can read the conspiracy in my mind. She sets the mid-weight package at the top of the basement steps for Tami to collect.

Tami doesn't have her bag with her at the breakfast table—for once she's left it behind. I rush downstairs before she hauls the massive cardboard box down to her room. Once through her door, I'm breathing like I'm some sort of marathon running criminal. I slide the closet doors open. No bag. No phone.

Under the bed. A ton of flattened cardboard boxes stacked up. Sheesh, how many packages has she gotten? There's a ridiculously tight stack squeezed between the floor and her bed. No phone. No bag. I go to the window, open as always. Weird, but used to it. No phone. No bag. The nightstand. No bag. No phone.

Under her pillow... phone. It's the one with the symbol. I fumble to get my own phone out and snap a picture of the symbol. I have to remind myself that I'm being thoughtful here and not being a spying jerkwad. It still feels wrong. Like an invasion of privacy. Maybe all interactions with Tami feel that way?

I slip Tami's phone back under her pillow and race out of her room —right into Tami's box at the door, being held by Tami. "Umph!" I fall on my butt.

Tami does a visual check of her room before lowering her gaze to where I'm sprawled. "What you are doing?"

"Oh hey." I need time to come up with something. I want to surprise her by knowing the symbol. "I uh..." She might think it's cool I learned something about her. "Was looking for my history book." Big emphasis on might. "I thought maybe you'd borrowed it." Because you don't read even basic English and that textbook challenges even me. I'm the dumbest reason giver.

Tami steps over me into her space. She walks to the window and touches the flapping curtain. Then she moves to the closet and bends to peek inside the only partly closed sliding door. From there, her eyes travel to the bed where all color drains from her face. If I didn't know better, I'd say even her hair pales.

"Okay, so I didn't find the history book. It must be in my room still. I'll go help Mom get ready for the lake."

Tami remains pale, and so very still.

"I'll make sure you get a lunch, okay?" No response from Tami. But that's not so unusual, so I move to my feet and head upstairs to help prep. Dad's off picking up Bevan for a lake day while we get everything ready.

"Be sure to pack enough lunch for Ben. He's coming, right?" Quieter she adds, "Lay off Tami, okay. She's in no mood to be teased right now."

"I am being nice. I even have a surprise." I say. "I'm going to learn one of Tami's favorite Japanese language symbols to show her that I care about her language too."

"Well." I can tell Mom's proud of me. "That is nice—and a great start to the holidays—being thoughtful like that."

Thanksgiving falls next Thursday. Dad and Howie picked up Bevan from his assisted living program in Silver City before we leave to the lake. I envy Howell in his car seat cocoon, and Bevan gets a personal aide who occupies the seat next to Howell. The rest of us are crammed on one bench like that's safe.

Bevan has his seizure helmet on, putting conversation on mute until both Ben and Tami acclimatize to the fact it looks like it's made of peach foamy brain tissue. Whenever Bevan moves his head to see something out the window, I have to dodge into Ben's personal space to avoid getting whacked.

Ben doesn't flinch, which is something, considering Tami looks like she's trapped in a horror movie. Her back, stiff as a rod, with her eyes cast down, boring a hole in the door handle like she's willing it to open and spill both Bevan and me out onto the highway. As soon as Bevan takes off his helmet, to reveal his scabby-red hairless-head, she'll be on that handle so fast—it'll be like an aircraft with a sudden cabin pressure change.

"How come I didn't get to invite a friend?" Bevan asks. "I haven't seen Max in forever." And there's the other awkward thing about me liking Max. He's my big brother's best friend even though Max boasts two years younger than Bevan. It's like all things weird are universally stacked against me.

The little shop where Max and I had donuts, when all life's problems seemed centered on Tami, makes my stomach swirl. Out of the corner of my eye I catch Ben staring at the mark across my face, like he's trying to convince himself it doesn't bother him. I feel like I'm cheating on Max, but it's not like he asked me out—or even texted.

No one answers Bevan's question right away, which turns into a drawn-out silence.

"So... Tami, how do you like the states so far?" Ben breaks the silence first.

Bevan swings his head wide in expectation of an answer. I flinch in response, and for some reason Ben grabs that hand. By no means was I waving a free hand in a 'hold me, hold me' sort of way. I've been putting so much energy into acting as neutral as possible without having to use the words 'friend zone'. I must have let my guard down when Ben addressed Tami, who still hasn't responded and I've had all this time to think about how weird it is that he's talking to her and grabbing my hand at the same time. Like the fact he's talking to her softens the impact of the action, which it does not.

I'm too busy being shocked at my Ben wrapped hand to say anything either. The question sort of falls off a tension ledge, leaving only the tension behind.

Apparently, none of us are into answering questions in this vehicle.

Bevan returns to staring out the window. His face moves back with everything we pass, as if the world still looks new and exciting. Maybe his regular seizures wipe out his brain patterns, so things seem fresh all the time, or at least need to be reclassified and sorted. His fingers reach toward a dog on a leash, lightly contacting the window. He pulls back as if he's been shocked by an invisible force field. I miss Bevan when he's not here.

"Almost there," Mom announces from the passenger seat. Even though it's still twenty miles out. "Tami, have you ever been to a lake before?"

Before Tami can answer I say, "She's from another country—not a barren planet. Jeez, Mom."

"Your mother is trying to start a polite conversation," Dad says. I want to point out that two polite conversations have already died in here.

Tami answers. "Yes." The conversation already buries itself, but that belated response feels like the stamp to seal this as the most awkward family outing to date.

Ten excruciating minutes of trying to ignore my hand sweating inside Ben's grasp, while also craning to look out any window so I don't have to make eye contact with anyone pass before the car really starts to stink. Literally stink.

Everyone on the back bench stiffens from the odor—trying not to stir it up to our noses, either afraid to ask who dealt it, or concealing the fact that they're the one who ripped a butt-bomb. Having grown up with Bevan, I'm familiar with his personal brand of noxious gas. It's not him. I'm pretty sure Tami robots with no working human parts—including the ones that produce gas. That leaves Ben.

"Pee-ew," Howell announces—meaning no one can pretend the gag-worthy smell doesn't exist.

"Howie, did you have an accident?" Mom asks once the stench makes its way to the front of the vehicle.

"Mom!" I shout, because Howie doesn't know to be indignant yet.

"Just crack a window," Dad booms over the battle that's passively been going since Mom invited Ben. "All the windows." He supersedes, using his master control to roll down every window in the SUV, including the sunroof.

When we finally pull into a parking spot by the lake, I have to climb over Tami and Bevan's aid in order to escape the car. Howie sticks in a web of safety belts strapping him inside the stink bomb until Mom manages to free him.

"Where are the oars?" Dad lifts the canoes from their straps on the roof of the car.

"Oh, you're kidding me." Mom joins the search.

"How long does your family usually spend at the lake?" Ben asks. I can hear the *this was a huge mistake* in his question.

"Don't worry," I say. "Something usually ends the day early. Like no oars for the canoe, and I doubt anyone brought a volleyball."

I have to duck as Mom slaps a ball toward my head. "I heard that." Mom laughs when I can't avoid getting whacked. So does Ben. Everything takes on a little brighter, less doomy, turn.

Bevan joins the laughter, picks up the ball. "Volley!" he yells. Bevan and Max became best friends because of their mutual competitive natures. They love to sports it up—challenging each other to how much more sportsing they are than the other. It's hilarious when they're together. Nothing like right now. Bevan hits the ball with all his strength. Right into Tami's face.

"Oh!" Her hands instinctively cover her nose. When she pulls her hands away to examine them, saliva rich blood puddles in her palms. She cranes her neck so no more red stuff can drip into the rocky sand. Her teeth are covered in blood. She doesn't scream, or cry, or gasp, or anything. I'm even more sure she's a robot.

Bevan continues to laugh like this moment rivals the most hysterical fun he's ever been a part of. Man, I've missed him.

"Tami." Ben grabs Tami, whipping her head forward by the force of his lunge—way too late to think he's getting her out of the way of the ball. "Lean forward and pinch your nose." By some miracle the bleeding lessens.

The rest of the family circles round Ben the nosebleed hero.

Tami swallows, clearing much of the gory scene from her teeth. "Okay." She waves us off toward the water.

Pretty sure I can't feel any lower about myself—until I hear someone shouting out on the lake. Sara.

"Lowry..." She yells from a small motor boat getting ever closer—arms waving like she's looking for a rescue from the coast guard. Pretty sure I'm the one who needs a rescue right now. "Tami!" She adds, to rising chants for Tami from the rest of the party on the boat.

Sara is here with a whole crew of kids from school, including a bunch of other foreign exchange students. Worst timing that could possibly happen, so of course its real life. And Sara looks amazing and happy—and the exchange students are having conversations with everyone—not sticking to themselves anymore. Because, they've been in high school long enough to make connections with the local kids too.

Mom leans over to me. "I sort of called Sara."

"You what?" Why are Moms so intrusive? I don't need her pulling all the strings in my social life. Sitting alone in my room on a Saturday beats surprise hang out any day.

"Don't get upset." Of course I'm going to get upset. "I didn't do this for you."

"Yet, here I am."

"I arranged friends for Tami." I smack my head. Mom knows nothing about high school and how weird it is to have someone's Mom arrange a play-date. "She needs to practice English before her test, and what better way than with friends?"

"Mom..."

"Besides, this gives you and Ben a chance to hang out one on one, if you wanted."

Mom! "You can't be serious."

Meanwhile Sara and a crew of exchange students (and the few locals up to going to the lake in November) continue to wave and exclaim. One glance at Ben, and I know he'd rather hang on the boat with kids our age, instead of getting stuck with my parents and me.

It's not long before they secure the boat to the dock and we're flooded with "Oh my gosh, what happened?" and "Tami are you alright?" "What did they do to you?" Like injuring Tami was intentional.

Bevan has yet to pause his boisterous laughter. Sara's used to Bevan.

"Hey, Tami, wanna come hang on the boat until your nose stops bleeding?" Sara offers.

Mom switches her attention to me, my face giving away much more than I want to say. "Uhh. Well..."

Ben bites his lip, like he's a puppy being left at the kennel while his family go ona butt sniffing vacation. Sara must notice. The next thing out of her mouth, "I mean, Ben and Lowry can come too, if... You know." Too late of an invitation.

Bevan has already walked over to the boat—completely oblivious to how many of the kids are pointing at his seizure helmet. It's an unusual lake accessory, for those not used to Bevan. I assume he's scanning the area for Max—wondering if his best bud will jump out like some surprise party. I'm secretly hoping for the same thing. Masato's on board, which means I might be able to ask him about the phone symbol. How do I casually bring it up so Tami doesn't notice? I want it to be a surprise that I've learned about her interests and language.

"No. It's cool. Go ahead," I say. I can always ask Masato at school. It's a little crowded on the boat, even though I sort of want to go, but also don't want to ditch my family. "We were about to start a game of volleyball anyway." Ben doesn't look like he's decided which direction to lean. All the air goes out of my lungs. "Ben, why don't you go with Tami. I mean—you know about bloody noses or whatever (because that's such a big deal sheesh, which I don't say) and I'll catch up with you."

"Yeah?" Ben says taking a step toward the dock.

I don't know what's going on with us anyway. "Yeah, go ahead."

"Okay cool." Ben supports Tami as they turn to face the boat. "I've never been on a boat before." He confides to Sara.

"Lowry, aren't you coming?" Sara calls from the doc.

Mom pushes me toward the boat. "You can't leave your date."

"Not a date, Mom." I remind her. "You invited him." Like everyone else on this freezing lake.

Ben's already assisting Tami into the boat by the time I run up the dock. I'm not sure what transition occurred, but Ben finally, definitely, shows less interested in trying to make 'us' a 'thing'. I'm confident Ben won't be sweating up my palm for the entire ride home.

"You didn't think I was trying to ditch you, did you?" Sara asks. "I just—you know—family time. It's a big deal at my house. I didn't want to upset your parents by inviting you away if it wasn't okay."

"No. It's totally cool," I lie. I rarely get to see Bevan anymore and even though I sometimes feel invisible when he's around, it's worse when he's not. Guilt over ditching him to hang with Sara's shiny new friends eats at my insides. I'm one of those jerks on a humanity awareness ad that ignores the kid sitting alone at a lunch table. "Totally cool."

Speaking of cool, my jacket remains back at my parent's car and the wind on the lake feels like it's blowing out of Siberia. Ben and Tami still have their jackets on. Would it be too much to ask Ben to lend me his?

"Anyone want to brave the water?" Sara asks the group, but she's looking at Jin and Masato in particular. Yi sports a bikini with no cover-up, despite the temperature being in the mid-sixties, because of course she is. That might be warm in Canada, but it's freaking Siberia of New Mexico to us. Yi emphatically shakes her head no to the 'jump in the water' invitation.

I join the unanimous "no's." It's too cold for water sports. Isn't that hypothermia temperature? I think it is. The water smells. Moss and fish mix with a metallic scent. Perhaps it's the wet hull of the boat? I don't know, but the smell isn't refreshing.

I work my way closer to Masato, to see if I can get a chance to talk to him about Japanese characters. We let the waves beat against the shell of the boat as we speed across the longest section of lake. There are a surprising number of water craft on the lake for November. Or maybe I don't visit the lake this time of year enough to realize how many people value recreation over personal warmth.

"Where's Max and Lacy and (I realize I've consigned myself to listing Violet, Derrick, Nathaniel—all by name and I don't want to take the time) everybody?" I ask Sara in an attempt to not think about the kind of attention Tami would get if she accidentally fell over the side.

"They had a group date, so I gathered everyone who could to come hang on the lake."

The jolt of the bow crashing against another boats wake knocks me off balance at the words 'Max is on a date.' It's not like he can't date. *No one ever said he couldn't go on a date. Why does it matter if he's on a date?*

Jin's at the wheel, aiming so we hit all the waves like some kind of Bond Villain. Masato, Quon, and Yi laugh like getting butt-slapped by the bench I'm on consists of the whole point of a boat ride.

"I don't know why I didn't think to call you and Tami." Sara says. "To let you know your Mom called me. It feels like I cheated on our friendship...with your mom." Probably assuming the seasick expression on my face has something to do with her oversight in sending me a heads up and less to do whomever Max is out with. "So sorry."

"It's been a weird week," I answer. Hoping that covers everything and our talk will end. My head hurts, Max on a date? Tami the drama queen and—Max is on a date!

"I seriously am. Really sorry."

"Don't worry about it."

Spray mists us all. Ben doesn't come to my side to keep me warm—he stays oddly close to Tami... And Yi. Or maybe Yi slides oddly close to him? Either way, it gives me a chance to slide my phone out in front of Masato without Tami looking over my shoulder.

"Hey, Masato, what does this character mean?" I show him the image.

He grabs my phone and stares at the picture for a minute, turns my phone on its side, which only makes the image right itself to how it had been oriented previously. "Huh, I don't know for sure—I think it's fire—or burn maybe?" He hands me back my phone. "My Korean's rusty though, you might want to ask Aiko or Yi to be sure."

"No this is Japanese," I say.

"I don't think so," Masato says. "Pretty sure that's Korean."

I stare at the picture on my phone. Maybe Tami likes Korean dramas? They're popular in the states, so it's not odd, I guess. When I look up, Tami has her eyes on me. I slide my phone back in my pocket, hoping she didn't notice, but also wondering if my knowing a Korean symbol will indicate I care about her culture, or not.

Another slam into the wake left by a jet ski. I reach out to hold onto something so I don't fall on my face—even though I'm already sitting—it's that bad. I wish I'd stayed on the beach with Bevan. Aiko points to bigger waves left by a bigger boat in the distance. Great. It's going to get worse.

There's no way to make this boat ride less awkward. We pick up speed, which makes the crashes even rougher. Someone needs to invent ship-shocks to absorb the butt-slapping pain of surviving on a boat.

"This is fun," I yell over the engine, and waves, and chatter.

"Yeah." Sara responds, then turns back to the guy she's sitting next to.

More jarring smashes, speeding on the surface of the lake, with spray coating all surfaces, causes me to lose my grip on a hand bar, my footing braced against the rubber mats on the ground and my wet butt on the white seats. I hear a group exclamation as the engine cuts off. The weight of the boat shifts to my side. "I'm okay, I'm okay." I pull myself back to my seat somewhat expecting a helping hand from someone who came rushing to my side, but no hand comes. I'm surrounded by bodies—all leaning over the side.

Jin kills the engine and I want to thank him for finally being considerate behind the wheel.

"Is she alright?" I hear Sara shout.

"I'm fine—I slipped. Don't worry about me." Except no one's looking at me—much less concerned for my well-being. The group scans the choppy water for signs of something.

"Where is she? Anyone see her?" Ben's voice rises above the others. On a ledge perched on the side railing, he's in position to launch into the water.

To be honest, he's handy to have around the more I think about it. I also realize I have taken him for granted and it's too late for me to appreciate him now. The bright side, he's about to save someone else, and Tami will realize Ben will save anyone. It's not special treatment because he likes her.

"I don't see her." I hear. Then I look around, realizing the only person missing is Tami.

I rush to the edge of the boat and search the murky blue gray water for dark hair and pale skin. "Tami?" This is all my fault, I'm sure of it. "Tami!" She's nowhere. She hasn't come up once—no bob—no splashing arms—not even a bubble.

Ben pushes off from the boat toward the cold lake.

30

Ben dives into frothy waves, splashing as he disappears below the surface. There's no way I'm going to stand back and let him be the hero of the day twice in a row. Without grace or agility of any kind, I climb onto the boat rail, slip, and fall back-first into the water.

"Lowry!" Sara calls after me. I don't hear anything once my head submerges. It's stupid cold in the water—as in, I might have made a huge life-threatening mistake. I have to resist gasping from the shock of instant icebox until my face resurfaces.

In addition to being insta-brainfreeze-cold, the water weighs a ton. Granted I have all my clothes on. Maybe it's a good thing I left my jacket behind after all, it would have added to the weight. Tami had a jacket on. Does she know how to swim? I slice through the water with my hands speeding my rise to the surface. Once my head pierces the waves, I scan for signs of where to dive, only concerned with finding Tami.

Ben's head pops up farther from me than I would have thought. Boat drift? Is there some equation to how much I need to swim in order to stay within a safe distance of the boat in case fatigue sets in? Am I expected to do math right now? It's all too much at once. Ben dives below the murky water again. So, I do too.

Something grabs my leg and pulls me down. Panic takes over my limbs. I rake the water for something to latch onto, to keep me from being sucked to the bottom of this weedy lake. Something yanks my shorts like it tries to climb me by my pockets. Lake monster stories fill my head.

Sunshine cuts through thinner rolls of waves on the surface and I reach as if there's a life raft in the thinner sections of water. The air in my lungs pounds against my chest, rushing up my throat and puffing my cheeks. I hold it in. If I open my mouth I'll suck in the entire contents of the lake in an instinctual scream. I forget how to swim and grab handfuls of bright water, pulling it toward me like I can grasp handholds to the surface.

Something ruffles the water to the side of me, but I can't pay that disturbance any attention if I'm ever going to breathe again—then it's gone—nothing holds me down or pulls against my clothes, but I don't get any closer to the surface.

My chest produces fire and drums, as acid climbs my throat.

I kick both feet. Forcing my fingers together I push my hands down, propelling myself up. It feels like so much effort with no reward of safety. My legs forget to kick for a second and I lose inches between me and surface. I go wild. My arms don't move together, my legs thrash in every direction—desperate to get to oxygen.

I'm out of air, out of thought, out of time. I can't tell myself to not gasp for breath anymore. My body won't listen. I'm crazy with desperation to get back on the boat. Why did I jump?

My arm smacks something hard, increasing my panic—am I under the boat? Did I somehow swim below it and now I'm trapped? I rage through my limbs like that's going to break whatever remains above me. The hard thing contacts my arm again. I spin and kick and twist and rage, fighting off whatever new threat on my life this fit of terror conceals, as I realize I'm losing—I'm losing.

Something clamps down on my forearm, if I could remember how to tell my other arm how to punch, this horror would be off me. It pulls on me. I haven't managed a breath since the last moment I was pulled down and here I am right back in doom's way. I can't stop it any longer, I suck in water in an attempt to breathe.

Liquid silences my effort, sealing my sinuses. Some weird instinct of my tongue causes that muscle to block my airway. Can a person choke on their own tongue? When they do my autopsy will the coroner say, 'this is a first, she didn't drown, she swallowed her tongue'?

I'm choking and gagging and spitting and swatting my arms wildly.

"Lowry."

I continue to swing and gag and fight my way to the surface. It feels like I'll never make it. I beat harder with my legs and arms.

"Lowry!"

I wretch, which makes fighting a lot harder—muscles seem to do some kind of instinctual freeze thing while my body vomits.

"Stop fighting, I'm trying to save you."

I don't recognize the voice, but I don't care either. I'm out of energy—except for the gagging and puking. That keeps coming no matter how tired I am, followed by coughing—so much coughing. I don't know how I got back on the boat, if I helped this happen, or if I was dragged here. All I can do... cough.

There's nothing left in my lungs or my stomach to expel, and yet my body insists on trying to get something more out. When I finally gain enough control of myself, instead of a thank you, the first thing out of my mouth is, "Tami."

"She's alright. Ben's got her."

Of course he did. I only made things worse. I look up to see who I'm talking with. It's Jin—the guy whose host family owns the boat. Also, the guy Sara seems to be trying to impress the most.

My attention shifts in search of Tami. Instead of catching her off guard, when I scan the deck to find her—her eyes are on me when I look up, then she turns her head to what I think is my phone. I feel my pocket—no phone, a pocket filled with water.

The boat slaps the waves again and I have to grab the rail so I don't fall over a second time.

"Whoa," Sara says, "Maybe you should sit down. I mean, that was really scary, what happened." She says it like a statement, but my head spins so hard her words turn into a question that runs in loop through my mind.

Tami has my phone? Someone grabbed me in the water—and stuck their hand in my pocket—now Tami has my phone. I'm not making this up, am I? Did she take it, or did she find it and bring it back in the boat to give to me? And if that's the case... Why isn't she giving it to me?

What happened? What just happened? What happened? I can't let it go. "What the heck just happened?" I scream at Tami, which wasn't how it was supposed to go in the pre-planned out version in my head. Everyone stares at me like I'm out of line. "What? You fell off?" I stand—even though my balance craps right now. My legs are shaking so hard and not from the cold.

"Lowry," Sara steps in front of me. "What are you doing?" She whispers, like the boat isn't ten feet long crammed shoulder to shoulder with teens.

"She grabbed my leg—pulled me down on purpose." I lean so I can point to Tami around Sara.

"No." Is all Tami says in response.

"Yes, you did! I jumped in after you, and what the heck?" I point to my phone in her hands. "That's mine—it was in my pocket." Stop shaking legs—it's not helping. Though I'm glad I invested in the waterproof case for my phone.

"This is uncomfortable." Ben's opinion—the last thing I need to hear right now.

"Is it Ben?" I say with more hip swagger than I should add.

"Okay, Low-low, I can see there's a little more to this than falling in the water." Sara reaches a hand like she's going to pat my shoulder or something. I jerk back—evading her touch.

"No, there's not," I say.

Tami continues sliding her fingers over the screen on my phone for a brief second, then lifts it in the air toward me. Ben takes the phone from Tami and holds it out for me—inches away.

“Forget it Ben—” I slap the phone, it clatters to the boat deck. The thing is, I could be wrong, but I’m so shaken by the whole thing. I’m not thinking things through. I still feel like I’m in danger of drowning.

“Hey!” Ben says.

“Shut it, Ben,” I say. “This is about Tami and me. She doesn’t like me.”

“I don’t believe that,” Sara cuts me off again.

“Stop talking over me!” I’ve never, not for the duration of our friendship, yelled at Sara in an upset way. Never.

“Sit down, Lowry. Before you fall off again.” If Ben could have said that without an eye roll—I’d still be pissed. But, now I’m ready to tie a rock to his ankle and throw it over.

“First of all, I didn’t fall over. I jumped.” Finger accusingly points to Tami, which feels great. “In the water, someone grabbed my leg and pulled me down—like held me down.”

“Shock and panic can make the situation feel more deliberate than it really was.” Ben says. “For example, during the Spanish War—“

“This isn’t debate team, Ben. This is real life, and she really held my leg and tried to pull me under longer than I could breathe.”

“But that doesn’t make sense, because she would be stuck under for that long too. Don’t you see how that doesn’t make sense?” Ben won’t get off my case. And Tami hasn’t said anything other than ‘no’. “She probably grabbed onto you, hoping you’d be able to pull her to safety.”

“Oh my heck,” a frustrated laugh escapes me as I push my wet hair out of my face. “That is so not what happened.”

Sara grabs my arms, pulling me toward her and angling me away from where Ben and Tami sit. “Lowry, this is all my fault, I’m so sorry.”

What kind of person thinks everything always falls under ‘their fault’? Does Sara literally think no one ever does anything wrong except her—all the time? Why does that make me more angry with her? Maybe that means everything is always all my fault, because I’m mad at someone who unselfishly takes all the blame on herself. Heck, I should let her take the blame—but I can’t!

"Why on earth would you think it's your fault?" I scream—because I've worked up to it in my mind even though everyone else seems really taken back by my elevated mood.

"I begged Jin to let you guys on even though there weren't enough life vests for everyone."

Jin pipes in, "Everyone's supposed to have a vest to be on the boat. But, I forgot to pack them in the seats—just food." Masato lifts a seat to reveal coolers—not life vests.

"This is sort of a traumatic event—shouldn't we tell Lowry's parents that Tami almost drowned?" Ben says.

"Oh man, my host parents are going to kill me if they find out I forgot the life vests so I could sneak beer on here."

Of course, the coolers are full of alcohol. This situation gets worse. My parent's will probably kill us too. All of our parents will, when all the information involving how this all happened comes out.

"Oh crap," Sara says, sitting next to Tami and putting her arm around her. "We're all in trouble." She looks at Jin. "We better go back to the dock."

Tami has been looking down for most of this conversation, but looks up at me. Her expression, neutral as ever. Not threatening. Not happy. Not gloating. I can't even tell if she's uncomfortable with Sara's embrace or not.

My phone slides around on the deck when Jin starts the engine and turns the boat around. I bend to pick it up. "Sorry." I say when I notice Ben waits for me to say something to him.

"Yeah," is all he says in return.

The rest of the time on the lake can be defined as patting Tami on the hand, stroking her wet hair out of her eyes.

On our return trip we bob on the lake, at a speed of 'shoot me now' slow, taking turns retelling how terrifying it was when Tami fell overboard. How heroic Ben was to dive in after her. And I keep my mouth shut about thc fact that I wcnt in to hclp too, and got pulled under the water, or at least it felt that way at the time.

Today revolves around Tami and her hero Ben.

When the boat gets closer to shore I notice red and blue lights flashing. My heart sinks. I know it has something to do with my family. Not that I'm so self-centered, it's just—it's been that kind of day. That kind of year, actually.

Mom waits at the dock. Being right hurts the worst. Something appears not okay. "Your dad went with Bevan in the ambulance. We'll meet them there."

"Where?" I'm still damp from lake water.

"The hospital, a gran mal seizure." Mom manages a choppy explanation. "Howie's already in the car, I need the three of you and we can go."

"Is it cool if I get a ride from Sara?" Ben asks.

It's totally rude, but at the same time, what's he going to do with my whole family in the hospital waiting room? "I guess," I say.

"Sara, are you down with that?" he asks.

She nods, her eyes already wide with concern for my mom.

"It'll be okay," I tell Sara. "We've been through this before." Bevan used to get these kinds of seizures all the time before the doctors increased his meds to the point that Bevan stopped talking much and used to walk around like a zombie. Come to think of it, he wasn't acting like medicated Bevan today.

Without saying anything, Tami disembarks from the boat and walks ahead of Mom to the car. She probably could have asked to stay behind and get a ride home. But, we all know how much Tami loves getting rides outside our family (or from Ms. Conklin).

"Everything go okay?" Mom asks me.

"Yeah. Why?" I ask.

"For one thing, you girls are the only ones with wet clothes."

"Ben's a bit damp too," I say defensively. "What? You didn't notice?"

"Fine. Don't tell me. But, if you two girls are fighting, I will find out. And I will do something about it."

Why do Moms always assume the worst thing? In this case, she's sort of right, but come on. "You can't force us to get along. There's no hug and say sorry for sixteen-year-olds."

Mom stops walking. “Tami’s going through a very hard time right now.”

“And I’m not?” I ask. “We’re not?” I gesture to the flashing lights and open car door. “We’re about to drive to the hospital.”

Mom gasps—actually gasps at me. “We’re all dealing with things, but that’s no excuse to be rude to anyone. Particularly not a guest in our home. And maybe, if you thought of someone besides yourself once in a while, you’d have a better relationship with Tami.” Mom’s voice drops like she’s going to be caught gossiping. “She failed a basic test for her program—they’re threatening to send her home early. You know failure isn’t acceptable for a lot of people in her culture...”

She’s probably right, but I can’t let her be right. “No. I don’t. I don’t know much of anything because Tami never talks to me, never tells me anything about her family, town, government, food, culture—whatever you want to call it.”

“And whose fault is that?”

Now I stop. “It’s not my fault.”

“You know how to use the internet. Learn for yourself. Maybe you’d understand her a little better.”

“Like you do?”

Mom takes two angry steps closer to me. I cringe anticipating a slap or something based on the expression on her face. “Get in that car and buckle you and your brother in. I do not want to hear a single word come out of your mouth for the rest of the day. Do you hear me?”

I roll my tongue across the roof of my mouth, but keep it shut because I’m not a total idiot.

31

Tami sits between me and Howie in the waiting room while Mom and Dad cross paths pacing the floor. The courtesy television hangs like a decorative piece of black construction paper—with enough dust to suggest it's less useful. Padded chairs line the walls, their fabric matches the stained commercial-quality of tightly woven carpet. There are dark stains on both the floor and several chairs, not instilling a lot of confidence. My family either chose the least populated section of the room, or the rest of the occupants are avoiding us.

"Sorry if I ruined today," I say, hanging my head.

Mom stops pacing. "What?" She comes and sits next to me with her hands on her own knees. "You did not ruin anything."

"It was supposed to be a family day. I left."

Mom moves one hand to my knee. "Honestly, Sweetie, it wasn't going so great even before you left." Her hand goes back to her own legs. She wipes her hands across her thighs several times before speaking. "What was I thinking? I can't force you guys to get along."

I nod, which earns me an irritated glance from Mom.

"Hon, you want to take the kids home?" Mom asks Dad.

"No." Tami says, pretty much all she's said all day. Instead of talking more, she's reverted to less English than ever.

Dad's shoulders relax. "I don't want to leave Bevan."

"Me either, but we have to think of how difficult this situation must be for Tami—she's never been around Bevan or seizures—." Mom whispers, even though we can all hear her still. "It's scary for someone not used to it."

"No." She repeats with no additional explanation.

"Are you sure?" Mom crouches in front of Tami so they're eye to eye. "I know this is a big deal."

Tami meets her eyes, but says nothing. Tami switches her focus so it's at nothing and everything at the same time again, effectively dismissing Mom. Something tells me Tami's seen more than Mom thinks. The girl hasn't been in a bubble her whole life. Maybe someone having a seizure isn't a big deal?

Mom stands again. She and Dad exchange a puzzled expression and we all return to our original worry condition: sitting, staring, pacing.

"Dobbs?" A man with a clipboard asks, walking into the room. Mom and Dad rush to him. I stand, but don't move closer. Tami doesn't move at all, and Howie watches all of us,seemingly unsure whose cue to follow. "Your son is going to be fine."

"Thank you, Doctor," Mom reaches out in an almost hug, but changes to a weird arm pat thing.

"I'm the technician," he says. "His file says he's been off his seizure medication."

The aid nods, like they're used to this sort of thing.

"No," Dad answers.

The technician pulls his lower lip to one side referencing the clipboard. "I have a parent signature from his care facility that indicates one of you okayed a trial without meds." Dad grabs the clipboard.

I'm guessing it's not his signature on there.

"He hates them." Mom speaks so quickly, I'm not sure Dad heard her right. His face goes white. "It's not worth it, if he can't even enjoy anything. It's like being in a coma."

"You took him off his meds without so much as telling me? Much less asking me what I thought?"

"I knew you'd say no," Mom says. Everyone else in the room watches them.

"You didn't give me a chance." Dad slaps a hand on the clipboard while the technician reaches for it back.

The technician regains the file and puts more distance between himself and my parents. "Should I come back?"

"Yes," Dad says at the same moment of Mom's "No."

"I'll come back."

"You know what?" Dad pauses. "Maybe *you* should take the kids home."

Mom's mouth opens and no words come out. I can see her eating up the guilt from the entire room. She's packing it in all her corners and silent places, gorging herself on it.

"I can drive," I chime in. "If you want me to take Tami and Howie."

The aid raises a hand without adding anything to the discussion.

"And her," I say. "Wherever you need to go." I'm not sure if I drop the aid at the assisted living facility, or her own apartment.

Still silent, Mom takes the keys from Dad's hand, then walks past me to Howie. She takes his hand and starts toward the exit. I wait for Dad to say something. Sorry. Anything. Mom is through the doors. "Come on, Tami."

Tami stands, breathes in the stagnant waiting room air, and walks ahead of me. When it's my turn to pass Dad, I shake my head so he won't say anything. The thing is, I don't think he was going to say anything anyway, and that's worse than thinking I prevented him from saying anything to me. I haven't been paying attention to my parents lately. Now I wonder if they've been paying attention to each other.

32

Dad brings Bevan home from the hospital late Sunday night—doped up like a kite that can't see two feet in front of him. His seizure meds are personality thieves. Since exchange students can't share rooms with host kids, Bevan moves in with Howie. I'm glad about that, because it means there's no chance Tami will be sneaking under Howie's bed ever again. Maybe I'll sleep better with Bevan back in the house.

The rest of the Thanksgiving break I stare at my messages and avoid my family. Nothing new as far as holiday behavior goes. Nothing new in my messages either. Nothing from Ben. Sara is silent. I want to text Max, but realize we'll probably end up chatting about his super-hot date last weekend, and I can't handle that right now. Violet was missing from the boat fiasco too—*please don't let it have been Violet out with him.*

We've definitely lost progress on the communication front. Tami reduces down to single word responses, Howie isn't speaking again. He isn't signing either. Not that I remember any of the baby signs Mom used with Howie the first two years after he was born. He's reverted to pointing and grunting—perfect imitation of Bevan back on his seizure meds.

Dad too has taken a vow of silence. He and Mom aren't on speaking terms after the waiting-room incident. If I talk to either of them, it's like I'm choosing sides. The house feels like a 'no words' zone. I'm reduced to whispering to myself to lighten the overall dark mood.

When Mom speaks normally it sounds like shouting. "I expect you girls to be caught up on homework by the time school starts again." This is the worst Thanksgiving break in the history of Thanksgiving breaks.

Tami holes up in her room most of the week, avoiding family interactions no matter how many times Mom invades her space. It gets so desperate I hear Mom say, "Let's play a board game, shall we?" to which Tami responds, "No."

Mom doesn't press again. An inch of dust settles on the games she bought a month ago. At the moment, I can't blame Tami. There's a 'do not disturb' vibe plaguing every room Mom and Dad occupy at the same time. A board game wouldn't go well for anyone.

Once Mom returns upstairs I slip out of my room and stand at Tami's door. She's hiding in her weird far corner, like she's afraid to get caught napping on the bed or something. I know I need to stop judging all the things Tami does differently as weird and uncomfortable, but sometimes her habits seem so unnatural—even considering she grew up with different social expectations. Who hides in corners all day at their house?

"Tami?" I whisper—a breath with punctuation more than her actual name, comes out.

A shuffling and click, followed by a low mumble, which I hadn't really noticed until the mumbling stopped, comes in response. I wait another second—listening. Tami says some words in hushed, frustrated tones I'm unfamiliar with, probably Japanese, but I honestly have no familiarity with differences in any languages. For all my knowledge, she could be speaking French.

Another rustling sound and the slide of the closet door on its tracks. Dang it. I should have burst in to see what was up, but that's also an invasion of privacy and I'm trying to rebuild trust between us, which I'm also constantly breaking. It's eating at me to know what's up, but every time I've rushed in to uncover some great terrible thing Tami stays up to—there's nothing but misunderstanding and me looking like a jerk.

"Tami?" I speak a little stronger than the first time with an added tap on the not fastened door, causing it to open even more. Tami rushes to her feet, shouting something at me I don't understand. "Sorry. I was— I'm checking if you're alright, you know, after the whole..." I motion a hand over my nose, signaling when Tami got hit in the face with the volleyball, which I hope she knows implies the lake incident and how I accused her of trying to drown me. I guess she probably didn't intentionally try to pull me under... Or whatever will make this less awkward for the rest of the school year.

"You knock."

"I know," I say taking a step back. "I did, sort of." I repeat the light tap. "I mean, I tapped."

"What?"

I know she's asking me what I want. Why I'm lurking outside her door like some kind of spy. "Uh. Just... You know." I point to where her phone lays on the floor. "Korean, huh?"

She looks at her phone, then at me. From the look on her face, I know she saw that picture on my phone. She doesn't look impressed that I went out of my way to learn about her interests.

"Fire, right?" I'm trying to extend a peace offering here, the least she could do was smile. "That's cool, you know. How you know more than one language—it's cool."

Tami stays stiff while she reaches out and pulls her phone under her butt, like my not being able to see it will erase its existence for right now.

"I hope it's not weird that I, you know." I flop my hand to where she's sitting on her own phone. "I was trying to connect with you—get to know something about you." Still no response from Tami. "I mean, I probably should have asked—you know, talked to you about it or something..." Seriously, not going to talk to me at all? I'm really trying here. "Anyway... wanted to... Say that." I flop my hand once more toward the phone under her butt. "So okay, cool."

I could say *I don't want Thanksgiving dinner to be weird.* But, let's face it. It's gonna be weird. Tami doesn't roll her eyes or huff. So that's nice. She licks her lips waiting for me. I take a couple steps closer to being out her door, then stop. There has to be some way for me to let her know I'm trying to be her friend and not invade her privacy.

"How's studying going?"

Blank stare.

"Need help?" I shrug my shoulders. "I'm decent at English, I mean, not like written parts of speech and stuff, commas confuse the bijeezus out of me, but other than that... If you need help."

Tami moves, extending her foot to where the door opens. She bends her knee, connecting her toes with the edge of the door, bringing it an inch closer to closed. Shutting me out.

"I'm down the hall." I point a thumb over my shoulder to my door, completely unnecessary. Then I swing my arms together in a clap. "If you need me."

She closes the door more so that my body prevents it from closing.

"I mean, out of everyone in the house, I probably speak the best—and most." I don't think anyone can argue with that point. Also, I'm impressed with how nice I'm being. I feel like a good Samaritan right now. I'm totally offering an olive branch of good will here. I step back so she knows I'm totally giving her the space she needs—respect of privacy and all that.

"The most. For sure," she says.

The door shuts all the way.

Wow. Did I hear her correctly? "Hey that sounded pretty good." I speak loud enough to pass through a solid metal door instead of a hollow fake wood one. This is awkward. Unsure if I should walk away, I opt to keep talking to the door. "Practically a native English speaker." I'm making it worse and I know it, but I can't pull out. "You must have been practicing."

#

Thursday hits like an upset stomach. Or maybe I do have an upset stomach. Mom has made a five-course breakfast for some reason. "What time did you have to get up to start all this?" I slide into a seat at the table and select a cranberry muffin and sausage link.

"I was up. It's no big deal."

"You're still planning on a turkey tonight, right?" Could she have forgotten its Thanksgiving?

"Already in the oven," Mom says.

Tami walks up the stairs scraping her slippers against every step—it's a slow process. Both Mom and I wait for her before speaking again.

"Got some more news," Mom announces.

I crinkle my brow and inhale another lungful of bacon air freshener. This meal has a motive behind it—I can taste it on the grease-laden air. I try to fade into the background so as not to distract the unfolding of Mom and Tami's interaction. I want as much truth as they're willing to reveal to each other, without being hindered by my presence.

"The Boston office called early this morning."

Dad enters the room from the living space. "No respect for time zones," he adds to Mom's news. Tami switches her intense visual focus away from Mom. Her eyes land on Dad long enough for her to tilt her head to the side—either weighing things or she has a kink in her neck. She shifts to the five-star banquet laid out on the table and counter. It's an impressive meal. Too impressive. This news out of Boston can't be good.

"They're sending a new test." Mom clasps her hands and bites her lip like she hopes this sounds like good news. "It'll be administered at school—not the library." Mom looks at all of us nodding at me, then Dad in turn. Like she expects me to be happy about this too. I have no idea what any of this really means. She wants me to play this up, but why? I lift my eyebrows to be supportive, feeling my brow furrow in confusion.

"Covering their asses, is what they're doing," Dad says.

"James!" Mom turns quickly to face him.

"There's no need to sugar coat it," he speaks louder. "They're not twelve."

"Fine." Mom swallows—like she can taste the bitter in the truth. "Your coordinator requested it. They're sending a new test, to make sure everything's done without any influence from that particular coordinator."

"From Japan?" Tami's alert now. She didn't seem too interested in the fact she has to take a new English test, but someone being fired has her attention.

"I think just the Boston coordinator. I can double check, if you want."

Tami nods her head then walks back toward the stairs—rapidly.

"Tami, wait." Mom closes the gap and puts a hand on Tami's shoulder. Her action meets with wide eyes and stiffness from Tami. Mom removes her hand. The gesture served its purpose to stop Tami long enough to get something more in. "None of this is your fault, okay."

Tami leans back and looks at Dad. Dad shrugs his shoulders, as if he's unsure what sort of reassurance he expects Tami to seek from him.

"You were sent here unprepared, and they're trying to cross their t's and dot their i's, so they don't lose funding, you know? We'll work this out." Tami straightens. She doesn't meet Mom's eyes again. She steps down the stairs increasing the speed of her retreat with each step. The sound of her door shutting comes shortly after.

I shove a muffin in my mouth and speak through the bulk, "Good breakfast."

Mom pivots to look at me, like I did something wrong.

Bevan enters the room—glazed over expression on his face and no helmet. Mom watches Bevan. It takes him several seconds to decide which chair to sit in out of a choice of two. The wooden legs screech against the floor as he pulls it back slowly and sits. He doesn't grab a plate or reach for food. He stares at the floor. For some reason, I always forget this part of Bevan when he's not here. The medicated, doped out Bevan.

I like the wild spontaneous version of him—the one that gets in trouble with Max on a three-a-day basis.

Mom licks her bottom lip, looks at Dad, then exits the room.

"Alright, Buddy. Let's load up a plate." Dad slaps a hand on Bevan's back, causing him to jolt. Dad pauses, letting out a pent-up breath. He grabs a plate and puts more food than any one person should be eating in one sitting and places it in front of Bevan. "There you go, Champ."

No one has ever called Bevan 'champ'. He and Max are competitive, sure, but it's not a Bevan nickname. I feel like a hostage to the scene. If I get up, I'll draw too much attention to myself. Whatever med they put Bevan on at the hospital, it's stronger than anything I've ever seen him take. Dad clicks his tongue, and then takes a bacon strip off Bevan's plate. "I'll take care of this one for you." He then returns to the living room with the parade on the TV and the security of Howie and no expectation of conversation.

I sort of want to join Dad in the comfort of one member of the family who isn't acting different than their long-established script. But, I'm a little afraid to leave Bevan alone. For once, school can't come fast enough. This holiday busts.

The rest of the day consists of silent eating. Tami joins us for turkey, two types of potatoes (sweet with marshmallows and mashed with gravy), stuffing, honey-glazed ham, fruit salad complete with out-of-season fruit, and deviled eggs. I have to say; the eggs feel the most fitting with how thankfully we're all glaring at each other during our beloved food gorging holiday.

It'd be healthy to avoid food the rest of the weekend. Instead we cling to meals like a social safety zone. Leftovers put something in our mouths to chew on, instead of discussing whatever underlying currents have us all uncomfortable.

33

Monday means the holiday's over—and our diets can begin. Except for some reason, Mom decides on a massive breakfast kick. Once again, she has a full spread out. I'm never going to lose the seven pounds I put on over the holiday at this rate.

Tami appears at the top of the stairs, carrying the largest delivery from Japan yet—stamps covering the majority of the cardboard. She sets it on an empty chair. Then I remember she has a 'retake' day.

"What's with the box?" I ask. Because seriously, who needs boxes that big? Unless you're shipping a small child. It's ridiculous-size and looks awkward to handle even without anything in it. I'm certain there are smaller transporting devices available other than the particular impossible to handle box she's hefting.

Before Tami has a chance to respond to me, Mom interrupts. "Hey, you." Mom's voice shifts from regular pitch to high octave. "I made some brain food for you—big test today." Well now the buttload of food makes sense, but Mom still isn't acting normal. "Eggs and bacon and fruit, and toast—"

I cut Mom off, "And sausage, and muffins, and yogurt, and grits, which are gross by the way, don't try those. Mom doesn't actually know how to make them, she likes the idea of them."

Mom steps in front of Tami, blocking me with her body as if she's a wall of silence. Its lame, but I shut up anyway. "I have a plate ready."

She hands Tami a heaping pile of food on a small white plate. Mom's hands shake, also abnormal.

"Is Dad home?" I ask. The vibe in this house so off, I can't read Mom's weirdness confidently anymore.

"Already left for work."

"It's six in the morning," I say. "He never leaves that early."

Tami turns her head slightly, taking Mom in from a different perspective, I think. She accepts the plate of food, sets her bag on an empty chair, and sits down to eat—keeping her eyes on Mom the whole time.

"Yes he does," Mom answers me. "It's not unusual for him to leave this early."

"Stop Mom, you're freaking me out. You're acting exactly like TV parent's hiding divorce papers."

Mom scrunches her face and shakes her head as if loosening thoughts from her brain.

"You are, aren't you?" I put down my muffin. "Because of the Bevan thing? With the meds?"

Tami's eyes dart between Mom and me like she's watching an intense tennis match.

"Don't be ridiculous."

"You're acting weird."

Mom picks up a muffin off the table and shoves it in her mouth while she's talking so that her words are muffiny. "It's Monday. Weird is reserved for all Mondays."

Mom's shutting me down, I need a work around, so I shift gears to get Mom's guard down on her own personal affairs—she always spills the beans when coming to the rescue of someone else anyway. "I thought you were testing today—why do you need a huge packing box?" I ask Tami.

"Art club." Apparently, that's all the answer Tami's willing to give, as she puts a delicate bite of pineapple in her mouth and chews like someone on masterpiece theater—very proper, I'm sure.

"Would you like help getting it into Lowry's car?" Mom asks, reaching for the box.

Tami almost chokes on her fruit. "No." Tami puts herself between Mom and the box.

What's the big deal about art club materials? "Top secret art supplies?" I ask, more to mess with Tami than anything, I lean toward the box. She flinches—it's definitely a defensive block. And now I *really* want to know what secrets hide in that box. "Come on, what's in the box?"

Tami grabs her bag, the suspicious cardboard package, and awkwardly opens the side door, balancing the box on her knee to free one hand, heading out to the car, without another word to Mom or me.

"She's going to have to wait a while, I'm not arriving an hour early to school."

Mom cranes her neck, observing Tami out the window.

"You know, Tami's not the only one acting weird," I say.

"I got a call this morning about the exchange coordinator in Boston getting fired."

"Tami's?"

"Uh huh." Mom tries so hard to spy without being too obvious. "It's not like the United States exchange office can put all the blame with the paperwork mix-up on Japan." Forging test scores rebrands itself as a 'paperwork mix-up' these days, I guess. Mom loses her balance, stumbles closer to the window, and waves. Obviously spotted by Tami from below.

"Smooth, Mom." I finish my muffin and stick two sausage links in my mouth like cigars. "I'm sure firing the coordinator has nothing to do with Tami and her top-secret art supplies. My guess—she stole something from the house to use in her club and doesn't want to get caught—might want to check if you're missing any beads or glitter glue. Heaven forbid you're short on fuzzy purple pipe cleaners for next week's craft session."

"I like c-crafts." Bevan sits at the table like he hasn't missed a meal here since he was five. Nothing odd about the fact he's been at an independent living facility for six months where Dad's going to drop him back off later today. He's going back with specific medication requirements and a new rule that both parents have to sign any changes to the medical plan.

"Of course." She waves a hand at me—dismissing our conversation. "Don't pay any attention to your sister. She's on her period."

"Mom!" I mean, I am, but how does she know that?

Mom switches into Bevan mode, which I'm familiar with. It's called 'Bevan needs me more than you right now' and it never ends. "How was your night?"

The medications rob Bevan of personality as well as the ability to process questions quickly. It looks painful for him to try to form an answer.

While Bev squints and contorts his mouth into a word, Mom rushes to the cupboard for a fresh plate. "Don't answer that." Mom waves a hand, erasing her question from the air. "How about some sausage and muffins."

And then it's clear to me. The breakfast wasn't for Tami. It's all Bevan's favorite foods. And he doesn't seem to remember that fact any more than I did when I first sat down. Maybe his meds have robbed me of memory of his personality too.

My appetite hits a guilt pit. "I better go drive Tami to school before she freezes to death out there." New Mexico in November freezes New Mexicans.

"Ask her if she wants me to purchase more art supplies? She shouldn't have to sneak things out of the house."

"Can I ask her art teacher? Tami isn't exactly the chatty type," I say.

"Sort of hoping to avoid that woman—probably forming more fun judgments because Tami's sneaking things for art. Like she's so much better than us." Mom shakes her shoulders and smoothes her hands over her unbrushed hair. "Just find out what supplies they need and text me. I'll drop some by the school myself, later today." She piles seven sausage links on Bevan's plate—way more than anyone should be eating in one sitting, like Dad on Thanksgiving. Maybe stuffing him with his favorite food reclaims him from the fog of overmedication. "—I'm going to bring the whole art section of Save-Rite."

"That'll show her," I say brandishing a power fist on my way out the door. "Don't want to be late being stupid-early."

"That doesn't even make sense," Mom says.

"Yes, it does."

Tami sits in the passenger seat. She's so rigid that she doesn't turn her head while her eyes follow me opening the door and sitting next to her. "Tense day, huh."

"I have a test."

"And art supplies?" I turn to lift a flap of the box. Tami slaps the cardboard closed before I can see what's inside. "Hey." I pull back. "What's with you and the box anyway?"

"I have a test."

"Yeah, you said that. But there's no way you're going to haul a huge package covered in foreign stamps into the testing facility—at least not without checking it out. They'd think you're trying to cheat or something."

"I have a test," she says again.

"I get it, I get it—you don't want to talk to me, geez." Frustrated she won't explain anything to me and keeps repeating the obvious, I change tack. "Why aren't we friends?"

Tami continues to stare forward.

"We didn't get off to a great start, but for a while there, I thought we might be mending things. I mean... If you think about it, me with my portwine stain, and you with your..." Oh crap, what was I going to say there? No politically correct word exists that can possibly fill in that blank. And now the time drags it out like a huge cold sore on my cultural sensitivity barometer. Say something. Anything—not anything. Something aware or diverse or... anything. "Well, you know." That has to be the worst possible thing I could've said.

Tami continues to stare forward. To be honest, with how I handled our communication gap, I can't blame her. I turn the key, and back out of the driveway.

Silence dominates rest of the ride, other than some rattling and metallic clashing sounds from the box. I'm still curious what Tami's hefting around, but she's so preoccupied with her test.

"Good luck today," I say when I cut the engine after pulling into a parking stall.

Tami looks at me sharply, then the box, then at me—like I've somehow violated the box's privacy.

"With your test."

She nods once, twists to collect all her things in one load, and opens her door.

"Yeah. Me too." I talk to myself. "Luck to me too on my day—the one where I don't do everything wrong, and say everything wrong, and wrong, wrong, wrong." I need to text my Mom an apology.

Sara's early today as well. What kind of luck do I have that my used to be best friend pops up everywhere—and we obviously want to avoid each other. Mostly because the lake experience was super odd. Mostly, I was super odd and now I'm embarrassed. Sara looks up from the corner of her eye, tries to act like she didn't see me. I shut my door as loud as I can, like I want to play this game of mute discomfort. I've perfected it at home.

The empty parking lot amplifies the slam of my door. Sara startles as her face contorts into a feigned delight to see me. Believe me, it'd be weirder if I let her ignore me.

"Hey, Lowry."

"Hey."

"You're early today." Sara looks around as if searching for some kind of distraction to get out of this conversation.

"You too." I slide my backpack over one shoulder and shift my weight.

"Crazy week, am I right?"

"Yeah. Crazy."

"How's Tami doing? I bet that was pretty traumatic for her."

"You know..." It was traumatic for everyone, sheesh. "She dried off alright, I guess."

"I mean with Bevan. And the ambulance."

"Oh." I nod. "Yeah."

Sara leans away. "Uhm. Okay."

"Did Ben say anything?" I ask lamely.

"Like what?"

"I don't know."

Sara looks uncomfortable, shifting her weight toward the building. "I mean—no. Not... What would he say?"

Quickly, I scan the parking lot for anything to distract this horror show of a conversation. And still it's empty. "That's cool...So he's not upset about the whole...Saturday was weird thing?"

Sara stares at me too long. "No... He didn't say that exactly."

Which suggests he did say something. "Well?"

"Do you really want to know what he said?"

"Yes." I practically shout.

"He said you're too self-conscious about..." She indicates her face—slashing a mark sideways across hers like my stain. "To even let him get that close to you."

"No. I'm not."

"That's what he said." Sara looks over her shoulder once again. "I told him that wasn't it."

Now I want to know what she told him.

"Hey, I gotta go. I'm helping with ESL tutoring and setting up a cultural awareness festival."

"Okay. Sure. Yeah." Because one affirmation isn't enough, I guess. Why am I so lame? "I have to go too."

We've been in the parking lot long enough that cars are starting to pull in. All the kids in clubs and on teams park and head toward the school—early morning practice and extracurricular hours to pad their college resumes. I don't fit in this group of early students, yet here I am—now standing alone in the parking lot.

So where do I go at this hour?

Debate. That's where I go. Hopefully no one else thinks of the same plan and I can nap for another half hour or so. Of course, Mr. Therault preps in the classroom because it's his actual classroom. Dang. Why didn't I think of that?

"Lowry?" Mr. Therault calls out when I try to duck back out of the class. "Everything going well in preparing for our meet?"

First of all, why call debate face-off a meet? Like it's held at a track or a lap pool? It should be a bee like spelling or geography. Or a math bowl. For crying out loud, why isn't it a debate bowl? "Uh. No?"

"It's not, huh?"

"I meant yes. As in, no there's nothing wrong."

"I didn't ask if there was anything wrong." He stands up from his desk and steps around a few chairs so he can assess me better. "I asked if everything was going well in preparing." He leans on a student desk-chair combo which slides under his weight. Then stands without leaning. "Is there? I mean. Anything wrong?"

"No." He's still standing here staring me down like some kind of emotion barometer.

"Okay." He nods slowly. "So you're all set for debating terrorism's purpose?"

"But that's stupid," I say.

Mr. Therault crosses his arms and squares his shoes. "Learning to argue uncomfortable perspectives in an intelligent manner, based on persuasive opinion, is a valid skill—and I'd add that it helps you better understand motivations of people you might not agree with."

I scoff and turn to leave the room. I can't remember why I signed up for this stupid club in the first place.

"Everyone should learn how to think like those they believe oppose their rights and beliefs."

Bull. I want to say, but I don't because he's a teacher and I'm a student. I step toward the door. "Learning how to think that way doesn't solve the world's problems."

Mr. Therault drops his folded arms. "But, Lowry, we're not here to solve the world's problems, we're here to argue them."

"So...Basically, debate is pointless?"

"There's purpose in discussion."

"To do what? Point fingers?"

"To bring people to action."

"But we don't do that. The action parts. We don't take any action, ever. We spit words at each other until the other team can't counter it—and we get a trophy."

"It doesn't have to be that way."

"But, it is." I walk away hoping he won't continue to debate me—on a side note, he's good at his after-school specialty—arguing.

35

I pass the art classroom Tami spends most of her non-academic time in and decide to try and check out the box Tami said she was bringing in. The classroom reminds me of grade school. Pictures are tacked around the room, decorating walls and cork boards with copies and repeats of the same images over and over. Art often feels like a master copycat class to me—maybe that's why I don't get it.

Sara, Violet, Yi, Aiko—everyone helping with the cultural awareness celebration or whatever, gathers in the classroom this morning. It's like a multicolor-crazy decoupaged space. Apparently, planning a foreign culture festival requires everyone I know to meet in the one place I don't expect them to be.

Even Nathaniel joins in the planning meeting—without me. I'm the friend who has an exchange student living in my house and I wasn't invited to this meeting. I mean, I was there when Sara first brought it up... And sure, maybe a bunch of the people eating lunch with us that day volunteered to help... And maybe I wasn't one of them, but still. I didn't even know they were doing this.

The only thing I don't see, include Tami or her box.

"That's weird," I say. Everyone's looking at me, I have to say something. "I was looking for Tami." I say. And truly, I could have sworn Tami came this way—and where else is she going to take her art supply box. But, maybe she didn't know about this either, and felt weird being here and not being a part of the meeting. Kind of the way I feel right now. "Don't mind me." I put my hands in the air—two palms face the group like I'm giving them double high fives in the air, which I'm not. It's really more of a surrender—I'm certain I'm guilty of something.

I back out of the room and flatten myself against a wall. Breathing fast and heavy. I wish I hadn't come so early this morning. Mornings at school are like Bizzarro High School.

Ms. Conklin passes me on her way to the room where everyone I know meets. She has a paper cup full to the brim with dark brown liquid. I need that liquid courage right now, but have nothing.

"Have you seen Tami this morning?" I didn't announce myself before I started speaking and cause the teacher—not my favorite teacher in the world—to startle, spilling her hot coffee all down the front of shirt.

"What are you doing?" she asks.

"I'm trying to help Tami haul her art supplies to class, but she ditched me."

The teacher grabs an oil cloth, kept in her back pocket, to dab the front of her clothes, looking at me sidelong. "Likely story."

"Why else would I be here? I don't even like art." That's a lie. I do like art. I don't like the teacher.

"I haven't seen Tami this morning. Her class isn't until after lunch."

"I thought she hung out here in her spare time." Like all my other friends do. No way am I revealing myself as the outcast of the meeting happening in her room right this minute.

"She's stayed after class a few times to finish a project, but that's about it. She doesn't get along well with the other exchange students—doesn't like social events much."

She could say that again. "You mean, she doesn't spend all her time here?" For someone who hasn't spent a ton of time with Tami, she sure acts like the prime resource on all things 'best for Tami'.

"Is there something more you needed?" Obviously, the cue I've overstayed my welcome—in the *hall*.

"Just. If you see her, can you let her know I was looking for her—to help her with the box."

The art teacher opens her eyes wide in some kind of 'yes, now leave' gesture that comes across more 'I'm crazy, if you don't want to learn more about that, get out while you still can'.

Unsure what to do with the rest of this early hour, I go to the library and curl up in a big comfy chair with my eyes closed. I can't sleep, but I hope anyone who recognizes me will assume I'm asleep and leave me alone until first bell rings. I'm not the only person with this plan. Chairs and benches fill fast as more students arrive early to school, or finish with early morning training, or council meetings—or whatever brings kids to school before actual school.

First class isn't a big thing. No one's alert. And the teacher doesn't seem to care. It's a Monday for everyone. Most students catch up on homework due in other classes when the intercom announces absent kids. I barely listen as they read the list.

"...Tami Watanabe..." read between names I don't pay attention to. Her first name doesn't stand out, but her last name, unmistakable. *That's my Tami.*

"Tami? But, she came with me. She's here." There must be some mistake.

She has a test today. That's probably it. She's missing first hour, because she's somewhere else taking a test—and she didn't know to let her first hour teacher know she'd be absent—for the test. Between classes, I'll let the office know that Tami is program-obligated to take some test her program sent. I'm surprised they don't know already.

"Hey, pssst, Lowry," a guy in my first hour class—who never talks to me, might I add—leans over in his seat. "I heard someone almost drowned at the lake... and you were there?"

Rumors already. This might be the worst Monday in the history of Mondays. "I don't know. There was a lot going on that day."

"I also heard Ben dumped you for Sara, or something?"

"What? Ben isn't with Sara."

"So he didn't dump you?" the guy asks. I doubt he's interested in me, so much as he's interested in the gossip.

"We weren't dating!" I say.

"Harsh."

What has Ben told everyone? There's no way we were dating, unless going on one date equals a promise ring to the guy. Sheesh.

I don't know if the guy says I'm the harsh one, or Ben is. I hope Ben comes off looking like the jerk here, but can't clarify before our first hour teacher intervenes. "Please stop talking and work on assignments."

We both duck our heads—like she doesn't know it was us talking so long as she can't see our faces. Too bad the desks in this room are too close together to not notice the glances from around the room. Everyone looks at me—and for once, I wish it was because of the purple slash stained across my face. Not because I'm a reject date. Or worse, with rumors flying this fast—maybe they all think I pushed Tami overboard or something crazy.

Once class ends, I rush to the door first. No more answering to 'pssst' today.

Testing during regular class hours usually takes place in the class that the test is for. Since Tami's exchange program requested an English proficiency test, I have no idea where to look for her.

"Three minutes till you're counted tardy," a teacher announces to the herd of students still navigating the halls. I nod and turn a corner.

Classroom plaques reveal subject and teacher occupying each room. I know Tami's been moved to an ESL class instead of the government, American History, and English Lit III courses that were originally required by her program. It was recently a big deal at our house.

"She's basically on an IEP, but as an exchange student," Mom had said.

"But, it's not about the grades. It's the opportunity to get to know another culture," Dad countered.

"But, living up to her obligations is part of obtaining that opportunity. Somewhere something went sideways here, and someone needs to be accountable."

"America prides itself on second chances, not lowering standards."

"When she's not prepared? There's no way she can do well in classes she can't understand." Mom says.

"Don't ask me. You're the one who agreed to have our special needs son taken off his life saving meds!"

"They're personality sucking meds—it was the right thing to do." Mom puts her foot down. "So is changing the contract for Tami." Stomping her foot so hard that Tami and myself, who were listening at the bottom of the stairs, jumped.

"This doesn't concern you," Dad shouts down to us. I'm pretty sure the slamming door after that signals Dad leaving.

Mrs. Fillmore ESL. Found it. I open the door to a red, black, and white color scale with some yellow thrown in to highlight things here and there. The sharp room, crisp with bold wording and uncluttered pin-ups of grammar rules. It's also filled with students. Mostly Hispanic kids and a few kids who were adopted from overseas while in middle school. No Tami as far as I can tell from scanning heads. The person I wasn't expecting to see—Max.

I try ducking out before I'm noticed.

"Lowry?" Max asks. "What're you doing in ESL?"

I could ask him the same question. He doesn't have any trouble with English, as far as I know. "Have you seen Tami?"

"No—I haven't. Not today." He squints like he's reading my thoughts.

More kids join the stare. It's stare at Lowry time—and the bell rings announcing I'm tardy for my next class.

"She's taking an English test today. I thought..."

Max crouches next to a group of students over a text—like they're having a huddle over a sports play. "You might want to check with the counseling center. They sometimes proctor tests, if it's not for a specific class."

I'm being dismissed. I get it. "Right. Thanks."

The counseling center resides on the other end of the school all together. To get there I'm going to have to pass a million classes, all of whom have teachers eagerly waiting the chance to make an example out of tardy kids to the rest of their students. Detention bookmarks my future if I choose to continue my Tami search now—or rush to class and say I had an emergency bathroom stop in hopes of avoiding a pink slip.

I risk it.

Ducking past doorways and across pods, in order to be less readily identified. My portwine stain makes it difficult to get away with much —easy to pick out of a criminal line-up, a decent deterrent for misbehavior. I make it to the counseling offices without incident.

"Tami?" I ask the first person I see in the offices.

"Tami?" The same secretary who I've spoken to every time this year asks me—like she still hasn't figured out who I am. She must be filling in at the counseling center today. "Last name?"

"Wanatabe."

"I'll check with the sign in sheet." She looks down a paper on the wall, dragging her finger along the lines and pen and pencil marks. "Did she have an appointment today?" Her finger comes away without finding Tami's name.

"Just a test." I shrug. "Part of her exchange program, I think?" Confusion sets in. What's going on? Where's Tami? The secretary nods and looks over her papers. "I have the test papers, but she hasn't signed in to for it to be administered."

Right then the intercom scratches to life announcing the students who didn't show up for the current period. Tami again announced among the absent, but not before *Lowry Dodds.* "If present, please come to the office." The intercom then rephrases the same statement. "All students on the absent rolls, please come to the office."

"Well, there you go," says the woman in the counselors offices. "She'll be headed to the office. If you need to get hold of your friend, that's probably your best option."

I don't point out my name was called too. "Thanks."

The main office isn't far from the counseling area. I don't know why they have those separated at all. Why have two sections of high school where no student ever wants to be? Oh wait. I might have described all sections of a high school.

Three students wait on a wooden bench against a far wall in the small waiting area in front of the secretary desk. I join them. We're each called, one by one, to clear our names from the absent roll—all praying we have a good enough excuse to not get a tardy on our record. Parents are called automatically when students are marked tardy. Even one time. There exists no grace period.

While I wait for my name to be called up to the desk, I bend forward to see if Tami walks by. Hoping she'll step through the door to clear her name any second—then I can go back to my cruddy day and obsess about what happened with Max. *Is he thinking about me? Does he think I'm a lunatic? Worse, does he think I made that Tami search up, to have the chance to run into him—and the rumor that Ben broke up with me.* Though that's not a rumor. It's true. *What if he thinks I was looking for him because, now that I'm rejected, I'm available...? How desperate I must appear?!*

Max would never be my second choice. I'm not good enough to ever be his first choice—or any choice. *Ever.* I bury my head against my knees.

"Lowry Dodds?"

"Present." My head snaps up.

"Not in class I take it," this secretary's known for joking with the students. Also, she knows my name.

"Do you know if Tami's been in today?" I ask.

"Mmmm." She gives me the look of 'pressing confidentiality issues, are we?'

"I drove her to school today." This reveal of information buys me nothing more than a half frown. "We sort of got in an argument, and I was supposed to help her unload a box of art supplies... and I didn't."

"What would you like me to do about this absence mark?" The secretary changes the subject on me.

"I need to apologize to Tami, if she's here. She was also supposed to have an English proficiency test today. I thought maybe she'd be in the counseling center, but she wasn't."

"ESL is where I'd look for that sort of thing, but back to you..."

"I already tried Mrs. Fillmore's room." I say.

"Sounds like she's absent."

"But." I stammer. "She should be here."

"I'm going to mark this as a tardy. It's clear to me, you weren't intending to get to class on time, or report to class before asking permission to look for your friend."

I don't argue. "Actually, I need to be marked absent."

"Excuse me? You can't check yourself out without a parent or guardian permission slip."

Dang it. "Fine. Tardy." I walk the three steps toward the exit. "When you call my mom can you mention that Tami isn't in school, and possibly missed her test for her program?.. And that it's possibly my fault because I was sort of 'on one' this morning?" I don't turn around to check if I get a nod. The secretary's chair squeaks under her weight as she rolls to her office phone. I glance at the clock. It's almost ten.

"Lowry." I spin in the direction of hearing my name. "Want to come with me for a donut run?" Max has keys. Right now, I'd do almost anything to get out of this building. And no matter how awkward things are between Max and me, there is no one else I'd rather escape with.

"Can I?"

"I'm a teacher aid for ESL this hour, I have this note that says I need to get donuts..." He produces a permission slip to leave school grounds. He waves me toward the large glass doors to join him.

What can I do about the beating in my chest—is my face flushed? Will Max notice the sweat on my palms? If I speak will my voice be full of question about his date over the weekend, or insecurity about what he might have heard Ben say?

I nod and follow Max toward the parking lot, through the glass doors separating high school from freedom and clamp my mouth so tight I'm pretty sure my lips will never recover.

Max says nothing when we transition to the mid-morning sun in our eyes. Life outside high school pushes on with cars passing on the main road and birds perched in trees near parked cars pooping on windshield and door handles. When I'm in the school it feels like everything outside freezes until I return to it. It's comforting to feel the rush of time, but also—why hasn't Max spoken to me yet?

His car isn't locked. I sit in the front seat aware of my knees too close to the gear shift. Pulling myself into a rigid line, I wait for Max to settle in. His comfort level hurts a little. He seems to not care how close I am, or am not. He wriggles to get the best fit between his butt and the seat, while pressing the brake and starting the ignition in one smooth—unencumbered by my proximity—motion.

"Where do you want to go for donuts?" he asks—like there are so many options in our town.

"By the dozen?" Because that's obviously an answer. *I'm such an idiot.* Max bunches his bottom lip in a puzzled fashion. "I mean, the store?"

He reverses, looking over his shoulder without stopping even one second to catch my eyes when his gaze flies over mine—and back again. I can't tell if it's him or me that blipped those split seconds away, but they're gone and I miss them.

"Isn't that your mom?" Max pulls onto the main road, passing a sedan that looks surprisingly like Mom's car. If the secretary called her, she arrived faster than expected. "And I'm pretty sure Bevan and Howie are with her."

I duck, so late after the car passes that it's a pointless gesture. Hopefully she didn't see me. Even if Bevan or Howie did, what are the chances they can successfully communicate that to Mom.

"Everything okay at home?"

"No. Yeah. Just..." *Is this not a normal reaction?* It seems like what any teen would do when leaving the school in the middle of the day and their parents are pulling in, right? "They called my name over the intercom, so you know."

"I don't know." Max keeps taking his eyes off the road to give me the 'you're acting like a weirdo' look.

Instead of a normal human explanation, I launch into a high-speed word vomit of things I'm not even sure relate to why I'm crouched against my knees. "I didn't help Tami with her box this morning, and she wasn't in art, and I might have been being a jerk so she ditched this really important test that's required by her program... What I mean is that the art teacher was all 'you suck at being hosts' and her box, by that I mean Tami's, wasn't even there—or anywhere, and then I lost her..."

"Whoa, whoa, whoa." Max pulls over to the side of the road. "Do you need to call your mom? Are you okay to be checked out?"

I pat my leg and realize I have no phone in my pocket. It's either at my house or in my car. "No."

"Are you sure? You don't seem like yourself."

"Yeah. I'm sure she's there to give Tami a healthy snack or something motherly." Max doesn't get back on the road yet. "I need a break from it all. I need this—to break some rules and not be at school right now. Think of me like you used to hang with Bevan." The ditching class part and all that.

Seconds pass with Max looking at me—he's not avoiding my gaze. He lets out a huff of air and I can't tell if he's taking me back to school or not when he pulls back into traffic. "Just so you know, I don't think of you the way I think of Bevan."

I turn as we pass the last option to turn left into the high school.

I let my head fall against the head rest—freedom. But, not freedom from Max.

Sirens blaze past our car.

"Something's going on at school," Max says.

"At our school?" I am the failure of all wording today—and this sentence cumulates all I can brain-up. Police vehicles, a fire truck, and an ambulance with lights swirling also race in the opposite direction of our car.

"Maybe we should go check out what's going on."

"Yeah. We should definitely check it out."

Mom enters the building. She's going to ask where I was (since I'm obviously not at school), what I was doing, why I didn't help Tami more this morning.

"Is that a SWAT team?" Max asks.

Maybe something really is going on at the school. And my mom and brothers are in there. I sit forward trying to get a better look at what's happening. "Can you pull up to the drop off zone?"

"I don't think so—they're motioning me away."

"Let me out here," I demand—like I have some authority, which I'm pretty nobody believes. Max stops the car anyway. I get out and run toward the glass doors.

"Stop!"

I turn to see police waving me away. "My mom's in there—and my brothers."

"Step away from the doors."

I don't go closer or farther. I stop. Inside the glass I see Tami. She has a vest on, which she didn't have on earlier, with wires and cords, and something in her hand, which she's holding in a punching grasp with her thumb pressing against the top of whatever it is. My brain isn't working. *What's happening?* "What's going on?"

"There's been an attack," one officer says. "Stay back."

I survey the building with a quick back and forth for smoke, or broken windows—or even a group of kids fighting—I mean, what does this guy mean by 'attack'? Nothing looks out of place. "What kind of attack?"

"Nationwide." Max at my side, pulls me back. His phone broadcasts some breaking news on social media. Bombings coordinated throughout the nation. Massive Terror attack.

This makes no sense. *Is this some kind of joke orchestrated by our demented debate coach? I can confidently say he's gone too far on this one.*

"...A terrorist cell. Made up of exchange students across the nation. Twenty minutes ago, the first school was bombed in New York, thirty seconds later five other schools across the country were bombed. Three more within a minute after that..." the newsfeed goes on, but none of the strings of words are adding up to meaning in my brain. *A large scale, coordinated... Exchange students?*

I look up at the building. "My mom's in there." I know I already said it. I can't think of anything to say.

"...We know from reported damage that the bombs have been placed throughout the year, positioned for maximum damage in areas of high foot traffic..." The breaking news keeps coming.

"Give me your phone." I take Max's phone without waiting for him to respond. I put Mom's number in the text field and write, 'r u ok?' Then I remember how Mom hates short text and erase it. I'm wasting time. 'Are you okay?' She doesn't respond right away. Then I remember she doesn't know Max's phone number, or that I'm using it. 'Me—Lowry. Left my phone somewhere.'

'I've been calling you all morning. They said you're absent. I'm in the office. Tami is...' the screen has wavy dot, dot, dot indicating Mom types, it goes away, she must be erasing, it's back, typing... 'Where are you?'

'Parking lot.' I cringe. Will she care I was ditching given the circumstances?

'Thank heavens you're alright.'

'What's going on?'

'Tami's about to blow up the school.'

This can't be real. Tami isn't with the news alert thing on Max's phone—that incident—that coordinated attack—already happened. It's in the aftermath now.

I show Max the message from my mom. In unison, we look up to stare at the image behind the glass. Tami with her vest and all its wires. It looks like she's going to blow herself up too. "I don't understand," I say to Max.

"My family's in there," he answers, which isn't an answer. We're both at a loss of what to do. "Turn it back to the newsfeed."

I hand him his phone. "...A coordinated attack across the Nation. Obviously planned to go off at the same moment regardless of time zones—and all within school hours for all locations."

But, our school isn't on the news. "Maybe it's not the same thing."

"...Survivors report a fellow student wearing a wired vest and detonator. When released, multiple explosions throughout the building were triggered." Max steps back from the building, but I move closer. "Tami!" I shout, like she can hear me. "Don't do this!"

Through the double layered glass doors, Tami looks at me. She's talking to someone inside before that moment. I follow the direction of where she was looking prior and see Howie. Little Howie happy to see her, and trying to escape Mom's grip from the main office doorway, where she's desperately trying to pull him back inside, in order to go to Tami. Panic shows in Tami's eyes. She didn't expect Howie to be here. I wish he weren't here. "Howie!" I scream in an entirely different register. "Tami, you can't. You Can't!"

"Please step back, we're handling this." An officer puts his hands on my shoulders to direct me toward Max, who has kept his distance. I'm shaking. This can't be happening. "Move behind the police line." We're both directed—pushed more like—toward emergency vehicles with their doors open and officers communicating on radios behind those doors.

Over officer radios I hear contact has been made with teachers inside the building. "...assume all exits are wired. Keep to window escapes and stay as far from the main office as possible..."

They're getting students out—that's fantastic. Except Mom and Howie and Bevan—they're in the office. I turn to the officer nearest me. "What about people in the office?"

He lifts a hand, showing me I need to be quiet and wait. Tension shows in his intentional and unwasted movements in every action. He has no time for my concerns, his focus engulfs every possible person in the building.

"Max," I plead. I don't know what to do, but Howie moves too close to Tami—and her death suit. Why is she wearing it? *This can't be happening.* And Max stays here. Right here. On his phone. A chime signals a response from whomever he texted.

"Sara's in the cafeteria. They're sending the students on that side of the building out the windows."

I nod. But, what about Mom, and Bevan, and Howie? Bevan switches to holding Howie. They trusted Tami. Why did we trust her? Then I wonder what reason we had to not trust her. There were things. Weird things that might have added up to something. But then again—*This?* Who thinks *this* is going to happen? Who ever thinks *this*?

This is crazy!

"Why is this happening?" I ask no one in particular.

"I don't know," the officer nearest me answers again—suddenly he has time to talk. "I hope I never understand why someone would do something like this. And children—attacking other children."

"Sara's out," Max says.

"Remind them to stay out of view from the main doors, if you can. We don't want to set this person off," the officer says to Max. Max nods and texts frantically back to Sara.

"Her name is Tami," I say. "This person is Tami."

"Well, Tami's the only one whose hesitated this long. Of all the known attacks today—only one hasn't gone off." The officer returns to his radio. Groups are visible in the distance, gathering in size running away from the high school. "Everyone's hoping there's a way to prevent this one."

Max shows me his phone. It's a text from 'You're All In Trouble,' Mom's nickname in Max's contacts. 'She doesn't want to do this. I can tell.'

I tap the officer on the shoulder. "It's from my mom. She's inside the office. We hosted Tami."

He squints at me, like he's determining how reliable I am. He lifts off his haunches a moment, to search the crowd. "We need a negotiator over here," he announces.

"We're trying to connect through the school—no luck," someone else responds.

The Officer at my side pulls out his cell phone and indicates he wants me to punch in my mom's number. I mis-enter the seven-digit sequence I've had memorized since I was five.

"It's an out-of-state phone, add the area code please."

I tap my number on his touch screen one more time, remembering to include the area code. He hands the phone to a new addition to the team, I assume it's the Negotiator.

"Here. Someone inside knows the girl. Get her on the phone—talk her through what to do, what to say." In response, several officers engage in hand signals, then hushed conversations across small groups and radio feedback. It all happens quickly, but also feels like a flutter of purposeful chaos. No one shows confidence in their eyes even though they have squared shoulders and tight jaws. The next thing I hear, Mom's on the line.

36

Mom sounds unnaturally calm given the circumstances. Only the smallest quiver detectible in her voice. "You want to talk to Tami?" she asks from inside the school.

"Just stay on the line ma'am." He puts a hand over the speaker on Max's cell. "What do I tell her to do?"

"You're not a negotiator?" I ask the uniformed man.

"I've had a little training, but I don't normally work with foreign teenagers or their host moms."

Of course, how many hostage negotiations has Bronzetown had in the last...forever? None that I can recall. Max puts his hands up like he doesn't know either.

"My family is in there—my three-year-old brother."

"Was he in there when this started? Could your family be the reason the terrorist hesitated in this case?"

Terrorist? It's Tami. And if anything, I'd think seeing us would encourage her to set off the bomb—or maybe me. "I don't know, I was ditching."

The officer looks at Max, like he's the bad influence in my life.

"He has a permission slip," I say in Max's defense.

The officer returns his focus to the call with my mom. "Does she seem to be conflicted about her actions? Maybe she has a connection with your family and that's what we need to draw on."

"Are you sure you want to be communicating through my mom?" I ask. Max shushes me.

The officer covers the mouth piece again. "She put me on speaker." He sounds irritated by this.

"Can you hear, Tami?" I ask. It looks like she's ranting up a storm from my vantage point. It's difficult to tell for sure, but I'd guess she was yelling obscenities from the expression on her face.

"I can't make out what she's saying." He turns to me again. "What nationality is she?"

"Japanese."

"You're sure?" He asks. I nod, not knowing what else I'm supposed to say. "Do we have a translator?" We all wait for someone to carry the message they need a Japanese translator. Then the officer has to make his way, as inconspicuously as possible, to the phone. So much time wastes in the waiting, but no one wants to make an uninformed move. Spooking Tami tops the last thing anyone wants right now. "I hit record." The officer on the phone speaks with the translator. "You want me to play it back?"

"Is she still talking?"

"Yes," the officer holds up the phone so the translator can listen in—being careful to not put his end on speaker.

"Is there a way to continue recording and allow me to listen back?"

More waving and hand signals. I'm worried they'll all disappear inside an armored truck and I won't be able to eavesdrop. Except this is a small town with few resources. I'm certain every police officer, fireman, EMT, and news reporter is already here. And no one has a fancy van decked out with expensive audio equipment.

"No." The translator takes the phone from the negotiator.

"Have you ever even negotiated anything before?" I ask. I'm depending on him to talk my family safely out of there.

"Of course."

"What?"

"Domestic disputes."

My mouth won't close. What if I don't get my mom and brothers back? All the other—connected—attacks are over. Horrible damage done. It's all over social media. I know because Max wouldn't stop scrolling. I don't have to look at his screen, his hand over his mouth in shock conveys enough. It's bad. Worse than bad. Our nation has endured the most seamlessly coordinated attack on the up and coming youth of the nation—the soon to be voters. The children of leaders, future leaders. We're meant to bend and weaken.

"Keep the terrorist distracted, we have almost everyone out," another officer sends a message down the line.

"Her name is Tami," I say.

"Why are they still here?" A finger points at me and Max.

"They know her. The host family is in there," the negotiating officer says. "Can we be certain the host family has no part of this?"

My feet forget to grip the earth for a second. They question Mom's involvements? Mine? Howie and Bevan, for crying out loud? Are they insane? I have to grab Max's shoulder before I tip too far sideways.

"Okay, it's not Japanese—she's speaking," the translator says. "Well, it is every few phrases, but she has a heavy accent—not fluent in Japanese."

"Can you understand what she's saying?" the negotiator asks.

"Something about the timeline or something moved."

"She failed her English exam," I say. By the looks I get, I'm not being helpful.

One of the officers gives me the 'shut up or I'm removing you from the scene' look. So I shut up.

"She's screaming for everyone to get back." Through the window, Tami motions her hand—detonator and all—toward my family. "Or maybe it's 'go home'."

"What?" I ask. Someone pulls me back so I have to listen more carefully, and maybe guard my tongue. I clamp my hands over my mouth and get to stay near the conversation.

The translator stops. He looks at me and Max and his expression panicked. "They can't be here. Get them out." He hands the phone off to the negotiator. "Someone get these kids out of here. Everyone out!"

"What'd she say?" I ask. Tears escape my eyes. I have no idea why they weren't falling before now. "Mom!" I shout toward the building, as if my words could bore a hole for my family to escape out unnoticed by Tami. "Howie, Bevan!"

"Get these kids out of here!" The translator pushes us back where more hands grip our shoulders and drag us behind more lines.

"What'd she say?" I shout this time.

Rifles raise along the front row of men crouched behind the line of cars.

"What's going on?" Breathing labors. "She's holding a detonator. They can't shoot her."

Max no longer looks at his phone. His eyes are glued to the glass doors. "She's not even trying to take cover," he says. "It's like she wants them to stop her."

"This can't be happening." I push my hair away from my forehead.

"Are you inside? How fast can you reach the device if we make the shot?" the question travels over the radio. We can hear the static doubt over the coms. One officer goes as far as placing his palm over his shoulder to garble the messages, but we hear. "Move in now, be ready."

"Text my mom," I tell Max. "Tell her—they can't be right out there."

One officer grabs Max's phone before he can send any messages. "You can't alert the target to any action."

"She wants to be hit—look at her. She's in the open." I shove my entire hand toward the doors—like I'm slicing reality with my fingers. My arm slaps down to my side.

"Do not alert the target to any action." This horrible plan happens. It's happening now. In front of Bevan and Mom and little Howie.

"Max." I know he can't do anything, but I want him to do something. "My family." He blinks. His mouth opens like he wants to send words out to comfort me, but then he closes his mouth again.

"Wait for my signal." The commands go on, without my permission. A fisted hand stands at attention, ready to belay a command. Every part of this moment feels separate from the rest. My feet no longer belong to my body. I can feel myself running toward the doors, screaming for Tami to stop this right now. But I'm not moving, it's the feeling of it all in my feet. My lungs burn as if they're being pressed under too much water and if I attempt to breathe I'll asphyxiate.

Someone creeps so close behind Tami, I'm sure Howie's waving at him, if Tami turns to look it's all over.

"Hold." The fist still tight in the air. "Hold."

Tami continues to rant in her language. I wonder if she learned English in her second language, not her first. Maybe that's why she's so terrible at it. Then again, maybe she faked the whole terrible-at-English thing so she'd get sent home and not have to do this awful thing. No one wants to do this awful thing, right?

I wish Tami had been sent home when she first did something weird, but we live in a world where we can't judge the things that make us uncomfortable. If we do, we're bad, or rude, or inconsiderate—or heaven forbid 'offensive'.

Admittedly, I don't know everything about being culturally sensitive, but I do know about gut feelings and my gut's been screaming at me since Tami arrived.

"Hold." The fist flinches, and with it several officers.

And I don't want her to leave this way. Not this way. Not like this. "No!" I shout prematurely. A shot goes off in response to my voice.

"I didn't say fire!" The officer with the fist screams over the crowd, but it's too late. Several more guns fire. Men in SWAT outfits inside the building rush at Tami—no, at her hand holding the detonator. They have to prevent her clenched fist from releasing the already triggered detonator.

I barely register that Tami's been shot. Her head bows forward. I don't see blood splatter like in movies. It's more like, there wasn't red on the glass and now there is. Two men behind her move in so quickly, I wonder if they were holding her before the bullet made contact. One slides his hands under her shoulders to hold her up while the other man has his hands over her fist holding the detonator. He puts pressure around the entire contraption while a third man runs silver tape over and they wrap it around and around and around her hand—making sure no pressure ever releases from the object she still holds. Her body crumples to the tile in front of Howie's innocent baby face.

All I can think, 'how will they get her to the hospital if her hand is still connected to the detonator?' *They're obligated to try to save her, aren't they?* The emergency vehicles around us aren't starting their engines.

"Everyone down!" My head gets shoved to my knees.

"It didn't go off," I say. "It didn't go off." *Someone help Tami.*

"It's not over yet." Someone presses my head lower, like low elevation saves lives. "Keep cover."

But, I can't. I have to know if my family gets out. As soon as there isn't a hand on my head, I rise to check the doors. Mom and Bevan and Howie are rushed through to the outside by large men with dark vests and yellow letters across their backs.

"They're out," I say to Max. He lifts his head, but we're both shoved down again. "Mom!" I scream from my low vantage point. She's not close enough to hear me. I keep screaming it, over and over. "Mom. Mom. Mom!" until someone pulls me farther away. Back from the lines of officers and the cars in their circle cover.

"I want all civilians as far away as possible while the bomb squad works." The negotiator shoves us away—toward my family. Max has his phone out again, frantically texting—probably everyone he can think of.

"Out of the parking lot too—it hasn't been cleared yet." A sergeant yells orders at another officer. "Someone get the dogs in here to clear this area."

Heads lean to shoulder radios—police chatter blurs different directions and orders. It's chaos while they clear safe zones.

"We have no idea how many explosives have been planted throughout the school. Someone make sure there's no distance default on that detonator before we move the body." I can hear in his words that the threat isn't over, but it's no longer immediate—it's no longer Tami. The urgency in her favor falters. It's what she's done, but she's no longer a part of it. They can't ask her where the bombs are. They aren't trying to work out a deal, or see if there are more attacks to come. Tami isn't in the equation anymore. And I can't process this fact.

I look at Howie and know we're all going to be in therapy for years to come. Probably the whole school. They're going to have to hire seven more therapists to cover everyone who needs to work through this.

The other thing I know—Bevan won't be going back to the assisted living home. We need something to worry over close at hand, something safe and familiar. We need Bevan. We always have. Probably more than he needs us. I'm not saying it's healthy or healing that we rely on each other in this way, but we do, and right now and for a long time after, we're going to need each other to worry over as a whole.

We wait for the bomb crew to move in with bomb dogs, who can apparently sniff out explosives. We're evaluated for shock while being pushed farther away from the building. Bevan moves to an ambulance to be monitored for seizure activity.

"I need to check on the rest of my family," Max says.

I understand. It's selfish of me to want him here and my family here. But, I still don't want him to go. "I don't have my phone." For some reason, I think he's going to make sense of my thoughts based on this statement. "How will I call you?" What am I saying? I feel raw and exposed. I'm pretty sure the stain across my face has gone fuchsia because I sound needy and lame right now. "I mean, yeah—tell Sara I'm glad she's okay."

Max holds up his phone with my Mom's text message thread still on his screen. "I can always contact your mom," he smiles, as if he wants to smile, but it feels inappropriate under the circumstances—and at the same time a huge sense of relief intoxicates me regarding Max being in front of my face. "Besides, I'm pretty sure I still owe you a donut."

"We're riding with Bevan to the hospital," Mom says. "Can you drive the car as soon as it's cleared."

I have to wait for officers to scour our vehicles. Tami rode in our cars —transported explosives to school while seated next to me—possibly next to Howie. I nod in response to Mom. "Yeah." I'll wait for the all clear. I turn to Max, also waiting. "A really good donut—like the best the store has to offer."

Emergency crews work their way through small groups, checking kids for shock or other medical concerns.

37

The week following the terror attack on high schools nationwide brought with it a lot of false information and drama. Not to mention new limitations on visas and international travel, which stinks because I've never been anywhere and might want to see something beyond the Grand Canyon one day.

It also brought more information about what happened with Tami. Tami wasn't her real name. She wasn't Japanese, though she did live in that country for a while before becoming an exchange student. Japanese wasn't her first language, and she had to learn English from Japanese instructors—double hard.

A North Korean orphan refugee in China, Tami was taught that she was hated for no reason at all other than her nationality. She wasn't treated very well it turns out. She was then adopted into a group of radical-terrorists based out of Japan, though not actually all Japanese in origin. She did have an older brother in her adopted home. He didn't accept the doctrine of hate and was banished from the family. Tami was told only that he had brought shame. The news reports about him revealed several defectors from the group that adopted Tami. They were identified now, post mortem. The news didn't say how they died.

It probably didn't help that she and I didn't hit it off right away. She had an idea of how Americans are supposed to be and it didn't include stained faces and seizure disorders running in families. I had an idea of what an exchange student would be like, and it didn't include Tami.

Maybe we would have been able to avoid the entire end of this year if we had accepted each other a little easier. Heck, along those lines, if Tami's entire childhood had a little more acceptance and a lot less sadness, maybe she would still be alive.

Tami received bits and pieces of materials in the boxes she got from her home country. Sometimes the parts she needed were inside licorice tubes, or feminine-pad packages. There were wires inside bras and plastics in school supplies. Never too much at once and never anything that an x-ray could easily identify. Always marked with the Korean symbol I noticed. The entire operation ran very smoothly, and depended on having the entire year to get everything into place. What they didn't count on was the students developing relationships with their host families.

I'm certain Tami tried to avoid getting attached to us. Howie was her kryptonite. *He is impossible not to love*—speech impaired and all. I did everything I could to keep him away from Tami, the one thing that stopped her from blowing my school and everyone in it to smithereens—I was trying to not allow her to get close to him. It's almost funny now—*I mean, it's not funny, ironic maybe.* Howie saved all of us in a way.

So did Tami.

She stopped turning in homework to try to get sent home. She failed her tests in order to be disqualified from the program, but all that happened was a rushed timeline for her and all the other exchange students expected to carry out the coordinated attack. It had to all happen at the exact same moment, nearly impossible to time perfectly—thus the minutes lost between some of the attacks throughout the nation. Some of the buildings weren't entirely wired, and some weren't done correctly—the result being that Tami forced the cell to make mistakes. It's impossible to know how many lives were saved due to her actions—her attempts to be sent home.

Pretty much the whole school enrolls in counseling. They hired an additional grief counselor who also specializes in dealing with high anxiety and PTSD. She's a busy lady.

One thing's for sure. The exchange student programs will be examined a lot more closely.

Derek, Nathaniel, Lacy, Sara, Violet and the rest of our friends who went to the fair together at the start of the year still wave in passing. Derek and Lacy, we're pretty sure, are already planning one of those 'high school sweetheart' themed weddings. Lacy is, I know that.

Sara acts a little uncomfortable around me, but not because of how our friendship shifted over the year. I'm dating Max.

Like dating-dating, understandably weird for her. I can't chat her up about my first kiss, which was with her brother, which she doesn't realize was at Sadie Hawkins, which she planned.

And right this second, Max drives me to Silver City to get the best donut he knows about. I want to call Sara and say *'Ah, I'm in the car all alone with Max and I can barely breathe because he's so hot!'* But I do want things to be back to normal with us. "I sent this to your sister." I wait for him to park before I show him the text.

"That's not funny—she's going to tease me about that for weeks." He turns into the parking lot where we first ate in Silver City, when we were escaping life. Except, now we're celebrating the fact we're still alive. "She'll probably throw water on me every day and say she's trying to cool me off."

"I might know how to heat you up again, if you get cold." To be clear, I do not intend that to sound as dirty as it did, but can't retract it now. "...In a not gross way."

Max lifts his eyebrows. "I'm going to start running through sprinklers and jumping into puddles until I figure out what the gross way is."

I lean in to kiss him, absolutely-certain that my heart beats so hard I'm going to miss and kiss his chin like a dufus. But, at that just right moment, Max puts a hand on my chin, rubs his thumb across the pinkish-purple section under his fingers and bends to meet my lips so I don't have to stretch any further. "Kissing you is never gross." He says it so gently, so sincerely that his next words throw me off a little. "You're going to have to try harder to gross me out."

When he walks around the front of the car to open my door, I can't help but think, *maybe Lacy isn't the only one who'll graduate high school paired off.* Then Max breaks my thoughts with, "Another brick."

And in fact—the building rebricks its entrance. So that the back door, once turned into the front door due to flooding, now looks like an inviting front entrance. Because sometimes the world makes things backwards, yet everything doesn't all end. And it's okay.

It's our job to recover and redefine.

And, when we're ready...rebuild...accept...

forgive.

ABOUT THE AUTHOR

Aften has a Master's degree in Education and currently works full-time as a Teacher of the Visually Impaired (TVI) and Special Education Teacher and Case Manager at Wyoming Indian Schools, serving primarily the Native Arapaho and Shoshoni tribes of Wyoming. Her family has experience hosting an exchange student several years ago. They still stay in touch with social media as well.

Aften has additional published YA works including KILLER POTENTIAL a YA Psychological Thriller, and CHEAT CODE a YA sci-fi thriller. She loves gardening and animals.

www.ingramcontent.com/pod-product-compliance
Lightning Source LLC
Chambersburg PA
CBHW060545310726
48982CB00009B/1375/J

* 9 7 8 0 9 8 9 5 0 6 4 5 8 *